Flame of Love

CLARISSA ROSS

CRIMSON
ROMANCE

F+W Media, Inc.

This edition published by
Crimson Romance
an imprint of F+W Media, Inc.
10151 Carver Road, Suite 200
Blue Ash, Ohio 45242
www.crimsonromance.com

ISBN 10: 1-4405-7293-3
ISBN 13: 978-1-4405-7293-7
eISBN 10: 1-4405-7294-1
eISBN 13: 978-1-4405-7294-4

Chapter One

London, September, 1846

As midnight approached, the thick, yellowish fog had spread throughout the city. It was now no longer possible to see more than a few feet in any direction, and the glow of the hissing gas lamps at the occasional street corner made no inroads against the almost impenetrable shroud of mist. It was no longer safe for pedestrian or carriage to be abroad on such a night. Yet there were a few of each still groping their ways to various destinations.

One of these was seventeen-year-old Fanny Hastings. The pretty red-head clutched her gray cloak about her and made her way along the winding, cobblestoned street in which she found herself. Since reaching Central London from Brenmoor an hour or so earlier, she had wandered about aimlessly. She had literally fled from Brenmoor Castle where she had been a maid in the employ of the Marquis of Brenmoor. As she clung to the small valise which contained all her worldly belongings she tried without success to chart a path for her future.

Now the result of her impetuous action was all too apparent. She was alone and friendless in the great city of London, which she'd only heard told about in grim tales by Marsden, the butler at the Marquis of Brenmoor's. And that worthy gentleman had not painted a warm picture of the teeming metropolis.

"London is a sinful city without a heart," the tall, dignified Marsden had warned her. "Best to avoid it altogether and be on the safe side!"

Marsden had been her superior in the busy household of the Marquis to which she'd gone on the death of her mother. Because her mother's cousin, Lily, had long been the cook in the grand mansion, it was there Fanny had gone when her mother's death had left her completely alone in the small country village where her widowed parent had toiled as housekeeper for the elderly scholar, Timothy Creighton.

Fanny, young as she was, might have carried on in her mother's footsteps as housekeeper for the fine old gentleman had not the same fever which carried her mother off also killed the old man in the early part of December. His tight-fisted nephew came to sell the house and settle the estate, and Fanny was given a few shillings and a stagecoach ticket to Brenmoor Castle on the outskirts of London.

Lily Kendall, a stout, kindly woman in her middle years, had taken her first startled glance at Fanny and exclaimed, "You must be Mary's child! You're the very image of her!"

Tears in her eyes, she'd admitted, "I am, dear cousin. I have come to you because I had nowhere else to go!"

The matronly spinster had taken her warmly in her arms and said, "And why should you turn to anyone else when Lily Kendall is alive and well! Don't you worry no more, the Marquis will give you a position!"

And so he had. Fanny, after a warm dinner and a good night's rest on a cot in a small attic room, had found herself nervously presenting herself to the Marquis the next morning with Lily standing in the background to give her any needed support.

Her Aunt Lily had warned her that the Marquis was often of uncertain disposition in the mornings. He was also a widower and a veteran of the French campaigns under Wellington. He had married shortly after his soldiering and his titled, frail wife had given him three sturdy sons.

The Marquis had not married again and was hardly likely to now that his three sons were full grown with the eldest twenty-four and the youngest twenty-two. His adoring wife had dutifully borne him an heir each year until her own health, sadly deteriorated, had doomed her to a few months of illness and then death. The Marquis had never recovered from the blow, and along with it he suffered from a leg wound received at Waterloo which had forever ended his riding days, causing him to use a cane and walk with a decided limp.

On that first morning he had sat at the desk in his study like the grim martinet he was. His hair was gray and thinning and he had the kind of strong, lined face with a prominent nose which somehow made the nervous Fanny think of an eagle.

The heavy gray eyebrows met in a frown and the Marquis commented, "You speak very well, girl. Not at all like one of the lower classes. Where did you get your education?"

"I was most fortunate, sir," she said. "My mother took care of a scholar and I lived in the house. As part of her wages he gave me lessons in any number of things."

"Consider yourself a lucky girl," the Marquis said in his odd, hoarse voice, a result of chronic bronchial trouble. "Do not lose your fine way of speaking. It may serve you well in life."

"Yes, sir," she said quietly, looking down.

"And you are an orphan you say," the Marquis went on. "May I ask what happened to your late father?"

Fanny looked directly at him now, her large green eyes wide. "My father was a strolling player, sir, a man of great talent. Many years ago he left my mother to search for employment in the theatre at Bristol. He never did come back. The letters my mother sent to him were returned so we presumed he had died."

The Marquis scowled and moved his cane a little. "I should say the fellow deserted her! That you and your mother were abandoned by this scoundrel of an actor!"

She protested hotly, "We have never thought of it that way. My mother always said he was a kind man with fine manners and speech. That is why I have wished to learn to speak well. I would like to be an actress one day!"

There was a shocked silence in the study as the Marquis glared at her in astonishment. Then her stout cousin Lily had bobbed forth to curtsy to her employer and say, "You must forgive the girl, sir. She is from the country and does not know what the life of an actress means. Her ambitions are moral even if her goal isn't! And she shouldn't be blamed for loving the memory of her father, sir. That surely isn't a bad quality!"

"Filial devotion!" the Marquis said. "I find no fault in that, Lily. But the pitfalls of a life in the theatre should be explained to the girl."

"I shall do it, sir, never fear!" Lily promised. "If you will be so kind as to take her on as a scullery maid I'll give her a proper training!"

"Very well, Lily," the Marquis said. "Fanny shall be our new scullery maid." And turning to her he had added severely, "Mind you pay attention to all your cousin tells you and forget that stage business! It could lead to your ruin!"

"Yes, sir. Thank you, sir," she'd bobbed her gratitude.

"We shall do our best to offer you a good home here, Fanny," the Marquis said. "Do the duties assigned you and you will have no problems." With that he waved them out.

So it had been settled. But as they made their way back to the kitchen Fanny had defiantly told the elderly Lily, "I shall work hard but I won't give up my dream of becoming an actress!"

Lily's round, fat face showed impatience. "Drat it, child, let me train you to be a proper servant first before you worry about anything else!"

And Lily had been an excellent tutor. Marsden, who had served at Waterloo as orderly to the Marquis and who was now his butler, also had shown a keen interest in her. The tall, long-faced man with frayed, gray side-whiskers and thin gray hair had shown her particular attention, perhaps because he and Lily were warm friends. At any rate, within a few months Fanny had been promoted to upstairs maid.

It was as upstairs maid she had first seen the three sons of the Marquis. There was Viscount George Palmer, first in line to his father's title, a young law graduate of Oxford, who had inherited his mother's good looks and fair complexion and also her indifferent health. He had recently returned from a long voyage to Australia and New Zealand to strengthen his lungs.

Then there was his twenty-three-year-old brother, Kenneth. He was darker in complexion and had his father's stern features. He was now the Reverend Kenneth Palmer, curate of the neighboring Brenmoor Cathedral. And the youngest, the twenty-two-year-old, Charles, who had recently taken his commission in the Fifteenth Cavalry Regiment, his father's old regiment. Captain Charles was quite as handsome as his oldest brother and also fair like him. He had a jolly disposition and was fond of practical jokes.

It was inevitable that Viscount George and Captain Charles be the favorites with the servants, while the Reverend Kenneth was regarded with some wariness as being whey-faced and unduly stern in his moral judgements of others. Unlike his two brothers, he had little friendliness about him and went back and forth to the Cathedral, spending scant time at home. Fanny had found him cold and a little frightening.

It was Viscount George who had first shown an interest in her. As a girl she had often attended the travelling shows which came to her village. One entertainer in particular had caught her fancy, a singer and dancer called Little Nell. Fanny attended her performances often enough to memorize all the entertainer's songs and dances.

She soon began giving her mother and the old scholar a sample of what she'd learned. They had been most enthusiastic in their reception of her talents. So it was not strange that after she'd been long enough at the Brenmoor mansion she began to entertain the other servants with her musical act, often at their insistence.

One night in March after the dinner had been served and everything cleared away Peg Grant, one of the other maids, a tiny, straw-haired girl urged her, "Do some songs and dances for us, Fanny!"

Fanny had been standing by the blazing fireplace and now she turned a questioning face to her cousin Lily. The stout Lily, in turn, had hesitated and then given Marsden a look. Marsden, regal at the end of the kitchen table with an accounts book in his hands, had nodded his assent. There was a burst of cheers and laughter from the younger servants, hushed at once by Lily.

"Very well, now," the stout woman had said sternly. "Let us have no row! If Fanny is to entertain us let us listen quietly like ladies and gentlemen!"

"Hear! Hear!" Marsden said, closing his accounts book.

Fanny took a stand at the end of the big kitchen and began her first song. It recorded the adventures of a dairy maid who caught the eye of the Squire and married him. She carried it off with spirit and ended it with a little dance.

She'd been so absorbed in her performance that she'd paid no attention to her audience. Now as she finished she was astonished to find that standing on the sidelines was the good-looking Viscount George. He was smiling with admiration and with the other servants hushed into silence by his presence, he came to her and congratulated her.

"You did that like a professional," he said. "I'm amazed."

"It's only a poor imitation, sir," she apologized, pink with confusion.

"Not at all," the handsome young George told her. "I've seen much worse in the Halls. Isn't that so, everyone?" He turned to the others.

"Fanny is a proper riot!" Peg piped up and clapped her small hands enthusiastically. The other servants followed her example leaving a smiling, blushing Fanny.

The young Viscount said, "There! You see?"

"They're much too kind!"

"Never," George Palmer said. "You are good enough to be a professional entertainer right now!"

"I'm quite happy here," she assured him, seeing that her cousin Lily was watching with bated breath.

"Fine!" George said, smiling. "But if you ever wish to change your work I'm sure someone would be willing to hire you as an entertainer."

It was her moment of glory. From then on the others kept requesting her to sing their favorite songs. She didn't mind since she enjoyed doing it and her secret ambition still was to become an actress, despite what she had heard about their ranks being filled with loose women not in any way highly regarded. Her ambition and her respect for her father's profession continued. And she continued to give her impromptu concerts.

Little did she guess then that her friendship with the charming George was to be the cause of her leaving the great mansion. There was not even a small cloud on Fanny's horizon at the moment as the harsh weather ended and spring came. But she had been impressed by the pleasant, young man and often thought about him.

• • •

From the thick, yellow fog behind her came the distant sound of carriage wheels and horses' hooves on the cobblestones. She had chosen a street of modest mansions with fine steps leading up to each and a door to the servants' entrance situated at one side beneath the steps with access by its own stone set of steps downward.

Hearing the carriage approach she pressed close to the wall of one of the houses and waited uneasily for the vehicle to pass. She had visions of wayward gentlemen riding in it and dragging her off the sidewalk and into the carriage. Everything terrified her at this late hour on this lonely street. She knew what a fool she had been to run off from her snug quarters at Brenmoor House to brave the threats of the London night. If she had been determined to leave she ought at least to have waited until morning!

Her heart pounded as the hackney cab went past and then, to her alarm, came to a halt a short distance beyond her. She pressed rigidly to the building, expecting someone to jump out and come running to pounce on her. But this did not happen. Instead she heard the sound of slightly drunken but happy male voices and a stout young man in brown coat and top hat stumbled out onto the street and bade goodnight to companions still in the cab. The cab moved on and he waved after it and then, staggering just a trifle, started up the steps to his door, fumbling for his key in his pocket at the same time.

Fanny was watching this small drama when to her horror she saw two sinister figures appear from hiding under the steps, a tall, ugly man in nondescript, ragged clothes and battered cap, and his singular companion, a bow-legged dwarf. The dwarf was wearing a battered stove-pipe hat and a coat too long for him, open and dragging on the ground.

The stout gentleman was still fumbling for his keys when the footpads came up behind him. The tall one quickly seized him by the throat and cut off any chance of his crying out by holding an arm tightly around his victim's windpipe. At the same time he urged, "Get at it, Snipe!"

Snipe, the dwarf, was dancing with excitement as he quickly went through the stout man's pockets and thrust all he found in the oversized pockets of his own greatcoat.

"Finished!" the dwarf chortled. It all happened in a matter of a few seconds.

"Better make sure he doesn't recognize us!" the tall one said hoarsely and to Fanny's horror took a knife from an inside pocket and plunged it into the stout man's chest. The stout man went suddenly limp and with a look of ecstasy on his ugly face the tall man let him fall onto the steps.

"Come on!" The dwarf, a macabre figure in the fog-shrouded street, was dancing again, with an expression of fear on his large ape-like face. He had short black whiskers which, along with rows of large white teeth made the simian resemblance all the more strong.

"Right!" the tall man said in a low voice, bending over his victim. "He's a goner!"

"This way!" Snipe, the dwarf, said tensely. And to Fanny's horror they started down the street towards where she was standing.

Sick and trembling from what she'd witnessed, she prayed that the fog would hide her sufficiently so that the evil twosome would pass on without seeing her. But it was too much to expect.

The dwarf came running awkwardly towards her on his short bow legs and then suddenly halted with a look of sheer hatred on his big simian face under the battered hat. He turned and in a shrill voice shouted, "Here, Martin! Someone here!"

The tall criminal was just coming down the steps and when he heard his companion's cry he came sprinting to join the dwarf. Fanny knew she would be dead in a moment if she remained there. She had no choice but to try and make a run for it. Catching up her skirt in one hand and clutching her valise in the other she turned and ran wildly back along the street with no idea where she might be heading.

"Crikey!" the dwarf shouted angrily after her.

"Got to get her!" Martin the murderer cried and dashed after her on the double with the dwarf coming along a poor third.

Fanny knew she could not outrun the tall, rangy Martin. Her only hope was to escape by confusing them. She turned at the first corner and then after racing down a short street turned again. They were not far behind. Then she was conscious of a church ahead and next to it what seemed to be an open field surrounded by an iron railing in which was a gate. She flung open the gate and raced into what she now recognized as a cemetery. She picked her way between the tombstones and finally saw a hedge which seemed to offer a hiding place. She flung herself onto the wet grass and crawled under the hedge to hide between it and the church wall.

She was sobbing now and her breath was coming in painful gasps from her unusual exertion. She'd barely hauled her valise in with her when she heard the footsteps of the murderers as they came running into the cemetery. She fought to silence her agonized breathing, fearful that they would hear her.

Martin, the tall one, gazed around with a menacing look on his coarse face. "I'd have sworn she came in here!" he said.

The dwarf, Snipe, was waddling among the headstones looking for her. He spoke up in his high-pitched voice; "I don't agree, Martin. A female isn't likely to come into this place of the dead!"

"No?" Martin eyed him with annoyance.

"She's not here," the dwarf said. "She tricked us by leaving the gate open, giving her time to run on."

"Maybe," the other one said.

"She'll be blocks away by now," the dwarf complained, still searching, and now close by the hedge where she was hiding, close enough so that he could have reached out and touched her. She held her breath and pressed rigidly against the stones of the church wall.

"I got a good look at her," Martin said. "I'll know her if I see her again!"

"So did I," the dwarf said, halting by the big man. "And if we *do* see her again we'd better manage more smoothly than this time. She saw it all! She can put our necks in the hangman's noose!"

"If we come upon her I'll not give her time for that," Martin said grimly. "We'd better get along and divide the swag."

The dwarf looked intently at the hedge and then seemed to change his mind. He moved away, allowing her to breathe again. Joining the tall man he said, "No use staying here! She won't come back! And there's at least a hundred pounds in that purse!"

"Good night's work!" Martin said approvingly as the evil couple made their way slowly out of the small cemetery.

Fanny didn't move until long after their voices and figures had faded away in the fog. At last she crawled out from her hiding place, wet, miserable and afraid. She gazed at the various headstones, crypts and monuments all about her and shivered. She did not much relish the idea of spending the night among the dead!

But her common sense told her that she had less to fear from them than she did from the living outside the fence. She stood there, still thoroughly fear-stricken, as the clock in the church tower sonorously struck the hour of one. She gazed at one of the flat-topped grave markers and debated stretching out on it to spend the night on this hard bed with the cold, yellow fog penetrating her body. It was a long way from her former warm room at Brenmoor. But there was no use feeling sorry for herself. She had brought herself to this unhappy state!

As she stood there she heard a slight creaking sound, like the movement of rusty hinges. It made her heart almost stop. Then she wheeled around in the direction of the sound and to her utter horror she saw the doors of the largest crypt moving. As they opened a fearsome apparition emerged, a thin man with a deathly white face in which were two sunken eyes, burning fiercely as they stared at her from the shadows of his gaunt face. The man wore a black top hat from under which flowed wild strands of iron-gray hair reaching to the shoulders of his black, worn frock coat and shabby trousers. She could only think of the creature as one risen from the dead!

"Girl!" The apparition was addressing her.

She drew back, terrified. "Who are you? What are you?" she quavered.

The ghostly one chuckled, showing gray uneven teeth in an equally gray, gaunt face. "The last question is of more moment than the first, I vow! What am I? A creature of the night! A wastrel of the streets, seeking comfort with my friends in this resting place of the dead."

"Your friends?"

"I have several," the apparition assured her. "From our vantage point in the tomb we saw you run in here followed by those two evil fellows."

"I saw them commit a murder," she said tensely, realizing that this was no spirit, but a human being like herself. "They wish to kill me!"

"No doubt," the ghostly figure said in his courtly way. "But they have gone now. So you are safe. I have emerged from the tomb to invite you to join my friends and me in a hot cup of tea and a warming fire!"

"Don't make fun of me!" she wailed, more conscious of the cold than ever.

"I assure you I'm not," the apparition intoned. He waved a claw-like hand gracefully. "Come a step further and observe for yourself."

Hesitantly she moved a little closer so that she was able to see down into the tomb and sure enough, there was a small blaze in the middle of the floor with sticks set up to hold a pot over it to boil. Gathered by the fire were three other figures, two very elderly women dressed in ragged clothes and a young girl of about her own age and in not so ragged a condition. The girl had jet black hair and a rather pretty face.

"There is a very good draught at the top which allows the smoke to go out and the fire to burn nicely," the apparition said.

She stared down into the eerie depths and in a low voice said, "I must be dreaming!"

"On the contrary," the gaunt-faced man said, "you are being rescued from your nightmare. Come along with me to a place of warmth and safety."

"What will they say?"

He assured her, "We have already discussed it among ourselves and decided that you should be given sanctuary. The church would normally be the proper place, but unhappily in the Anglican tradition the verger has locked it. So we have to make do with the hospitality of those who have gone before us."

As he went over this preamble Fanny carefully picked her way down the moss-covered steps and entered the tomb. The wave of warmth gave her a new feeling of hope. She deliberately ignored the shelves on either side with their dusty coffins and the cobwebs which streaked up from them to the level of the roof.

The two old women were huddled by the fire with their eyes closed. But the girl smiled up at her and said, "We're not spirits, though we may seem to be so."

"Thank you for allowing me to join you," she said. "My name is Fanny Hastings!"

The dark-haired girl laughed and said, "More likely it would have been mud if those two blokes had caught up with you. Mine is Moll! The last name don't count!"

The man with the skull-like face and long gray hair smiled as he settled down by the fire after having carefully closed the doors to the tomb. He said, "Her reason for not giving you her last name is because she does not know it."

Moll was pouring out a cup of tea and she stuck her tongue out at the gaunt man in black. "That for you, Mr. Hodder!" And she handed the tea to Fanny.

"Thank you," Fanny said gratefully. She sipped the tea and felt she'd never tasted anything so good.

"My name is Silas Hodder," the man with the burning eyes said. "I am a beggar by profession. And so is Moll. The two old ladies are somewhat beyond even this lowly profession and so live largely on our bounty."

"Share and share alike," Moll said piously. "Charity is a grand thing!"

"Amen!" Silas Hodder said, nodding.

Fanny stared at them in amazement. "But doesn't it hurt your pride to beg?"

"Not at all," the man said. "I consider myself tops in my profession."

"Oh, he's very good, he is, I promise you that," Moll agreed, her hands clasped around her knees and a smile on her pert face.

Fanny said, "Can't you get regular work?"

"None that would pay as well and be respectable," Moll told her.

"London is a cruel city," Silas Hodder warned her as the two old ladies continued to sleep by the fire. Fanny now noticed the gin bottle on the ground between them, empty as she might have suspected. The two old ones had downed it without doubt and were now blissfully at rest.

Moll followed her glance and laughed. "No tea for them! Gin is their mother's milk and nothing else will do."

Silas Hodder said, "I was once a businessman of some wealth and great respectability. I was swindled out of my fortune by scoundrels and I made a vow to even the score with the world by extracting a good living from it. And I have!"

Moll gave him an admiring look. "He's really brainy, Mr. Hodder is. He put me on my game as well."

"I'll explain my own tactics first," Silas Hodder told the dark girl. And then to Fanny, he continued, "I sleep rather late in the day. Then I make the rounds of the best taverns. I am, as you can see, shabby and peculiar-looking; I also smell rather high. When I enter these respected places I conduct myself most quietly and gentlemanly so there can be no excuse to evict me. I seat myself amid the most prosperous looking group and look as doleful as possible. Naturally I make them very uncomfortable."

"And then?" Fanny asked.

"One of them will query me about my business there. I tell them I have come merely to sit in my haunts of yesteryear. To be a shadow at the feast and think of more prosperous days. I note that I once had a suite of offices in the City and then I bring out a box of matches (without offering them for sale). Most of the fat-bellies have a fit of conscience and thrust coins in my hand as I leave. All I do is sit there dull-eyed. When I've made all I can in one tavern I move on to another."

Fanny said, "Don't they become familiar with your routine?"

"Makes it all the better," the skull-faced man said. "I become a sort of charge to them. If I don't appear they worry that my health has broken completely or I have taken my life as I've frequently threatened, and my demise will be upon their conscience. I make the same rounds in the evening until about ten. Then I return here."

She listened in amazement. "And this makes you a good living?"

"More than that, it allows me to bank a little each week," Silas Hodder said with satisfaction. "Soon I shall be able to retire and take up my status as a true gentleman!"

"Ah, you never will!" Moll told him. "Not you! The greed has got you! You won't ever give it up."

"What about you?" Fanny wanted to know of the girl.

Moll said, "I don't know. Mr. Hodder made me what I am. He showed me how to turn over a few pounds a week. He reads the death notices and he picks out names of married gentlemen in good circumstances. Then I makes a call on the dead man's widow. I tell her what a dear gent he was and how he made love to me on the quiet and promised to marry me. I sniffle a lot at losing him but tell her there's a good side. I will have the child he gave me. And it's then they bring out their purses and give me a little something to keep quiet and go on my way."

Fanny was shocked. "But that is so cruel! You make those poor widows unhappy by thinking their husbands were unfaithful. And you do harm to the reputations of the dead husbands!"

Moll chuckled. "There's more to it than that. Some of those widows didn't have much use for their husbands in any event. And they're properly surprised many a time that the poor old gent was able to get me with child, since he hadn't been able to do it for them. The way I see it, I give those dead chaps a gamy reputation that should make them happy!"

"No one is really hurt," Silas Hodder said. "I carefully select the cases. No grieving young widows are ever included."

"And all four of you sleep here every night?" Fanny said.

"We do," Moll replied. "The old girls spend most of the day under an arch on the embankment not too far from here. But come nightfall we all head for our tomb."

"A touch of the vampire, you might say," the weird old man said with amusement. "Naturally the church people are not aware of our making such good use of the facilities or they would evict us. As yet, our dead comrades have made no complaint of any sort."

She glanced warily at the dusty coffins with their cobwebs and said, "I can tell that. Is it healthy down here?"

"As healthy as most places in London," Silas Hodder said. "My physician assures me no disease lives on in such places. The coffins are well-sealed and the tomb makes a comfortable place for us on nights such as this."

Moll said, "We have just room for one more. You can join us if you like. You've got to keep out of the way of those two blokes!"

Fanny gave a deep sigh, thinking of all that had taken place since she ran away from Brenmoor on this eventful evening. She said, "The tall one will kill me to silence me if he ever finds me again."

"I wouldn't trust the dwarf either," Silas Hodder advised. "He has a wicked look."

Fanny's pretty face was shadowed with the evil memory of what had happened. She said, "I saw those two murder a man only a few blocks from here."

"Many such murders occur here in London every night," the man in shabby black warned.

Moll stared at her with interest. "How do you come to be in London on your own?"

"It's a complicated story," Fanny said, staring wistfully into the fire.

"You're nursing a broken heart! I'll vow to that!" Moll declared.

Fanny gave her a surprised look. "How sharp you are to realize that!"

"Part of my trade," Moll said proudly.

"Have either of you heard of the Marquis of Brenmoor?" Fanny asked.

Silas Hodder replied at once, "He has a large estate just outside London. I think he has three sons and a fine stable of race horses."

She told the odd, old man, "You're right on all points." And then she went on to explain about her mother dying, her cousin Lily being the cook at Brenmoor and how she came to be there. She also told them of her stage ambitions and of meeting young George Palmer.

In a moment she had lost herself in the pleasant reverie of her second meeting with Viscount George Palmer. It had happened on a night in mid-April. The Marquis, who held many shares in the British East India Company, was having an entertainment to honor a certain Prince Aran, the Oxford-educated son of a Maharajah in the northwest of that vast and mysterious country.

Cousin Lily was in a state about the food, since the Marquis had commissioned a special menu for the Prince who was a Hindu and would not eat any beef dishes. Fanny herself was busily involved with the preparing of extra rooms for overnight guests. The great ballroom was festooned with colorful garlands and other decorations. There was to be a dinner, dancing and a musical entertainment.

The only one in the house who was not excited was the Reverend Kenneth Palmer, who disapproved of the Marquis catering to a man he felt was a heathen. Fanny had overheard him in conversation with his father in the lower hallway.

The young curate had informed the old man, "I shall be absent from the party, father. I trust you will understand."

The Marquis had leaned on his cane and said tartly, "I expect you to attend. My guest of honor, the Prince, may be offended if you are not present."

"I do not share your enthusiasm for heathen royalty," the young man snapped back. "The Bishop is putting me up for a few days. I shall return here when this pagan orgy is over."

"I call that most inconsiderate of you, Kenneth," the Marquis had rebuked him.

But, as Fanny had expected, the rebuke had done no good. The bigoted young man was not influenced by his father's words. On the other hand, Captain Charles and the Vicount George entered into the preparations with enthusiasm, as did Dora Carson, a daughter of a distant poor relation of the Marquis whom the old man had adopted as his daughter.

Several times Fanny had been assigned to act as personal maid to the pleasant young woman. And on the evening of the party for the prince Fanny found herself acting in this capacity for Dora once again.

Dora was slender, twenty-two, quietly attractive. Her large brown eyes and olive skin were her best features and she wore white as often as possible to emphasize her coloring. On the exciting night Fanny stood behind her fastening her gown as Dora studied herself in the mirror.

Dora, surveying herself with a smile as Fanny worked at the buttons, said, "They say the Prince is charming and a ladies' man."

"You should soon know, miss," Fanny said.

"I have seen likenesses of him. I would not call him handsome by our standards but he has a noble look and a regal bearing, I'm told."

"Is he returning to India soon?"

"Yes," Dora said. "His father is ill. He may soon to be the Maharajah and his friendship is important to the British East India Company. Otherwise you can be sure the Marquis would not go to all this fuss."

Fanny finished and stood back. "There! You look ever so nice, miss!"

"Thank you, Fanny," Dora said, smiling at her. "You must look in on the party tonight."

"I shall be serving," she said. "And then later some of the other maids and I will watch from the balcony where we won't be seen."

Dora stood up. "Believe me, you're lovely enough to be a guest. And you speak so nicely. You really shouldn't be a servant."

Fanny said, "You mustn't be deceived by my speech, miss. I have very ordinary origins. I'm in my proper station in life."

Dora placed an arm around her. "My dear Fanny, my origins were no more notable than your own until the Marquis adopted me!"

"But you do have his blood."

"So little of it he would like to see me marry one of his sons," Dora said with a wry look.

Fanny was surprised. "Truly?"

"Yes. You mustn't whisper a word of it to anyone else. But the Marquis thinks I'd make a fine wife for a minister. And I can't abide that awful Kenneth! He's such a prig!"

"I agree!"

Dora's eyes gleamed mischievously. "I wouldn't mind being his daughter-in-law if he encouraged a match between George and me."

"The Viscount!"

"Yes," Dora said. "He's the pick of the three. I'm very fond of him."

"What about Captain Charles?" Fanny ventured.

Dora shrugged. "He's not like Kenneth. He has a good nature. But he lacks George's brilliance and charm."

Fanny smiled a little sadly. "I quite agree with you, miss."

"So you have been taken with him too!" Dora exclaimed with delight.

Fanny smiled ruefully. "He's the hero to every maid and scullery girl in the house. No denying the Viscount is the favorite."

"I'm sure of that," Dora said. And then confidentially, "Of course, the Marquis is playing politics again, even with the lives of those dear to him. He's deeply anxious for George to marry Virginia Andrews, the daughter of Sir Matthew Andrews."

Fanny found herself feeling shocked, as she had not heard of this before. She said. "Is she apt to make him a good wife?"

"She's pretty enough," Dora said. "But that's about all. She is flighty and shallow! The sort who flirts with every man at a party but cares for none of them. She only cares for herself."

"It doesn't sound promising," Fanny suggested.

"It's a shame," Dora sighed. "And the worst part of it is that Virginia just might entice George into marrying her!"

"I hope not," Fanny said, surprised at how strongly she felt on the subject.

"So do I," Dora said as she prepared to go down to the party.

•••

The ballroom of the great mansion was filled. Fanny was doubling as a serving girl. She went to the kitchen where she hastily donned an apron and different cap and then, equipped with a tray of dainties, went up to the ballroom to serve the guests.

At one end of the room an orchestra was playing. The notables, including the Marquis, the Indian Prince Aran and Dora and Viscount George stood at the other end of the great room receiving the guests as they came. There were red and blue uniforms resplendent with gold braid and bands, in contrast to the more soberly hued formal coats of civilians and the ladies in flowing gowns of every shade of the rainbow.

Conversation was loud and animated. The Prince, in native costume of pale salmon-colored silk and a turban in the same shade, was the center of attention. He was a young man with a short black beard. His eyes were black and sharp in his narrow brown face and his nose rather pointed. He was not truly handsome by Western standards, yet he had a certain quality about him.

Fanny did not take her tray to him as the group were still receiving. But she found herself blushing as his glance fixed on her and his eyes seemed to follow her about the room. Her tray was empty and she was about to go downstairs when a hand caught her by the arm. She turned to see that it was Viscount George.

The young man guided her to an alcove off the ballroom and whispered intensely, "I must have a word with you!"

Chapter Two

Startled by the sudden display of interest the young Viscount was showing in her, she looked up at him and asked, "What is it, sir?"

The handsome George smiled. "You're trembling, Fanny. There is no need to be alarmed."

The music was playing in the background and she felt that all the eyes of the elegant ladies and gentlemen must be upon them. She said, "I have my duties, sir. We're ever so busy. You are keeping me back!"

He still kept her cornered in the alcove as he told her, "You'll do no more serving this night!"

"What do you mean?"

"Prince Aran has taken an interest in you, which does not surprise me since he is a keen admirer of feminine charm," George told her.

Her cheeks crimsoned more deeply. She recalled that the guest of honor had been rather greedily following her with his keen, black eyes. She said, "I'm much flattered. But I still have my work to do."

"No, listen," the young Viscount said. "Seeing his interest in you I told him of your talent for song and dance. And he has requested that you be included in the entertainment which is to begin in a few minutes."

Her pretty face showed distress. "Oh, sir! You shouldn't have said anything!"

"Too late now," George said cheerfully. "Better make up your mind to put on your act for all of us."

Becoming more uncomfortable as the moments passed, Fanny protested, "I can't, sir! The Marquis would surely not approve of it. Nor would my cousin, Lily."

"I can't answer for your cousin Lily," the amused George said. "But I can assure you my father is quite in favor of it. I have come here to make my request with his permission. You see, catering to the Prince ranks above everything else."

She glanced beyond him at the crowded ballroom and told him, "I'd never manage! I'd be bound to faint!"

"We'll take that chance," George said. "I want you to put on your best dress and then take your place by the platform. When the time comes I will introduce you."

"Must I? Please let me be free of it!" she begged him.

Staring at her George saw she was in earnest. "By Jove, you are the modest one!" he exclaimed. "But there is no way out of it now! The Prince is thin-skinned, easily annoyed. My father must encourage his every whim!"

"I have no proper dress!" she wailed.

"Never mind," George told her. "I'll fetch Dora and she'll fit you into a gown of hers. You're the same size!"

"Miss Dora!" Fanny said in dismay. "I can't ask to wear her dress!"

"I'll take care of it," the Viscount promised.

And he did. Within the space of a few minutes she found herself whisked upstairs again in Dora's company and with the help of one of the other maids being fitted into a fine yellow silk gown.

Dora stood back and studied her. "You do look really splendid, Fanny. We'll just fix that flaming red hair a little. I feel sure that is what attracted the Prince's attention. Dark haired girls are no novelty to him, so I'm quite out of the running!"

Fanny was almost in tears as she stood there with the two of them fussing over her. "And I'm quite out of my depth!" she said ruefully. "I shall make a proper fool of myself before all those people!"

"Nonsense!" Dora said as she expertly pinned Fanny's hair on top of her head, allowing a few stray ringlets to escape in studied artlessness. "George tells me he witnessed your dancing and singing and you were very good. And he says your ambition is to be an actress?"

"Yes," Fanny admitted. "My father was on the stage."

"So that is why!" the other girl said with interest. "Otherwise I would discourage it! But if you wish to be an actress you must learn to face all sorts of people. Be glad the Prince is charmed by you! Go down to the ballroom and when your turn comes do George and me proud!"

Fanny managed a forlorn smile. "Well, if you feel that way, miss."

"I do!" Dora said. "You'll never look prettier, will she, Peg?"

The little maid said, "You're ever so lovely, Fanny! No one would know you was just a maid!"

"I know!" Fanny said grimly. "Well, if I have to face it I may as well get it over with!" And she picked up her skirt so as not to have the hem trailing the carpets and getting soiled.

"That's the spirit!" Dora cried and escorted her out of the room to the stairway.

The concert part of the evening was already under way when Fanny came to stand in the anteroom just off the ballroom, as a stout soprano was singing some frantic, high-pitched song about the beauties of an English garden. It went on for what seemed to Fanny an endless time, with the elderly male pianist anxiously accompanying the soloist with great energy.

The plump singer ended on a fantastically high note on which her voice noticeably cracked. Not taken back by this, the woman bowed to the loud applause which followed, giving a slight curtsy in the direction of the Prince. Then she marched off grandly, followed by her accompanist clutching his music. They went past Fanny without noticing her.

George suddenly appeared with a mild-looking older man at his side. He said, "This is the pianist with the orchestra. You describe your song and how you sing it and he will accompany you."

Fanny knew fresh despair. She told the pianist, "It's a number Little Nell made famous, called The Dairy Maid and The Squire'."

The pianist nodded. "You're in luck! I know it! You set the tempo and I'll follow along for both the song and dance!"

George's eyes showed a merry twinkle. "So you see! All your problems are settled!" And he marched out to the ballroom while she remained in the ante-room with the pianist.

George was greeted by applause. He smiled and accepted the good-natured laughter and ovation. Raising a hand, he began to speak; "Thank you, dear friends! I fear I must disappoint you. I shall not be entertaining you this evening. But I do have a special treat and surprise for you—a mystery lady who does a most spirited imitation of the famous soubrette, Little Nell! I have seen this pretty young woman perform and I can promise you some exciting moments! And some entertaining ones!" He bowed again and with a smile on his face came to the door, gloved hand outstretched, and led Fanny out to the brightly lighted ballroom. There was a loud burst of applause from the guests at the other end of the room.

Once on the stage she lost her nervousness. All she could think of now was her song and dance. The pianist had taken his place and was looking in her direction. She nodded to him and he played a short introduction to the comedy song.

Fanny had gone through the performance so many times before that she was completely at ease. The piano background was a big help, especially when it came to the dance steps. She sang and grimaced like Little Nell and was heartened by hearing the audience laughing at the right times. When she ended her lively dance the staid group went wild! She had to return four or five times to bow and the applause only ended when the orchestra began to play.

The first to reach her in the anteroom and congratulate her was the young Viscount. He seized her by both hands and smilingly told her, "I was proud of you! And the Prince seemed to be enjoying himself for the first time this evening."

"I'm glad I didn't trip on my skirt and fall down," she said.

"No chance of that!" George declared. "And I must say you look damnably pretty in that gown!"

"Borrowed finery," Fanny protested. "I must get upstairs and take it off. I have to return to work. They're short of servers!"

The handsome Viscount shook his head. "Not at all! You have done your work for the night. Now the Prince wishes to personally congratulate you. I'm to present you to him!"

"Please, I'd rather not," she said, weakly.

"You must or the Prince will be offended," George warned her. "Then father will be upset and there'll be the Devil to pay!"

Her eyes widened with concern. "What can I say to him?"

"Just answer him as you would anyone," he said. "You speak nicely. Just be your natural self!"

It was not an easy request. And when George brought her before the brown-skinned Prince Aran she felt herself weak at the knees. Only the fact George was at her side gave her the courage to carry on. She felt that everyone else in the place was watching and whispering.

Prince Aran's black eyes fixed on her with the same hunger as before but now there was admiration in his face and manner as he said, "You are most talented, Miss Hastings, in addition to being a beauty!"

"Thank you," she said. "It was only a vulgar, comic song, hardly suitable for a gentleman such as yourself."

The Prince smiled. "Truly I have too little comic relief in my life. I'm too sober a fellow. Your amusing song was just what the evening needed."

"You are most kind, Prince Aran," she said, lowering her eyes.

The Prince went on, "Most people are so in awe of royalty they are inclined to overlook the fact that we have average tastes. Or else, they think that Indian royalty must be savages, to be entertained only by dancing girls or trained cheetahs. This might be true of my father, the Maharajah, but I have remained in this country long enough to have cultivated Western ways."

George told her, "Prince Aran and I attended Oxford at the same time."

Prince Aran nodded. "George understands me. He is my good friend. Soon I will be returning to our kingdom in the hills of India and I shall much miss all this."

Fanny said, "It is to be hoped you return soon again, Your Highness."

"That depends," the Prince said. "My father is old and not at all well. If I succeed to his throne I shall not be so free to travel."

"That would be a pity," she said with sincere sympathy.

Their eyes met and she was once again aware of his charm. Though his face was narrow and his skin brown, his features were well-formed with the exception of the rather large nose. His beard was short and suited him and she could guess that he had won the hearts of many females in his brief life.

The Marquis came up and bowed to her. "You did well, miss."

"Thank you, sir," she said.

Leaning on his cane the Marquis turned to the Prince and said, "I really must tear you away from this lady. Lady Andrews is asking to be introduced to you."

Fanny was certain this was a strategy on the part of the wily old Marquis to get the Prince away from her. It would be embarrassing to him if the guests suspected the Prince was becoming too familiar with one of the household's servant girls and that they had been hoaxed in accepting her as a mystery entertainer when she was merely a maid in the house!

The Prince seemed to suspect this also. His brown face took on an ironic expression. He told the Marquis, "Very well, I shall go with you." And then he turned to her, his eyes making direct contact with hers and offering a message which sent a small thrill through her. He said, "I promise, Miss Hastings, to see you again before I depart for my native land."

"You are most kind, Prince," she said.

He bowed and left them. The old Marquis hobbling along with the aid of his cane went across the room to make the promised introduction of the Prince to Lady Andrews.

George gave Fanny a knowing smile. "I must admit you've made a conquest in the Prince."

"I'm sure he'll promptly forget me," she predicted. "He meets all manner of pretty girls!"

"None any more so than you," he replied. "I had to have him notice before I became so aware of you!"

"Mr. George!" she said shyly.

"I mean it," he said studying her.

At that instant an attractive, blonde girl came rushing up and tapped him on the shoulder, saying, "George! Your memory grows worse! This is our mazurka!"

"Sorry!" he said awkwardly.

"We cannot waste a minute!" the girl said and tapping her fan against his shoulder once more she drew him away with her. She only gave Fanny a slight glance and that an unfriendly one as she left her standing there alone.

A voice in Fanny's ear said, "That beauty was the flirtatious Virginia Andrews! Note how charmingly she took George away from you!"

She turned in astonishment to see it was George's soldier brother, Captain Charles Palmer, resplendent in his red tunic, blue trousers and yards of gold braid. She said, "Mister Charles!"

"Don't be afraid of me," Charles begged her. "I've been wanting to congratulate you but George and the Prince have been keeping you to themselves."

She was truly upset now. She said, "I must go, Mister Charles. I have no right to be here!"

"You have every right here tonight, Fanny," Captain Charles said, taking her by the arm so she wouldn't run away. "Surely you must have heard about Cinderella. She won a Prince by merely having her foot fit a glass slipper. You have done much more! Entertained the entire company most amusingly!"

"I did so on command," she said. "And with that over I ought to leave."

"Pray remain a moment or two with me, or I shall think I'm a poor fellow whom the ladies all despise."

"Not at all," she protested. "I like you, Mister Charles. All of us do below stairs."

"Just so long as you do," he said, his pleasant face showing one of his good-natured smiles.

"I'm wearing Miss Dora's gown!" she said, with naive pleasure.

"Dora's dancing her pretty head off with a fellow officer of mine," Charles told her. "She couldn't care less what you're doing. But I think you have eyes only for brother George. Isn't that true?"

"Mister Charles!" she reproved him though she felt her cheeks redden.

"Don't be ashamed of it, all the girls like him," Charles said frankly. "I hoped you might be the exception who inclined more to me!"

"You're making fun of me, sir," she accused him.

"Never, Fanny," the young officer said sincerely. "I swear I would not do that. Joke with you, yes. But make fun of you, never! I think you're the loveliest female here and I say it is a wry twist of fate that you are one of the household staff rather than of the gentry!"

"I'm sure you mean to be kind," she said.

"I do," he added quickly. "I should like to be your friend, Fanny. And I'll start by giving you some good advice. Don't give your heart to George, my girl; he's already promised to wed Virginia Andrews. And her father, Sir Matthew, and my father, the Marquis, are bound to make the match happen."

"So that is why she took him away so quickly," Fanny said.

"She does not tolerate his enjoying the company of any other pretty girl. She did not know you are a servant so she saw a threat in you. She is a haughty baggage and if she'd guessed you were a maid she would be making a protest at your being present here at all."

Fanny quickly pointed out, "So you merely prove what I have said. I ought not to be here!"

He shook his head. "I'm suggesting what the shallow Virginia would say. She's not worthy of your concern!"

"But your brother is going to marry her!"

"And will regret it!" Charles said grimly. "But that is the way with families. When they decree a union it must be or we are considered traitors to our class!"

She said, "I fear I do not understand."

"Better you don't," Charles said. "Now, I have no need to marry anyone. I'm the youngest son, not even the second as my brother the Reverend Kenneth is! I have no hope of inheriting the title so I am comparatively a free man, able to fall in love with the girl of my choice!"

"I hope you find her," she said.

His blue eyes held a merry twinkle. "Perhaps I already have!"

"No. You are merely playing a game. Saying pretty words to flatter me!"

"Don't believe it," the young officer said. "I would truly like to know you better, Fanny. So I beg you not to become too serious about George. I don't want to see you made sad."

"Thank you," she said. "I will remember your good advice."

It was then that Dora Carson and the young officer with whom she was dancing came up to join them. Dora at once came to her and said, "You were a great success, Fanny. Everyone is talking about your talents and wondering who you are!"

Fanny gave the pretty dark girl a plaintive look. "And I'm terrified, Miss. Please see me out. I'd like to leave now!"

Dora showed mild surprise. "You truly wish to leave the scene of your triumph?"

"Yes!"

"Very well," Dora said. And turning to the two young men, she said, "You must excuse us while we retire a moment to refresh ourselves for the balance of the evening."

Charles and the other officer bowed. And Charles called after them, "See that both of you return!"

In a few minutes she was back in Dora's upstairs room and the dark-haired girl was helping her out of the borrowed gown. Fanny said, "I'm ever so obliged, miss. The young men were keeping me there and I didn't know what to do!"

Dora stood holding the gown and smiling at her. "You ought to be flattered. You were entrancing! They were charmed! I saw how quickly Virginia Andrews dragged George away from you! She wasn't about to lose her Viscount to any mystery lady!"

Fanny was now in her maid's dress again. She smiled grimly and said, "She did give me an ugly look as she took him on the dance floor! I can't say I like her type!"

"She's a silly, shallow, spoiled girl!" Dora said with a sigh. Her lovely face shadowed. "My only fear is that she'll ruin George's life!"

"Why don't you marry him, miss?" Fanny said impulsively.

"The old Marquis would never allow it," Dora said in a weary voice. "You were a Cinderella tonight, Fanny. But all dreams don't come true that easily."

"You love him, I can tell!" Fanny said with concern.

"I don't allow myself to think about it. It's hopeless! I must go back downstairs," Dora said, tossing the gown on the bed and rushing out of the room.

Fanny watched after her sadly. Dora was hopelessly in love with the handsome Viscount and it could come to nothing. In a moment of rueful introspection she realized they were both in the same plight. For surely George meant more to her than any other young man she had known. Not that she'd been exposed to many others. He had become special to her. His brother, Charles, had offered her good advice. She should curb her feelings now so the hurt would be that much less.

Having reached this wise decision she made her way back down below to the kitchen. Cousin Lily was seated by the kitchen table drinking from a tankard of ale. The rush of the evening had ended and the exhausted Lily was taking her first rest. Some of the other kitchen help were gathered near her. On seeing Fanny they shrilled out their praise of her performance.

Peg came up with her freckled face glowing and said, "I watched from the gallery! You looked and acted like a real lady!"

Lily sighed over her ale and gave her a worried look. "I hope you didn't step above your level tonight, my girl. If the Marquis himself hadn't ordered it I would never have allowed you up there to take part in that nonsense!"

"They seemed very pleased," Fanny ventured.

Marsden, resplendent in his best butler's livery, had come into the room and now he walked over to Fanny and patted her on the arm. "Most entertaining," the butler said in his dignified way. "I understand Prince Aran was enthralled. You'd better mind yourself, my girl! Those heathen Princes can be a danger!"

Cousin Lily looked shocked and told the butler, "There now, Marsden! Don't be putting ideas into the girl's head!"

The old veteran of Waterloo chuckled and gave one of his frayed, gray side-whiskers a tug as he winked at her and said, "The Prince also has commented on the excellence of the food and is seeking the identity of the cook. I shouldn't be surprised if he spirited the both of you back to India with him!"

The stout Lily burst into pleased laughter. "You are a one, Mister Marsden! You truly are!"

The party was late ending and Fanny was safely in bed in her attic bedroom as the last of the carriages rolled away. There were still a number of house guests at Brenmoor so all the staff would be busy for at least a few days. When the Prince and his entourage left the busy time would be over.

She lay there on her hard, narrow bed in the dismal little room and stared up into the darkness thinking of the magnificence of the evening, of the grand fashion in which the gentry clothed themselves, enjoyed themselves and fed themselves. It was another world, one which would forever be closed to her after this brief experience. She had no doubt that later in life when she was married to some quite ordinary man she would remember this night and the glory of it. And prominent in those memories would be the handsome George! With a sigh she turned and almost immediately fell asleep.

• • •

There wasn't an idle moment the next morning. Cousin Lily was busy preparing trays and having them sent up to various rooms. Fanny found herself in the ballroom helping to take down the decorations under the watchful eye of Marsden. Everything of value had to be salvaged for future parties of the kind. She and Peg carefully packed away the lanterns and removed the garlands. When this task was over she and many of the other girls went upstairs to tidy the rooms and make up the beds, as the guests were mostly all downstairs by this time.

As luck would have it, Fanny found herself assigned to the room occupied by Virginia Andrews. The vivacious blonde had apparently been the last to rise. She was still seated at her breakfast tray which rested on a table by an open window overlooking the gardens. She was wearing a white lace negligee and her face showed a certain weariness. There were dark circles under her eyes, marring the lovely face of the previous evening. Fanny was surprised by this.

Virginia gave her a haughty glance and said, "You didn't knock before you came in!"

"I'm sorry, miss," she apologized. "I did. You may not have heard it!"

"Don't lie, girl! I despise liars," Virginia said sharply.

Fanny backed away. "I can return later, miss."

"You jolly well better," the girl at the table snapped. Then she pointed to the dresser. "There's a bottle of gin there! Pour me out a glass and bring it here!"

Fanny wanted to get away but she did not dare ignore the orders of the already irate young woman. She was shocked that Virginia should be drinking at breakfast—it was not a promising sign. She went to the dresser and found a partially empty bottle of gin and some small glasses. She filled one and carried it across to Virginia's breakfast table.

Fanny no sooner put the drink down than the blonde girl took a large gulp of it. Then her eyes fixed on Fanny and she put aside her unfinished drink to ask, "Have you served me before?"

She shook her head. "No, miss."

"Your face seems familiar, I vow!"

Fanny was trembling. "I'll return later!" And she turned to go.

"Wait!" Virginia cried out and she jumped up from her chair and seized Fanny's arm and wheeled her around. The blonde girl's face was distorted with rage as she went on, "I know you now! You're the 'mystery singer' of last night!"

Fanny pulled free of her and stood pale-faced as she asked, "Will there be anything else, miss?"

The blonde girl laughed nastily. "What a joke! Wait until I tell the others! It was a *maid* whom George foisted on us last night as his mystery lady! Special attraction for the Prince!"

Fanny turned once again and rushed out of the room with Virginia's harsh laughter ringing in her ears. She went to another room to work, still trembling from the ugly scene. She could not understand how anyone with Virginia's beauty could have such a cruel, hateful nature.

It was mid-day before she returned downstairs to help in the kitchen. She said nothing to anyone about her confrontation with Virginia. But while she was polishing silver Viscount George suddenly appeared in the kitchen. He paid his respects to Lily and then came directly to her and took her aside.

"I know about your meeting Virginia," he said grimly.

"I'm sorry she found out," Fanny said unhappily.

The young man frowned. "It was not any fault of yours. She is the one who has behaved most unsportingly!"

"Did she tell all the others?"

"Those who are still here," George said. "Happily, most of them are my good friends and really didn't care who you were. So no real harm has been done except that I'm bitterly disappointed in Virginia."

"She evidently felt resentment at being deceived," Fanny said, trying to make the best of it.

George sighed. "She behaved in her usual selfish fashion. You mustn't feel badly about it. And you won't have to worry about seeing her again. She's leaving for home within the hour."

"It didn't matter," she said quietly. "Perhaps there was something to say for her side of it."

"I can't agree with that," the Viscount said. "I wanted you to know I'm most deeply grateful for last night and for the way you've accepted things today." With that he left.

As soon as he'd gone Cousin Lily came up to her to ask, "What did the young Viscount want?"

Fanny said, "He thanked me for last night." She felt telling more would only complicate things.

Lily's round face showed concern. "I can't have him popping into my kitchen whenever he likes. It keeps the staff on edge. I hope that settles it!" And she waddled back to the table where she was arranging vegetables on a huge platter to go upstairs.

Fanny also devoutly hoped it would mark the end of George's interest in her. And for a while it seemed that it would. Then the following day there was another rush as word was given out that Prince Aran and his entourage were leaving. Fanny was in the drawing room polishing the beautiful mahogany and rosewood furniture when Peg came hurrying into the room and up to her.

Peg's freckled face was serious. "The Marquis wants to see you in his study!"

"The Marquis!" Fanny echoed, nervously twisting the dustcloth between her hands.

"I'll take that," Peg offered. "He said you was to come at once!"

"I'm not even neat!" Fanny worried. "I've been working all morning." She gave the cloth to Peg and smoothed her apron and adjusted her cap. "Will I do?"

"You always look first class," Peg consoled her. "I just hope he's not going to give you the sack."

Fanny sighed. "Anything is possible. This is getting to be a strange house."

She quickly made her way to the book-lined study of the old Marquis and found him standing near the doorway waiting for her, leaning on his cane. He was not alone. Prince Aran, in a dark coat and trousers and a white turban was also there, as was

Viscount George. She needed only to glance at George's face to see that he was troubled about something.

"Come in, my girl," the old Marquis said in his hoarse voice. "You know the Prince and my son. No introductions needed. Do sit down for a minute." He indicated a large leather chair.

She sat gingerly on the edge of the big chair. Looking up at the Marquis, she said quietly, "Yes, sir?"

The old man seemed embarrassed. He cleared his throat. "Yes!" he said. "Rather difficult to know where to begin. The fact is, you have made a most commendable impression on the Prince. He considers you a young woman of great talent!" He pointed his cane at the Prince. "I suggest you take it from there, Prince Aran."

The Prince nodded impassively. "Very well, if that is your wish." He turned to Fanny and in a grave voice said, "I have an offer to make you."

"An offer?" she said in surprise.

"Yes," the Prince said, his brown face showing no expression and his voice completely even in tone. "I believe you would be useful in my palace to teach some of my brothers and sisters English. Also to instruct them in the ways of the Western World."

"But I am not a governness!" she protested.

"You could be," Prince Aran said. "I'm willing to pay you any reasonable sum and guarantee your passage back to England at any time you find the post or the conditions of the country unpleasant."

She could hardly believe her ears. It was indeed a most generous offer. It would lift her from the level of a servant to an honored position in the household of a Prince. But she had no desire to leave England for India. Her ambitions were to make her name in the theatre and London was the place for that. Also, despite the Prince's cautious approach she wondered if her position would truly be that of governness, or if once she was in India the Prince might suggest something less proper. For all his calm demeanor, she had seen his greedy eyes on her the other night and she worried that he might have thoughts about making her one of his concubines.

Slowly, she replied, "You honor me with your offer, Prince Aran."

"I have given much thought to this," the Prince said soberly. "I think you would make an important contribution to my household."

The old Marquis coughed again, and said, "You understand this is entirely between you and the Prince. I have merely asked you here at his bidding."

George, who had been rather nervously standing in the background, now stepped forward. He looked at Fanny directly and said, "What my father means is that we are in no way involved in the offer. We are not encouraging you to accept it nor does it have our approval."

Prince Aran's black eyes took on a sharp look as he snapped, "Are you saying you disapprove? And are you speaking for yourself, Viscount, or for the Marquis as well?"

George met the Prince with a stern face. "I first speak for myself. But I would assume that my father is in agreement with me."

Prince Aran glanced at the old man. "Marquis?"

The Marquis scowled and shifted his weight on his cane. "I'm not sure this girl would be as useful as you think, Prince. India is not an easy country. Her health might suffer due to the change of climate."

Prince Aran's tone was now icy. "That is your only concern, Marquis?"

"Oh, quite!" The old Marquis said awkwardly. "I should say it is up to the young lady to make such an important decision. And perhaps she should have more time to think about it."

"Most certainly," George agreed.

The Prince smiled coldly. "I fear that is impossible. As you know, I leave here in a few hours. My ship sails in the morning. If Miss Hastings decides to honor me by accepting the position she must make up her mind immediately and prepare to leave at once."

"You're giving her no time to think it over," George said. "That is hardly fair, Prince."

Prince Aran shrugged. "I would have expected more consideration and assistance from you, Viscount. We are comrades from our college days."

"I must be honest with you," George said firmly. "I think you are asking too much, too hastily."

The Prince turned to Fanny again. "It would seem, Miss Hastings, that this solely depends on you. Let me assure you once more of the high esteem in which I regard you. And I offer my regrets that I have had to make my offer so belatedly."

She knew that the Marquis was unhappy about the offer but desperately trying to humor the Prince. George was less concerned. But it was plain that neither father nor son liked the appearance of the Prince's proposal.

She said, "I thank you, Prince. But I cannot make such an important decision on such short notice. I am honored and will consider it. If you wish to write the Marquis later I will be glad to send you word of my final answer."

The Prince showed no emotion. Calmly, he said, "I regret the position is only open to you now. The future is another matter. I regret you have decided against it, but I accept your decision." He bowed and turned away as if the matter were ended.

The old Marquis pointed to the door with his cane. "That is all, my girl. We will need you no further."

She rose and hastened from the room. A moment later George followed her out into the corridor, closing the study door after him. He grasped her arm.

He said, "You gave me some bad moments. I was terrified you'd accept! Did you think my father and I wanted you to?"

She smiled ruefully. "I think you made it quite clear you didn't. I fear you have lost a friend in Prince Aran."

"Then let it be," the young Viscount said. "Father will handle him and try to get him in a better mood. I'm not at all sure that his intentions were as honorable as he pretended."

"I doubted that also."

"Fanny!" he gazed at her with undisguised admiration. "I have come to care deeply for you. I realized that there in that room just now!"

She tried to pull away from him. "You mustn't," she whispered. "You are betrothed to Virginia Andrews, and even if this were not so, you are a Viscount and I'm only a servant!"

"Confound Virginia! I have no patience with her!" George said vehemently. "And as for the rest of it, there has to be a way!"

"Please let me go!" she urged him. "Someone will come and see us!"

"I must talk with you more!"

"Later!" she said in an effort to get away.

"Tonight," George said at once. "In the gardens! Meet me by the arch of roses."

"Perhaps," she said, pulling away from him.

"Midnight," he whispered, and kissed the hand he was holding before he let it go.

She rushed down the corridor in a state of confusion. She had endured one surprise after another. No sooner had she settled the matter of the Prince than she was faced with George and his declaration of love. The unhappy thing was she also loved him. If there were any hope for them she would gladly take him from Virginia. But it would be no victory if she ruined his future! She must not cause a conflict between father and son.

In mid-afternoon she watched from an upstairs window as Prince Aran took his leave. It seemed to her he was coldly formal in his goodbyes to the Marquis. She also saw that George was not present. The Marquis shook the Prince's hand and an unsmiling Aran entered the closed carriage. As she watched it drive off she could not help wondering what her future might have been if she'd accepted his offer.

For the rest of the day she worried about whether or not she should keep her rendezvouz at midnight with George. One part of her nature warned her against it, while the other urged her on. He had asked to talk with her more about his love for her and in the end she decided to give him a chance to do this.

Midnight came and she cautiously emerged from her room and made her way down the back stairways to the ground level of the old mansion. Then she went out into the gardens. It was a pleasant night in early June and the air was warm and fragrant with the aroma of the various blooms in the large, well-tended gardens.

The arch of roses was some distance from the house. She made her way there quickly. Once a cat darted across her path, a gray blur moving swiftly in the moonlight and vanishing in the bushes opposite. It gave her a start but as soon as she realized what it had been she went on. But when she reached the arch she saw no one there.

She stood there in the silver of the moonlight wondering why George hadn't come. He had seemed much too serious to lightly change his mind. She was standing there debating whether to return to the house or not when he suddenly appeared, coming up the gravel walk toward her.

Fanny ran to him and he took her in his arms. He kissed her ardently and held her tightly to him. He said, "I was detained. My father is still in his study worrying about Prince Aran. He gave me a long lecture about handling Indian royalty!"

She looked up at him. "Did he think I should have gone with the Prince?"

"No. But he enjoys blaming it all on my bluntness," the young man said. "Let us forget about it. We have other more important things to discuss."

They found a secluded spot by the bushes where he spread her cloak on the ground and they both stretched out on it. Again they were in each other's arms.

After a period of kisses and caresses, she said, "I love you, George. But we both know it's no good!"

"No," he insisted. "Give me a little time until father gets over his present distress. Then I'll tell him about us."

"He expects you to marry Virginia!"

"I shall tell him it's hopeless! That I love you! He thinks you are a most unusual girl. I'm certain he'll relent and give us his blessing."

"You truly think that?"

"I do," he said. "You must leave our service and take up residence somewhere else with a chaperone. After a suitable time our engagement will be announced. No one need connect Miss Fanny Hastings with the servant girl here."

"Virginia Andrews will!"

"I think not," he said. "She does not know your name. And let us hope by then she will have found someone else and have forgotten all about us!" He kissed her again.

"George, I do love you so!" she breathed softly.

"I'm parched for you," he whispered in her ear and at the same time began feverishly to unbutton her gown. She gave him no opposition and soon he was fondling and kissing her bare breasts.

Her misgivings were lost in her ecstasy as their naked bodies joined in a frenzy of passion. She felt the firm thrust of his manhood and in her eager response forgot all else.

When their passions were spent, he continued to hold her closely to him. He was not her first lover, but her previous venture with a shy country lad at home melted into nothingness compared to this. She knew their affair was unwise but she could not help herself.

Chapter Three

The weeks which followed were incredibly happy ones for Fanny. Her romance with George continued and they plotted to meet frequently at various places. On her days off they had a rendezvous in an empty cottage on the estate. In the evenings they often met in a corner of the large gardens. And, becoming more bold as the affair continued, it occasionally happened that George made his way to her small attic room late at night.

The question of the future was always with them though George tried to avoid it when he could. He urged her to be content with their present happiness and in time he would talk to his father. But somehow the talks never seemed to come to pass and though this troubled her, she did not dare to nag him about it.

In the back of her mind there was still her girlhood dream of going to London and making a career for herself in the theatre. This exciting fantasy had sustained her through some of the hard days of growing up and once again it loomed in her mind as a possible alternative, should George not be able to marry her.

She was deeply in love with the young Viscount and she hoped that in the event he did not marry her there would be no match between him and Virginia. She had formed a far from favorable opinion of the blonde girl. If George were reckless enough to enter into a marriage with the shallow and bad-tempered Virginia, Fanny knew he would be bidding farewell to any chance of happiness.

The weeks went by quickly and the romantic conspiracy between Fanny and the young Viscount continued. In late August there was a garden party on the grounds of Brenmoor and once again the household staff were unusually busy. She could not help but notice that Virginia, in a pale blue gown in the latest style and wearing a wide brimmed hat of blue with trailing silk ribbons to match, was much in evidence at the garden party, and that a good deal of the time she was on the arm of Viscount George.

The young man did not seem at all unhappy in the company of the shallow, vivacious girl; in fact it seemed to Fanny that he was enjoying himself. Since he was called to London on a mission for his father the next day she did not have a chance to discuss this with him. But the next evening she heard a discussion in the servants quarters between her cousin Lily and Marsden which set her to thinking. She was seated in a corner of the big kitchen near the two and could not help overhearing what was said.

Marsden, settled back in a rocking chair with a pipe in hand, told the stout cook, "I happened to be in the drawing room this morning when the Marquis was talking to the Reverend Kenneth."

"I saw the Bishop was here for the Garden Party," Cousin Lily said with a smile as she kept busily knitting on a sweater which she wanted finished before the autumn came in.

"It was not about the Bishop they were talking," Marsden said. "The Marquis was discussing the coming public announcement of the Viscount's marriage to Sir Matthew's daughter!"

Cousin Lily halted her knitting and leaned forward. "Did you really hear them discussing that? I was beginning to think it might not happen for some reason."

The dignified Marsden said, "That is what the Marquis was saying. That the marriage had been delayed too long. He wants it to happen at once and he was talking to the Reverend Kenneth about using the Cathedral for the ceremony."

"That would be proper," Cousin Lily agreed solemnly.

"Reverend Kenneth did not seem enthusiastic. But then you know he and the Viscount don't get along! No love lost between those two brothers."

The cook sighed. "The Reverend Kenneth is so filled with Christian indignation, nearly everything offends him. He thinks George leads too loose a life!"

"Aye," Marsden agreed. "Now, Charles and George get on a deal better. They are truly fond of each other. But that Kenneth is an odd one!"

"It is so!"

"At any rate, the Reverend Kenneth promised to speak with the Bishop after the Marquis pointed out that the Queen and her consort might actually attend!"

"Victoria and Albert! Think of that!" Lily said with awe.

Marsden gave her a critical glance. "And why not? The Marquis and Sir Matthew are both advisors to Her Majesty. She should be at the ceremony which unites the two families."

Cousin Lily said, "Then it is only a matter of setting the date!"

"It is!" Marsden said, emphatically placing his pipe back in his mouth.

Fanny fled from the room and made her way upstairs. Her eyes were brimming with tears as she stepped out the service entrance to a deserted section where deliveries were made during the day. The news had shocked her, though she might have expected it. She could not entirely blame George for not telling her, for it was possible that he knew as little about this latest development as she did. His father might well be forging ahead with the wedding plans, expecting to discuss them with George when all was settled.

She was sure it was the end of their happy summer romance. Tomorrow was her afternoon off, and as usual, she had promised to meet George in the deserted cottage at the other end of the estate. He had assured her he would be certain to be back from London by then. Her throat choking with pain, she decided she would keep the rendezvous, but it would be the last. She must begin to make other plans.

When she had recovered from her first overwhelming sorrow she went inside and started slowly up the stairs to her room. On the first landing she met Dora Carson on her way down. The pleasant poor relation of the Palmer family halted to speak with her.

"You look pale, Fanny," the dark-haired girl said.

Fanny said, "I expect I'm tired after the party yesterday." She hoped the signs of her tears didn't show.

"It did make a lot of extra work for the staff," Dora agreed. "Thank goodness such affairs don't happen too often."

"That is true, Miss," Fanny agreed.

Dora leaned forward to her confidentially to add, "From all that I hear we may be faced with another special occasion soon!"

"Oh?" she said.

Dora nodded. "The Marquis is getting impatient! He is trying to rush the marriage between the Viscount and Virginia Andrews!"

Fanny said, "You have heard this?"

"It's a fact. So be prepared!"

Fanny said bitterly, "If he must marry, why must it be that silly miss with her love for gin!"

Dora looked shocked. "How do you know that?"

"About the gin? I saw her at it in her room!"

Dora's pretty face shadowed. "It is all too true. People have begun to notice and talk about her frequently drinking too much. And one so young! I'm sure her parents are hoping marriage will cure her!"

"It won't!" Fanny said unhappily.

"I agree," Dora replied with concern. "If only George would wake up and assert himself before it is too late. I fear he'll go through with it meekly because of Virginia's pretty face and the family's desire to please the Queen. Her Majesty has heard of the match and approves of it!"

"Bother the Queen! She ought not to interfere!" Fanny exclaimed.

"You do have spirit, Fanny!" Dora said with a smile of admiration. "Well, never mind, perhaps it will all turn out better than we think."

"I hope so, miss," Fanny said, the irony of it being that despite all this, Dora did not guess that she and George were lovers.

• • •

The next day Fanny could hardly wait to finish with luncheon and leave the mansion for a few hours. The luncheon dishes finished, she went upstairs and washed and changed into a simple but attractive print dress which was George's favorite. Surveying herself in the mirror in the hall as she went downstairs she thought moodily that she was certainly not stylish like Virginia, although she carried a tiny white parasol against the sun and wore a small straw hat decorated with blue flowers. As she stepped out the side door Captain Charles came riding up on a dappled gray mare. He waved to her and dismounted. She didn't want to talk to him as she was on her way to meet George but he handed the reins over to a lackey and came directly up to her.

"By Jupiter, you look lovely this afternoon, Fanny," the young officer complimented her. "You ought to have dressed like that for the Garden Party instead of wearing your maid's uniform!"

She managed a small smile. "But I am a maid, sir."

"So you are," he agreed. "And a pretty one! Where are you off to?"

Trying to hide her blushing, she said, "To shop and see some friends!"

Charles winked at her knowingly. "See some friends! Now what might that mean? Some young man, I'll venture!"

She looked at Charles, immaculately turned out in his uniform, and thought how much he resembled George, though he was less handsome. She said, "There are other things in life besides men!"

"True!" Charles agreed, holding his riding crop in his hands. "But don't deceive yourself! The game between male and female is most important! You'll find yourself playing it whether you wish it or not!"

"I shall remember that," she promised.

"I was thinking of you yesterday during the party," he said. "Wishing that you might brighten the dullness of the affair by singing for us as you did that night a few months ago at the party for the Prince."

She said, "I shall not likely forget my place again."

"You did not forget your place," he protested. "It all seemed quite right. You were the equal of any lady present. I still remember you in that dress."

"Thank you," she said. "Now, I really must go."

"Have a pleasant afternoon, Fanny," the young man said. "I wish I could go along with you."

"That would never do, sir," she said.

"Perhaps not," he declared with a sigh. "Why is it such a stuffy world, Fanny? Things would be so much simpler if it weren't!"

"I'm sure I'm not wise enough to answer that, sir," she said. "Good afternoon!" And she hurried on her way.

Ten minutes later she was walking quickly along the narrow woods road which led to the isolated cottage. It was shaded and pleasantly cool here and she closed her parasol and held her bonnet in her hand. She hoped that Charles had not guessed her destination or whom she was meeting!

The cottage door was open and her pulse began to beat more quickly at the prospect of seeing George. She hurried to the doorway and saw him standing inside with his arms stretched out to receive her. She was filled with a mixture of pain and joy as she ran to him. He held her close to him, his lips on hers.

Releasing her, he said, "Every minute seemed an hour! I rushed to get back from London. I've been waiting here more than a half-hour."

"I was delayed," she said. "Charles met me on the way out and kept me talking."

The Viscount raised his eyebrows. "What did my brother want?"

"Nothing," she said. "He just talked in a friendly way."

"Do you think he had any idea you were coming here to meet me?"

"I can't imagine why he should," she said, looking up into his handsome face wistfully. "Would you care very much if he did know?"

"I'd be proud!" George said with a sudden smile, taking her in his arms again. "I've an idea Charles has his eye on you as well. It's no good! You're spoken for!"

"Am I, truly?" she asked.

"Truly," he said. And, his arm around her, he took her into the bedroom of the cottage.

She offered no resistance. She had thought it over and decided they would have this final beautiful moment before she told him of what she'd heard. She trembled as he undid her clothing with a skill born of familiarity. He had also become familiar with her lovely body and the areas of eroticism which most excited her.

In a few moments their naked bodies united in the expression of their passion which had become so precious to them. Fanny was brazen in her enjoyment of the coupling. When it was over they lay together on the narrow bed delightfully exhausted. George slept for a little.

When he wakened she had dressed and was sitting on the bed beside him. He frowned. "Is it so late? Must you go so soon?"

"I do have to leave," she said. "And there is something to discuss before I go."

The handsome Viscount leaned on an elbow, a single sheet covering his slender body. "What is wrong, Fanny? Something! I can tell."

Then she told him. She finished with, "Have you been deceiving me all along? Have you always known this marriage was to happen?"

He sat up and seized her by the arms. "How can you believe that of me, Fanny? You know it is only you I love!"

"You were attentive to Virginia at the party yesterday."

He made a weary gesture. "Only to please my father!"

"Perhaps you will also marry her to please him," she suggested.

"Never!" he said.

She looked at him directly. "You have never told him about me?"

He hesitated. "No."

"Do you intend to?"

"Yes," he exclaimed, his handsome face showing his unhappiness. "I agree I have put it off too long, and I give you my word that I shall face him with it and have it settled."

Quietly, she said, "I have enjoyed this as much as you have, George. You do not have to marry me because I have given myself to you. I do not hold you to any bargain!"

"You do not need it," he said. "I have never felt for Virginia what I feel for you. To marry her would be a sham! I want no part of it!"

She could not doubt his sincerity and she threw her arms about him. Their embrace was long and deeply felt. And when she left him she once again hoped they might share some sort of future together.

This hope was bolstered by the fact that in the weeks following there was no announcement of a marriage between Virginia and the Viscount. She continued to meet George secretly and they kept their usual midnight trysts in her bedroom. When she asked him if he had spoken to his father, he told her he had managed to postpone the wedding with Virginia on the grounds that he loved another. As yet he had not revealed that the woman he loved was Fanny.

"My father is old and quick-tempered," George warned her. "I must do this gradually. I understand him. It is the only way."

She accepted this as reasonable. The shock of learning that his son wished to marry a servant in his house would be difficult for the proud old man.

Then something happened which terrified her. The Reverend Kenneth Palmer continued to divide his time between his duties at the cathedral and living in the old mansion with his family. He moved about the great house like a grim raven in his dark clerical garb and white collar. His hawk-like face was always set in a grim expression and often as he talked with anyone he fingered the golden cross he wore around his neck as if to ward off evil, worldly spirits.

Fanny felt he reserved some of his most formidable frowns for her. Yet she was startled when he came upon her suddenly in one of the shadowed upper corridors as she was coming from doing up a bedroom. The ascetic young cleric seized her by the arm and spoke to her in a low voice.

"You are a daughter of wickedness!" he hissed at her.

Tensely, she tried to draw away from him. "What do you mean, sir?"

"Don't try your evil wiles on me, girl!" he snapped. "I know you for the harlot you are!"

"Sir!" she reproved him.

"Do not deny it," he said, his eyes shining fanatically, his face distorted with hatred. "You are the sort which brought about the fall of Sodom and Gomorrah!"

"You are raving!" she protested.

"No!" he cried. "I know whereof I speak! I have seen my brother coming from your room after sinning there with you! Not once but several times!"

"You sneaking creature!"

"Do not scorn me! I am a servant of the Lord!" he went on wildly. "And you are a scarlet woman!"

"I will not hear you any longer! Let me go!" she sobbed.

"You will hear me and then I shall release you," the Reverend Kenneth said in the same low, hissing voice. "I have not spoken of this to my father or anyone else. Not for your sake or for my brother! George is a wicked person! I despise him! But I must think of my father!"

"You will be sorry when I tell George," she warned him.

"Yes," he said. "Tell George! Tell him your bedding with him must end, else I will reveal all! You will be sent out into the streets where you belong and George will be disgraced before my father!"

With this warning he gave her a final baleful look and went on down the stairs. She stayed in the sanctuary of the dark corridor until she had recovered her composure. Even then she was dreadfully worried. She was to meet George in the garden that night and she could barely endure the hours before she could tell him what had happened and warn him of the intentions of the Reverend Kenneth.

Once again there was moonlight, but Fanny was in no mood to enjoy it. All she could think of was contacting George and telling him of the ugly encounter with his fanatical brother. She fairly raced along the gravel path until she came to the arch of roses. George was waiting in the shadows as usual.

She let him take her in his arms and kiss her. Then she hastily told him, ending with, "I think you should talk to your father before he does."

"I agree," George said grimly.

"Your brother hates us both," she warned him. "He will not hesitate to harm us!"

"Kenneth takes his priestly vows too seriously," the young Viscount said with disgust. "Why does he try to interfere with our lives when he knows so little of the problems we face?"

"He considers himself the Lord's servant."

"A poor errand boy for the Almighty, I fear," he said. "Kenneth has always been jealous of me. He is a strange, twisted person. I regret he entered the Church. He will do it little credit."

Fanny said, "If he goes to your father it will make your task of telling him you plan to marry me doubly hard."

"I have been too long getting around to a frank discussion with my father," George admitted.

"Let us pray it is not too late now."

"I think not," George said. "Tomorrow morning will find me before my father, declaring my intentions regarding you." He again took her in his arms and they remained in a long, ardent embrace.

Fanny felt afterwards it must have been the intensity of their emotions which plunged them into a world of their own removed from anything beyond themselves. She heard nothing as they embraced until angry words cut through the stillness of the night air.

"So I have found you!" It was the old Marquis come upon them.

George released her quickly and took a step forward to confront his father. In a quiet yet steady voice, he said, "I am sorry you discovered us this way, sir!"

The Marquis angrily drummed his walking stick on the gravel. "From all I hear, I could have done worse! Found you in bed with this strumpet!"

"Do not say such things, father!" George cried.

"I shall speak the truth," the Marquis declared in his hoarse voice, thick with anger now.

"I know that Kenneth has gone to you with his tales," George said desperately.

"It is good someone warned me," his father replied.

Fanny stood in the background feeling that her silence was the most valuable contribution she could make at this moment. George continued to stand between her and his father.

George said, "It is all my fault, sir. I should have told you about this earlier!"

"Told me you were sleeping with one of our maids! I vow you have more brazen nerve than I've given you credit for!" the old man cried.

"Listen to me," George pleaded. "It is true Fanny and I are in love, and have been lovers, for that matter. But that is because she is the only woman in the world for me, the only one I shall ever marry!"

The Marquis leaned on his cane and stared at his son in blank astonishment. Then he said, "I swear this is worse than a vulgar business of bedding! You have lost your senses as well! You are daft!"

George moved to Fanny and placed his arm about her. "I love Fanny, father. And I ask your permission to marry her! I told you I did not want to marry Virginia because there was someone else!"

"Daft!" the old man muttered in a stunned fashion.

"I mean this, father," George said.

The Marquis stared at him. "Gad, I believe you do!" Then he addressed himself to her. "Young woman, what have you to say for yourself?"

"There is little I can say except that I love George," she told him.

"So you love George!" the Marquis repeated her words with grim irony. "That is fine news, fine news, indeed!"

George said, "I beg you to make the best of this, father!"

"The best?" the old man sputtered. "There is no best!" And then he turned to her again. "Young woman, may I ask you to retire to the house. Wait for us there in the reception hall. I wish a few words in private with my son."

George protested, "You do not have to go, Fanny. All that we have to say can be said in front of you!"

But Fanny shook her head. "No! Your father is right. You must be free to discuss the situation without my being here."

The Marquis said, "Thank you for your good sense, girl."

She told George, "I shall be waiting inside as your father asked. I beg that you do not have harsh words between you on my account."

With that she hurried away leaving the two men standing there facing each other in the moonlit garden. Nothing was said within her hearing as she made her way back along the gravel walk. She was still stunned by what had happened, though she had feared something like it for a long while. At least the whole sorry business was now in the open and George had been noble when he had finally faced his father. What would happen next?

The old house seemed strangely quiet as she entered it and began to pace restlessly in the reception hall. The Marquis had requested that she wait there and he was not only her employer but also her prospective father-in-law! The enormity of this suddenly hit her. Was it possible that she, a servant in the house, could all at once become wife to the man who would one day inherit the title and own it all?

She knew what Cousin Lily would say. The stout woman would scold her for being so bold as to hope for such a match! Marsden would simply stare at her and mumble about the strange changes in servants. As for Peg and the other maids, they would consider her improving her station in the world, but at the same time they would think she had been a traitor to them. She had pretended to enjoy being their equal when all the while she had aspired to higher things!

Her pretty face was shadowed as she halted in her pacing to stare at the portrait of some ancestor of the Marquis whose bewigged likeness hung on one wall of the reception hall. What was wrong with trying to get ahead? Nothing, except her ambition had never been to make a fine marriage and rise socially; she had wanted to become a popular actress in the theatre. So, in a way, she was actually being untrue to herself. She sighed and wished that George would come. He had a way of talking and making things seem right.

The sound of the front door opening made her turn and look for George to appear. But it was the old Marquis who entered, not the young Viscount. He was leaning more heavily than ever on his cane and she thought he appeared older than ever before. He closed the door and then limped over to her.

She asked, "Where is George?"

"He's run off somewhere," the Marquis said in a grim tone. "We had a quarrel and he just ran off!"

"Ran off," she echoed him, not knowing what to think.

The Marquis gazed at her with his sharp old eyes. He said, "I'm sorry. He undoubtedly will be back when his temper settles. I understand your disappointment."

"I hoped he would return with something to tell me," she said.

The old man sighed. "I understand." Then he gave a second sigh and told her. "I doubt if he'll return in a hurry. If I know him, he's gone to the stables to have a horse saddled and he'll ride off to the village tavern and drink for a while."

"I see," she said.

"In the meantime, I think we should talk," the Marquis said. "Come with me to my study."

The old man limped down the wide corridor to the oak-panelled room and she followed him with a heavy heart. She was worried about George and about the situation in which she found herself. She followed the Marquis into the study where a lighted lamp burned on his desk. He waved her to the leather easy chair in which she had sat that other time when Prince Aran had made her an offer to go to India. Perhaps she should have accepted the brown-skinned man's proposal, however dubious. At least she would have avoided this pain and embarrassment!

The Marquis sat heavily in the chair behind his desk and stared at her in silence for a long moment. Then in his hoarse voice, he said, "George ran off just now because I refused to consider his marrying you. Does that surprise you?"

She sat very still. "No," she said in a small voice.

"I expect not, you're sensible enough," the Marquis went on. "Of course George told me he'd marry you in any event. And when he returns that is what he will tell you. There can be no question that he cares for you."

"And *that* you can do nothing about, sir," she said in a tone of bitterness.

The Marquis nodded his head. "You are quite right! I cannot change that. I wish I could."

"And I truly care for him," Fanny said.

"I haven't a doubt of it," the gray-haired old man said. "Not a doubt!"

"I do blame him for not telling you sooner," she said. "I urged him to do so."

The Marquis raised his eyebrows. "I'm glad to hear that. I approve of frankness. A most important quality. That is the great thing about Her Most Gracious Majesty, Victoria; she is an utterly frank woman."

"I would not know, sir," she said.

"That is just it," the Marquis sighed. "There are so many things of which you are unaware. Shall I tell you what will happen if George defies me to marry you? I think you should know."

"If that is what you think," she said, waiting to hear what he would say.

"Very well," the Marquis said. "My first choice would be to disinherit George and have the title go to my second son. But I cannot do that. Kenneth has chosen to be a priest, he is a strange young man whom I cannot understand, unfit to one day become Marquis. Charles would do. But he is my third son and the last in line for the title. So while I will turn my back on George, he will remain my heir."

"Because you have no choice."

"Exactly," the old man said. "The family will be ruined. I will have to resign my position at Court as advisor to Her Majesty. There must be no taint of scandal near the throne."

"Would a marriage between George and me be so scandalous?"

"Yes," the Marquis said firmly. "Not because you might not make a suitable wife for him. I think you would. But a man of title cannot marry a servant in his household without becoming a sensation in the yellow press! Now, if you left us, made a good marriage with some rich man, later to be widowed…then my son might woo you with only a small sensation as the result. But to raise you from maid to Viscountess will cause a furore!"

Fanny listened, realizing he was putting all her own fears into words, fears she'd fought against because of her love for George. But George was also the Viscount Palmer and nothing would change that.

Quietly, she asked, "You think I will harm George if I marry him?"

The old man eyed her sadly, "You will ruin him."

"You believe that?" she asked tensely.

"He will have no future. Nor will you. You are both bound to be barred from society. You will live here in this great house as privileged prisoners. It will be dreadful for him but infinitely worse for you. For, as time passes, you will know that you were the cause of it all."

Tears blurred her vision so the lined face of the Marquis seemed more like that of an ancient eagle than ever. In a choked voice, she said, "Could that be why he delayed so long in going to you? Because he knew, that ultimately, our marriage was not practical?"

"I think that may well have had a great deal to do with it," the Marquis agreed. "George is not a coward nor a cheat. He proved that tonight by his defence of you. And he will marry you for all I have warned him against it."

Fanny sprang to her feet. With all the dignity she could muster, she said, "You have made it clear to me, sir. I see now that George and I were lost in a romantic dream! You need not worry. There will be no marriage between us!"

"I pray there won't be," the Marquis said lifting himself up and leaning on his cane again. "But I think George is too deeply committed. He will insist on marrying you!"

She moved towards the door. "This time I will have the final say," she told the old man. And with that she ran out sobbing.

Writing her curt farewell note to George and packing was a nightmare she only barely remembered. In her note she told him she'd realized her ambition to become an actress was more important to her than marriage. It was the only thing she could think of that seemed reasonable. She begged him not to come looking for her as her plans were made. She would never see him again.

Her innate strength of character helped her now. Once she had made up her mind that her love for George would condemn him to a miserable existence she kept firm in her decision to run away. It was the only answer. And a test of her love! She could not believe she would go through such a painful experience again.

She left another note for Cousin Lily thanking her for her kindness. And then she crept out the kitchen door and quickly made her way along the gravel path to the road leading to the village. She began to walk swiftly along this road and as she tired, her pace slackened a little. Then she heard the sound of a horseman approaching from the village. She peered ahead and was able to make out the figure of a man on horseback.

It was bound to be George! In a panic she rushed to the shelter of some tall trees at the side of the road and stood there completely motionless until George rode by on his way back to the house expecting to greet her. She made sure he was a good distance away before she resumed her journey to the village.

The night was still young and though the road was lonely and she'd heard spine-chilling stories of thieves and murderers preying on travellers like herself, she kept on. She tried to put such thoughts out of her mind. Eventually the lights of the village tavern showed ahead.

The tavern on the outskirts of the village was the place where the stagecoaches stopped on their way into London, only ten miles distant. She had some money tied in a handkerchief and hung around her neck under her dress. It wasn't much but it would see her through a few days at least, until she was able to find some work in the great city.

She hoped that a late stagecoach might be still passing through on its way to London. But when she reached the inn yard she saw that it was empty except for a wagon with a single horse between its shafts. She was debating venturing inside and enquiring about transportation when a fat old man in top hat and long coat came out of the tavern.

She approached him, asking, "Has the last stage left for London?"

"A full hour ago," the fat man said, around a large gray mustache. "Why do you ask?"

"I'm looking for transportation to London tonight," she said. "I have an aunt who is very ill and needs me."

"Bless my soul!" the fat man said in a hearty voice. "Well, it so happens I'm leaving now to drive to London. I can't make the same time as a stage and the journey won't be all that comfortable but it will cost you nothing!"

Fanny felt relief and gratitude. "You are most kind, sir. And I trust you will not think me a bold hussy if I accept your offer! My aunt is so desperately ill and time is so precious!"

The fat man looked sympathetic. The brandy which she smelled on his breath must have put him in a mellow mood. He said, "You need have no fears of me, miss. I'm a family man!"

"I could tell that at a glance," she said. "You look most respectable, air."

"And I am respectable," he said, pointing to the wagon. "You will see my name inscribed on my wagon, Thomas Trimble, Silent Sewing Machines. I have my main shop in London and a few days a week I travel in the nearby villages to offer my wares."

"It sounds like a fine business," she said.

"It is," the fat man agreed. "Twenty-one shillings pays for it all. Finest sewing machine on the market if I do say so. Unsolicited testimonials by the dozen!"

"I shall be honored to travel with you," she said.

"Then come along! Mustn't lose time," the fat man said, taking her valise and leading her over to the wagon. "My missus waits up for me these nights and if I'm very late she always worries!"

Fanny was anxious to be on her way, fearful that George might find her gone and come after her in spite of her note. He would be bound to come to the tavern first. So she was glad when the fat man clambered up onto the seat beside her, gave the reins a flip and started off on their way to London.

A small lantern swinging from the side of the seat provided their only light. The wagon was a good one and the horse trotted along at a brisk pace. Fanny could feel the great city gradually getting nearer. They passed other wagons and a few coaches coming out of the city. There were good natured shouts exchanged between the drivers on the dusty road as the vehicles passed.

She found herself caught up in the adventure of it all. And Thomas Trimble proved an entertaining companion. He had a great repertoire of anecdotes. He told her, "There's an Irishman lives in the attic of my building. Something of a drinker! The barman asked him where he lived and he said, 'Sure, if the building were turned topsy-turvy, I'd be livin' on the ground floor!' A grand old reprobate, is that Irishman!" The fat stomach of Thomas Trimble wobbled with laughter.

She said, "You must meet many people making the rounds with your sewing machines. You must be a good judge of character."

The fat man nodded as they drove along in the darkness. "You've hit the nail on the head! I never judge people on their appearance alone. A coat out at the elbow may be buttoned over a generous heart!"

"That is so true," she agreed.

"Nor do I think a pretty face is all that important, though I must say you're the prettiest lass I've had in my company in many a day!"

"Thank you," Fanny said.

"A handsome woman pleases the eye," Thomas Trimble said. "But a good woman pleases the heart! The one's a jewel, but I say the other is a treasure!"

"How wise you are," she flattered him.

The fat man looked pleased. "I've lived a good while and I've kept my eyes and ears open often when my mouth is shut. A good rule to follow and one that leads to wisdom!"

The conversation continued along these lines until they entered the outskirts of the city. The road gave way to cobblestoned streets and there were buildings on every side. It was now late and the city was mostly asleep. Even at this hour there were some carriages and wagons in the streets and a few furtive figures on the sidewalks.

A heavy fog had met them a few miles from the city and now that they were in London it had thickened to a dense, yellow mist. This made everything seem weird. It had also become cold and Fanny clutched her cloak about her.

"My place is in Stark Street," Thomas Trimble told her. "We're close to there now. Where does your aunt live?"

"Very near here," she said. "If you'll let me off at the next gas light."

"Is that a fact," the fat man said. "I'm glad she's near. I'd like to take you to the door but my missus is waiting."

"I understand," she said. "The next gas lamp will do well. I can quickly walk to her home from that corner."

Thomas Trimble halted his wagon at the gas lamp and saw her safely to the sidewalk. The fat man urged her, "Walk fast, my dear. The streets of London are filled with dangerous characters at this hour." Then he drove on and left her.

She really had no clear idea where she was except that she was in an area of most respectable homes. She had never been in London before and as she groped her way in the fog she heard a carriage coming up the cobblestone street behind her.

•••

Now she stared into the dying embers of the fire in the tomb in which she'd found refuge with Moll and Silas Hodder and the two old women, who were still asleep, as she'd told the others her story.

She said, "It was then I encountered those two killers and ran here to this graveyard to hide! And you were kind enough to give me refuge!"

Chapter Four

Fanny was ready to believe that London was a city constantly wreathed in fog. The next morning the same heavy, yellow mist gave everything a ghostly air. She, along with the four other vagrants, cautiously emerged from the tomb and made their way out of the tiny graveyard to the street. Had the verger arrived early enough to witness their leaving he would have been bound to consider it a mass resurrection!

On reaching the street the two old women lurched off by themselves, shawls over their heads. Silas Hodder watched them go with a resigned expression on his gaunt face. "We only see them at night," he said. "Around dusk they'll come back to the tomb again. What they do in the meanwhile I can't guess!"

Moll gave a little laugh. "And perhaps it's best not to try! One thing is certain, they always raise the price of a bottle of gin!"

"That they do," the tall man in the black top hat and suit agreed. He gave Fanny a smile. "Now we shall go and have our breakfast. And perhaps we can think of some employment for you."

Thank you," Fanny said. "I'm quite prepared to buy my own breakfast and treat the two of you, as well. I have almost two pounds saved."

"Keep it, my dear girl," Silas Hodder warned her. "You will have sore need of it to exist in London, especially if we can't think of some gainful work for you."

"Mr. Hodder has a first class place for us to eat and it's all paid for," Moll told her with a smile on her pinched face. The girl looked more attractive by day but her clothes were terribly shabby.

Silas Hodder showed a smile on his skull-face framed by shoulder-length gray hair. He said, "I guarantee you a breakfast as fine as you'll find anywhere in London! Even the toffs can't do better!"

The three of them made their way along a series of narrow streets in the thick fog. The streets were filled with people now and Fanny was stunned at seeing so many people in such a hurry.

"Is the city as busy as this every day?" she asked.

"Every day and a good part of the night," Moll assured her. "Greatest city in the world!"

"Give pause!" Silas Hodder told the girl. "You have not seen Paris. As a *boulevardier* of some experience I can vouch for the many offerings of that city!"

"Wouldn't hold a candle to London, I'm sure," Moll said firmly. "Those Frenchies could never match us!"

They waited for a dray to rumble by and then hurried across a narrow street to find themselves staring at a sign, "Branscomb the Baker." Silas Hodder led them in a side door which led to the rear of the premises. They entered the busy kitchen and sat at a plain wooden table removed from the hurly-burly of the oven area. Two fat men and six or seven boys kept filling the great ovens with items to be baked and taking the savory-smelling food cooked out.

An elderly woman in apron and dustcap brought them plates with bread and cheese, along with a large pot of tea. The dried-up face of the old woman broke into a tremulous smile as she said, "Right on time, Mr. Hodder! You are a gent who keeps on a schedule."

"Early training, my dear," Silas Hodder said with pride. "I have a guest this morning, a Miss Fanny Hastings, lately come to London."

"Pleased to know you, miss," the thin woman greeted her. "You're welcome! Eat hearty!"

The cheese, bread and tea were fresh and Fanny wolfed her share down. The old woman came with another half loaf of bread for them and an extra chunk of cheese. Silas Hodder carefully divided it among them.

Fanny asked him, "Do you know the owner, since he is so generous with you?"

"Know him, my girl! I may say I'm employed by him," Silas Hodder said. "Between my engagements at the various pubs I tread the streets for two hours in the morning and two hours in the afternoon bearing the yoke of yonder sign upon my shoulders!"

Fanny glanced up the wall where he'd pointed and for the first time saw a sandwich-board sign folded and leaning there. It was painted white and in large red letters announced, "Branscomb's is Best! Fine Bakery 10 A Canon Street."

Moll smiled at her across the plank table. "In exchange for being a sandwich-board man, Silas is given all he can eat and free meals for any friends he brings along. I come with him regular and so can you."

Silas waved an expansive hand. "All paid for!"

"That's very good," Fanny agreed. "So right off you both have free bed and board!"

Moll turned up her nose at the mention of this. "I'm not saying I enjoy sleeping in a graveyard but in winter the nights are cold and Silas manages to keep our tomb nice and warm."

"Nothing wrong with graveyards as resting places," the gaunt-faced Silas said. "For some, it's eternal rest; for us it is a more pleasant temporary arrangement."

"Breaking us in for what's to come!" The sharp Moll burst into laughter at her own sally.

Silas remonstrated with her, raising a protesting hand. "No unseemly humor, girl. Be grateful. Now let us put our minds to what our new found friend, Fanny, can do to earn a living."

"She could try my game," Moll said. "I can teach her the tricks!"

Fanny at once said, "Thank you, Moll. But I haven't the nerve for it. I could never carry it off!"

Moll grinned. "Not much to it. A bit of sniffling and a mention of the Dear Departed. Then a sad smile for the babe to come. By that time they're thrusting a sovereign or two in your palm and pushing you out the door."

Silas Hodder said, "I'm sure Fanny is seeking something a trifle more…respectable."

"I would like to make my way on the stage," Fanny said. "My late father was an actor and I have always wanted to follow in his footsteps."

"The stage," Silas Hodder repeated. "Now let me see. I must know someone connected with the theatre."

"All those blokes you meet in the taverns are well connected," Moll agreed. "At least one of them must have a friend on the stage."

Silas Hodder's skull-like countenance suddenly brightened. He thumped a fist in the palm of his hand and exclaimed, "I've got it! The very thing! You're as good as hired!"

Fanny couldn't believe her good fortune. It made her almost forget her pain at leaving Brenmoor and George. She exclaimed, "You mean you can find me a post in the theatre?"

Silas nodded. "I can! It is not actually in a regular theatre but in the entertainment profession! I can assure you of that! The owner of the establishment is an old friend of mine, Mr. Gilbert Tingley."

Moll showed amazement. "Of course! I never thought of him! The very man." And to Fanny, she said, "Gilbert Tingley's Emporium of Wonder is the finest thing of its kind in London!"

Fanny said, "Emporium of Wonder? What sort of show is it?"

"A compendium of the bizarre and the unusual," Silas Hodder said grandly. "In short, my girl, a collection of mechanical and human freaks!"

"Freaks!" Fanny said in dismay.

Moll nodded happily. "You ought to see the fat woman! A mortal sight! Weighs close to four hundred pounds, they say!"

Silas Hodder said, "Tingley is a model employer. He pays well, considering he charges only a penny for a walk through his place, and the people in his show live in rooms upstairs, very good rooms, and eat in a community dining hall in the basement. Three wholesome meals a day!"

"It's a kind offer," she said. "But even if Mr. Tingley would have me it isn't exactly what I'm looking for. I'd like to try to find something in a regular theatre."

Silas Hodder and Moll exchanged looks. Then the gaunt man told her, "Fanny, let me impress upon you that everyone in London is not as kind as I am. This is a hard city for a young girl. And for a young female looking for employment in the theatre the risks are monstrous!"

Moll agreed soberly. "What Silas is saying is true. I near wound up in a house of shame when I came here. I would have but for him."

Silas continued, "My advice would be to take a job with Mr. Tingley if he can find a place for you. Get to know London, and in your free time look for this stage employment you are seeking, with the knowledge you have both work and friends behind you."

Fanny listened and realized the truth of what he was telling her. If she took a job in the freak show, doing goodness knows what, she would have time to learn something of London. She would also make some contacts of at least a semi-theatrical nature. As it was, she would exhaust her small savings in a short time while she looked for work. And as Moll pointed out, she might end up in some desperate plight.

With a small smile for Silas, she said, "You are most kind. And I will accept your help in this."

"You'll not regret it," the gaunt man promised. "The Emporium of Wonders is closed in the mornings, so you would have all your mornings to study the city and look for better work."

Moll said, "You're a beauty and if you have any talent you'll get on the stage one day! You talk so nice!"

Silas rose from the table. "I must go on my rounds with the sign. Moll will stay with you and you can meet me outside the Duke's Tavern at sharp two this afternoon!"

Moll looked delighted as she confided to Fanny, "I'll take the morning off and show you some of the shops the toffs patronize!"

Fanny said, "I'd like to see the Houses of Parliament and St. Paul's Cathedral."

"I'll show you them, too," Moll promised.

And she did. The morning went by swiftly. Fanny had her first experience of using the crowded, rough-riding horse cars. But Moll did know her way around the city and they covered a great deal of ground. They had a lunch in a small restaurant which served good food in plain fashion and in humble quarters. It was a far cry from the grandeur of the tables at Brenmoor but Fanny saw it as a different and exciting existence.

At two o'clock they met Silas Hodder outside the plush Duke's Tavern. He was in a good mood and confided to them, "I have done well this noon. My gentleman friends of better days were most generous. You've brought me luck, Fanny. Now let us see what I can do for you."

They left Molly to begin her own day's work and walked along a series of mean streets until they came to a short side-street which had a dead end. Here over a grubby three-storey building was a painted canvas sign, "Emporium of Wonders—Freaks of the World! Open daily except Sunday from 2 p.m. until 9 p.m."

Silas Hodder knew the building and took her to a door in an alley which was unlocked. He led her up a dingy flight of stairs and knocked on a battered wooden door which bore a small white board on which was printed in plain black letters, "Gilbert Tingley, Manager." Silas gave her a knowing look and then knocked on the door.

A high-pitched voice cried out, "Don't bother me now! I'm doing my bills!"

Silas leaned close to the door and spoke loudly in reply. "It is Silas Hodder and I have news of advantage to you!"

A sound which might have been a groan came in answer to this statement. There was a shuffling noise and then the door was opened by a little man with a black mustache wearing a plaid vest and brown tweed trousers. He had a stoop and he peered out at them as if he were short-sighted.

A look of annoyance on his pinched face, Gilbert Tingley asked, "What is it you want to tell me, Silas?"

"What sort of hospitality is this? Are you not going to invite me and this charming young lady in, Gilbert?" Silas Hodder said in hearty fashion.

Appearing pained, the little man stood back for them to enter. "All right," he said peevishly. "I might as well put the bills aside since I don't have enough to pay them in any case."

Silas said, "May I present Fanny Hastings, a brilliant young actress from the provinces, temporarily at liberty. I have assured her that you are always on the lookout for talent."

Gilbert Tingley listened to this and then stared at her with his pale blue short-sighted eyes. He said, "You have a pretty face. What about experience?"

"I sing and dance a little," she said nervously.

"No good here," he said abruptly. "Have you ever been a freak?"

"What an absurd question to ask this lovely girl!" Silas Hodder declared.

The little man's Adam's apple bobbed above his hard collar and bright red cravat. He said, "Nothing absurd about it! Sit down, both of you! All Gilbert Tingley asks is a plain answer to a plain question! *Has this girl ever been a freak?*"

Fanny sat in the nearest chair and Silas chose one by the impresario's roll-top desk which was littered with papers, presumably bills. She said, "No, sir. Never!"

"Right!" The little man said. "Do you think you *could* be!"

"I should try very hard," Fanny promised.

"Proper spirit," the little man said, sitting at his desk. "I put it to you this way. Lodgings and board found and five shillings a fortnight! What do you say?"

Silas Hodder spoke up, "She says yes, of course. Not a generous offer, but then she is a beginner."

Fanny asked worriedly, "What sort of freak do you propose to make of me?"

Gilbert Tingley studied her with his weak eyes. "You are fortunate I happen to have a vacancy. We have just lost our mermaid. Ran off with a fish peddler! He kept coming to see her night after night! She seemed to fair fascinate him! I should have seen the danger and discouraged him from coming. But I didn't, and now we've lost a star attraction."

Silas said, "You are saved! Fanny will make a beautiful mermaid!"

Fanny was still dubious about the project. She wanted to know, "What sort of costume must I wear?"

Gilbert Tingley was all business. "A fishtail which fits about the hips and hides the lower portion of your body. Made by the top theatrical costurner in London. The scales are that real you have to see them to believe it! A most gorgeous tail! For the upper portion you wear a rose-tinted, tight-fitting vest to show your maidenly form to advantage!"

"But it is a modest costume, Mr. Tingley?" she said anxiously.

"Nothing is revealed, miss, but your two bare arms and your neck. The rest of your upper parts are outlined in a way to cause the male eye to stare and enjoy, and the lower portion is a work of art. You recline upon a platform painted bright blue to suggest the sea."

Silas Hodder gave her a look of encouragement. "It is a great opportunity, Fanny."

She felt it was much less than that but at least she would be safe and cared for in this place. She still hadn't recovered from the shock of being pursued by the ugly little dwarf and his equally unpleasant companion the previous night. She had seen them kill a man and she would never be safe from them if they caught up with her.

Another benefit of playing a mermaid occurred to her. It was entirely unlikely that George would look for her in a museum of freaks. It would be an ideal place for her to hide for a time.

She said, "I'll accept the post, Mr. Tingley."

"Excellent," he said. "I'll show you to your room and have our wardrobe mistress, who is also our housekeeper, fit you to the fishtail!"

So Fanny's future in London was launched. She thanked Silas Hodder profusely and he promised to return and see her when she made her first appearance that evening. He then left and Gilbert Tingley took her upstairs to a tiny cubicle of a room. But it was clean enough and Fanny was satisfied. The owner of the freak show left her to rest a little. But shortly after, a big, red-faced woman with the smell of gin on her breath arrived with the elegant fishtail.

"Have to be taken in a good bit," the big woman said, breathing heavily while she fixed pins in what appeared to Fanny a rather sensational costume.

"What about the upper part?" Fanny worried.

The big woman frowned as she went on with her pinning. "Do you have a blouse what fits you tight?"

She considered. "Yes. A white one. My best."

"Cut the sleeves off and wear it," the woman said. "Nothing here that would fit you."

"*Must* I cut the sleeves off?"

"No other way," the big woman told her flatly as she stood back to judge the fitting of the fishtail. "Mr. Tingley likes his mermaid to show a bit of flesh. The arms are safest, though a low cut bosom is good."

"I'm sure the blouse will be fine. It has a rather low neckline," Fanny said.

The big woman pulled the fishtail off and said, "Time for the noon meal. In the cellar. Community table. Give you a chance to meet the others."

Even before she reached the bottom of the dark stairway leading to the cellar she was able to smell a pleasant aroma of food and hear loud talking and laughing. When she stepped down into the big room with its long plank table and chairs all along it, she found herself faced by the strangest group of people she had ever met.

Looming in the forefront was the Fat Lady who smiled at her amiably, and next to her was a man so thin and doleful Fanny knew it had to be the Human Skeleton. Across from these two sat a black man with a shaved head and some kind of bone through his nose, undoubtedly the Wild Man from Borneo! Next to him sat a midget, perfectly formed and pleasant looking but not more than three feet tall. There were a lot of others at the table whom she could not identify at a glance but later found to be a Fire-eater, Tatooed Lady, Pincushion Man plus a Bat Lady with webbed hands!

Gilbert Tingley was seated at the head of the table like a proud father to his collection of freaks. He saw Fanny and came down the room to greet her. He seated her in a place of honor on his right, while the webbed-handed Bat Lady, who appeared to be his lady friend by their conversation, sat on his left.

The little man rose and with a twitch of his mustache said, "Important announcement! Beginning this evening, Miss Fanny Hastings, an actress of impressive experience despite her youth, will appear with us as the Mermaid Lady!"

There were cries of approval and a round of applause. Fanny felt touched that they had received her so kindly and smiled her thanks, blushing delightfully all the while.

The beef which was served was delicious, as was the rest of the meal. The kitchen was at one end of the big cellar which made the serving of meals easy. Nor was drink excluded as Mr. Tingley saw that a mug of ale was placed by every plate. Fanny was slow in drinking hers.

"Drink up!" her new employer urged her. "A small bounty which I offer my people."

"You are too generous," she told him.

The little man shook his head. "Not at all! Gilbert Tingley has a large heart! I would do more if conditions allowed it!"

The Bat Lady, whose features showed signs of good looks long faded, offered a simpering smile and assured Fanny, "You will find Mr. Tingley a joy to work for. I would retire if he gave up the Emporium."

"Thank you, my dear," Gilbert Tingley said fondly taking one of her webbed hands in his. It was obvious that his bad vision allowed him to delude himself that he was courting a beauty.

"You speak very nicely, Miss Hastings," the Bat Lady said. "No doubt your training as an actress has given you a desirable accent."

"My father was also in the theatre," Fanny replied, for something to say.

Gilbert Tingley frowned. "The entertainment business is in a sorry state. The freak shows have been hurt by too many fakes. Offering two-headed babies made of clay in bottles filled with liquid and trying to pass them off as real. Disgusting! Gilbert Tingley offers only genuine freaks! But we suffer from the chicanery of others! Still I shall carry on, come what may!"

There were more cheers from the table at this and Fanny saw that they were a warm-hearted and emotional lot of people who regarded themselves as a family. She could not have imagined such a place or such people but here she was in the midst of them, about to become one of them. Life was indeed filled with strange twists!

• • •

That evening she made her appearance in the main room of the Emporium of Wonders. During a short interval when the show was closed to visitors she discreetly took her place on the wooden platform provided for her and with the assistance of the house-keeper-seamstress, pulled on the now snug-fitting fishtail. She had adapted her white blouse for the upper portion and was assured by the fat lady on the platform next to her, that she looked "ever so pretty!"

It took her a little while to become accustomed to the customers who sidled by gawking at her in various states of awe. Following Gilbert Tingley's instructions she preserved a demure dignity and gazed soulfully off above the heads of those who had paid their pennies to see the various freaks. She pretended not to hear the comments which varied from humorous to lascivious.

A brace of sailors from the Royal Navy came in and jocularly declared they were going to gather her up and carry her off to their ship. But a dignified Gilbert Tingley put in an appearance and they moved on with merely a parting wink for her.

Later in the evening Silas Hodder and Moll arrived and stood admiring her. "You look born to it," Moll enthused.

"You do have an air, Fanny," the gaunt man told her. "We're going to miss you in the tomb tonight."

"You livened things up with your story and all," Moll agreed.

"I shall miss your company," she told them. "You must come here when you can and keep in touch with me."

"Never fear," Silas Hodder assured her. "I'm going to continue to search for a more suitable position for one of your beauty and talents."

Even though she felt he was merely saying this to be kind to her, she appreciated his words. So began Fanny's sojourn with the freak show. In time it all began to seem quite normal to her.

She made particular friends of the Fat Woman and the Human Skeleton, who happened to be man and wife.

October came and the nights were cold. In the melancholy autumn weather her own thoughts took on a gray turn. Her mind often went back to Brenmoor and her life there. For just a short while she had been so supremely happy. But she sadly realized that the old Marquis had been right. The gentry would never have accepted a servant as wife to the Viscount. She and George had been living in a romantic rose-colored dream, tinted by their passion.

She often met Moll and together they made trips to every part of the city. She became very fond of the beggar girl who lived by her wits in spite of her dubious profession. Sometimes Silas Hodder would join them and they would have fish and chips at a favorite place of his.

Fanny's life was settling down to a comfortable routine, it seemed. But it was not to last. In the first week in November Gilbert introduced a new attraction called "The Mechanical Man". It was a metal man seated on a large box and when a switch was turned the man lifted up its hand and removed its blue top hat; the hat was then returned to place and the man's eyes moved in a most interesting fashion.

The new device was to be installed on the other side of the Fat Lady and she much resented it. Privately she told Fanny, "It's a fraud! And Tingley has always tried to avoid such fakery before! I'm shocked by this! You know, there's a dwarf hidden in the box at the bottom. It is he who manipulates the metal man with wires and levers! Mechanical Man, indeed!"

But Gilbert Tingley found the new addition attracted some extra business so he was enthusiastic about it. Fanny did not pay much attention to it until one evening after the museum closed she saw a new operator make his way out of the door at the back of the box. She thought she would faint. It was none other than the ugly little Snipe, whom she'd seen help his partner, Martin, in the murder of a man her first night in London!

She had come down from her platform and was standing with the Fat Woman. She pretended not to notice Snipe and hoped he wouldn't recognize her. But she saw in a moment that he had. He stared at her hard and then turned away, pretending indifference. She had not been deceived by this and began to worry about whether he was living in the house.

Gilbert Tingley came by on his closing rounds and nodded pleasantly to her and the Fat Woman. "Good evening, ladies," he said.

Fanny took advantage of the moment to step up to him and ask, "This new dwarf! The one operating the mechanical man! I'm sure I've seen him before. I believe him to be a criminal!"

Tingley's mustache twitched and his mild face showed surprise. "I think you must be mistaken, my dear. His name is Snipe and he seems very good at the task assigned him. Dwarfs are not easy to come by, you know!"

Upset, she said, "I saw him and another man attack a gentleman on his doorstep one night. I'm sure they killed him. Snipe knows I'm a witness and I fear he may do me harm. Is he going to live here?"

"Yes," Tingley said. "But I'm certain you must have made an error. Snipe is a mild little man. Reserved, but not a criminal type."

Fanny suspected he was arguing on the dwarf's behalf because he'd hired him cheaply and wanted to keep him on. She worried, "How can I protect myself?"

"I am always here," Gilbert Tingley told her. "If the chap bothers you, come to me. Keep the bolt closed on your bedroom door at night and think no more about him."

She tried to follow her employer's advice but it did not work well. Snipe was around a good deal and while he avoided her company he made her fearful. When Moll came by she told her about her problem.

Moll wrinkled her brow and said. "I'll ask Mister Hodder what he thinks you ought to do."

"I wish you would," Fanny said. Silas Hodder had not been around to see her often of late. She missed his good advice.

But before Silas put in an appearance two frightening things happened. One evening the other murderer, Martin, came to visit the freak show. He spent a long time standing staring up at her with a grim look on his coarse face. By the time he moved on she was a nervous wreck. She knew he had come at Snipe's request to check on her and make sure she was the one whom they had pursued to the cemetery that night.

His visit increased her terror. She was afraid to leave the emporium even on her free mornings. When Moll came over she stayed in her room and talked of her desperate situation.

Moll said, "Silas is trying to find you another post to get you away from here. In the meanwhile, he says you must stay away from the dwarf."

"No fear of my not doing that," Fanny exclaimed in disgust. "But will that Snipe leave me alone?"

"He's a wicked little creature and no mistake about it," Moll agreed. "I should say you'll have to depend on Gilbert Tingley."

The Fat Woman had a poor opinion of Tingley's prowess as a protector. When Fanny mentioned him in this role, the woman's many chins wobbled with annoyance. "Tingley spends most of his time boozing in the office. Don't count on him for anything!"

Fanny was astounded. "Is he a secret drinker?"

"It's no secret to us who know him well," the Fat Woman said indignantly. "That's where most of the show's profits goes. He spends more than he should on drink and then blames us for not drawing more crowds. I knew that Mechanical Man would bring trouble. But I didn't think anyone so nasty would come along as that new dwarf!"

Fanny's terror was becoming acute. She felt she must make some change whether Silas Hodder was able to find her another job or not. Twice she passed the little dwarf in the dark corridor on her floor and each time he had glared at her malevolently but said nothing. At mealtimes he sat at the end of the table a distance from her but she was always aware of his menacing presence.

Several nights later after she'd gone to bed Fanny fancied she heard someone try the latch of her bedroom door. But the bolt held securely though it gave her only a modest feeling of relief. In her unhappy plight it was inevitable that she thought of Brenmoor once again and of George. She began to fantasize that he would appear at the emporium some evening and take her away with him.

The climax came one stormy night in late November. Rain beat down in torrents and the wind howled at the single window of her room. She lay awake because of the storm and all her fears assailed her in the near darkness of the cramped area. She closed her eyes in an effort to make sleep come, trying to ignore the sounds of the angry storm.

Then her whole body tensed as she heard something else. A new and strange sound, as if someone were scraping at the window. She sat up in bed and stared across in time to see a figure dangling from a rope by her window. It was the dwarf, Snipe, who had let himself down from the roof on a rope and was now in the process of opening her window. He had clearly chosen this night so the sounds of the storm would cover his evil actions.

She screamed and leaped out of bed just as he managed to raise the sash. The rain beat in as his small feet sought the window ledge while he clung to the rope with one hand and flourished a knife in the other. The gleam of satisfaction on his monstrous face showed his intent.

Screaming again she looked around wildly for something to protect herself with. The only thing she saw was an ancient broom. She seized this and holding it by the straw end plunged the wooden handle into the dwarf's body as he stood on the window ledge. He uttered a cry of pain and fear and she quickly rammed him again with the broom. He lost his balance and grabbed wildly for the rope as she prodded him with all her strength yet another time.

Snipe was screaming now. He missed grasping the swaying rope and toppled back to vanish into the dark and rainy night. The rope swayed back and forth before her open window, mute evidence of the drama which had taken place. Without bothering to close the window despite the rain which was now flooding her room she ran to the door and unbolted it, heading to Gilbert Tingley's office for help!

As the Fat Lady had predicted, Tingley was not only asleep in his swivel chair but muddled by drink. The appearance of a hysterical and drenched Fanny soon brought him around. He went back to her room and saw that her story was not fantasy. Then he closed the window and he and a worker went out to see if Snipe had survived his fall.

Fanny was not surprised to learn that he hadn't. Snipe had most effectively broken his neck. The event caused a sensation among the freak show people and led to the retiring of the Mechanical Man as an attraction.

A police official who investigated the dwarf's death confirmed all her fears. The elderly man from Bow Street told her, "We've been looking for this little chap for months! He and a dangerous oaf named Martin are wanted for murder."

"I was there the night it happened," she said. "I saw them do it."

"That's likely why Snipe tried to get into your room and finish you off," the police official said sagely.

"I'm sure it was. And there's Martin still at large!"

The constable said, "I know. But I wouldn't worry about him too much. We feel he's left London. And if that's the truth you are relatively safe."

Fanny gave a small shudder. "I don't think I shall ever feel safe here again!"

And this was the truth. Memory of what had happened and the fact that Martin knew where to find her, tormented her. She spent all her working hours in the show fearful that any moment the ruffian would appear and try to murder her. She felt so strongly about this she sent Silas Hodder an urgent message by way of Moll.

Silas proved he was still her staunch friend. A few nights later he came to see her just as the show was closing and brought another gentleman with him. This neat man in his worn but well-cut brown frock coat and trousers was much in contrast to the shabby gaunt-featured Silas with his long, unruly gray hair.

Silas introduced him, "This is Mister Barnaby Samuels, of the Samuels Repertory Company. He is about to launch a theatrical tour and by a strange stroke of luck he is in need of a young woman to play principal parts."

Barnaby Samuels bowed to her. "Silas has praised you highly, Miss Hastings. I would like to hear you recite a little if you will."

Fanny, taken by surprise but nevertheless eager, said, "I shall do a poem which appeared in the daily paper a while ago, if I may. It is about a little match girl."

"Go ahead," the courteous actor-manager said. He had thinning, white hair and a noble face which had been refined by time. Still, he had the air of an actor and she was sure he'd once been a leading man and was now probably a competent character actor and director.

She nervously ran through the poem standing beside her platform on which her fish tail reposed. The Fat Lady and her thin husband had lingered to listen, and gave her loud applause.

"Now there is true talent," the Fat Lady said emotionally.

"Without a doubt!" her husband echoed.

Silas Hodder turned to the actor-manager in triumph and asked, "Well, what do you think?"

"She will do," Barnaby Samuels said in his superior way.

"*Do!*" Silas said with scorn. "She has the makings of a star!"

"Perhaps. It will take much time and training to learn that," Barnaby Samuels said. Addressing himself to her, he asked, "Can you leave here and join my company on Monday night? We are taking the evening run of the London-Liverpool Railway Train. We shall stop at our first destination, the town of Rigby. I can offer you good parts and my personal help, plus your expenses and a percentage of the company's profits in which all the cast share equally."

Fanny didn't need to think about it. "I can join you," she said. "I'm certain that will give Mr. Tingley time to find another mermaid."

As a matter of fact he didn't even have to look for a replacement. Moll had become so enchanted with the freak show people and their way of life that she decided to abandon begging and offered herself for Fanny's replacement. In no time at all she was being fitted into the gorgeous, scaly fishtail.

Fanny's parting from the company was an emotional one. Gilbert Tingley held a special dinner for the occasion on Sunday night. He even went so far as to substitute gin for the usual ale provided. As a result there was much weeping, a great many predictions of a bright future for her, and a touching speech delivered by Tingley himself.

Moll was at the table as a new member of the show and Silas Hodder sat at Fanny's side as an honored guest. Everyone heard the freak show owner through with polite silence and when he finally raised his glass and said, "A toast! To Fanny Hastings and her good fortune!" everyone lifted his glass and drank. Then they clustered around her, the women embracing her and the men shaking her hand. It was a truly gala event.

Fanny had been instructed to meet the actor-manager and his company at the railway station, where he had promised he would have a ticket for her. She was all excitement at the prospect of really starting her acting career. No longer would she have to sit silent and immobile on a platform wearing a fishtail while people stared and commented. Now she would be playing real characters on a stage!

Fanny had yet to learn that Barnaby Samuels, although basically honest, had been having a run of bad luck. Several times lately his companies had been stranded in remote villages. And on his return to London he had only barely managed to scrape enough cash together to get a company started on the road, but no extra capital to sustain it through bad weeks of business. That was why he was paying his company on a percentage instead of a salary basis and why he had been so quick to hire her, since she was inexperienced and could not ask for a guarantee.

Silas Hodder had no knowledge of the precarious state of the actor-manager's finances and thought he had provided his protegée with a great opportunity. He was so proud of what he'd done that he insisted on hiring a hackney cab, picking her up at the Emporium of Wonders and taking her to the railway station.

"You have become like a daughter to me," the strange old man confided as they rode through the busy streets to their destination.

She said, "I'm ever so grateful to you! I shall try to merit your confidence by becoming a great actress."

"I'm sure that you will," the happy Silas said.

"But I shall worry about you. You won't have Moll to look after you. Are you going to go on sleeping in that tomb?"

"I'm thinking of securing more normal quarters," Silas confided. "You remember the bakery where I take my meals?"

"Yes."

"They have a small storage room which is not always in use," he said. "I have reason to believe I may soon be able to sleep there. It is bound to be warm in even the coldest weather."

"That would be ideal!" Fanny said, brightening. "Now I will not be so troubled."

The gaunt-faced man closed his thin hand over hers. "You are a dear girl," he told her.

Fanny had only visited a railway station once before, when she and Moll had been making their tours of the city together. Now Silas Hodder guided her into the busy, noisy place. Travellers were moving about in every direction, asking for information, clutching their pieces of baggage and generally looking confused.

Solemn, whiskered officials in uniform called out loud (and generally incoherent) instructions. Silas guided her along the tile floor of the gas-lit, high-ceilinged main station to the gates. The open iron gates gave access to a number of wooden platforms and trains were coming and going on the rails between the platforms.

The belching, puffing engines squealed along the tracks and came to a halt with a screeching of brakes. Fanny and Silas Hodder proceeded to Platform Four where the attendant had directed them. And there, along with a number of other waiting travellers, she saw the actor-manager, Barnaby Samuels. He was wearing a gray suit with a gray cape and a matching top hat. He motioned for Fanny and Silas to come down the platform to him.

They started down just as they heard the sound of a train approaching behind them. Fanny glanced around to see an engine with a long row of carriages after it coming along that very track. She decided it must be the train they were waiting for. Before she could mention this to Silas walking beside her, she was horrified to see the ugly face and figure of the killer, Martin, loom up ready to shove her in the path of the oncoming train!

Chapter Five

Fanny cried out in terror as Martin bore down on her. She stumbled back as he seized her and prepared to hurl her on the tracks before the oncoming train. Then from out of nowhere someone came bursting between them. Fanny was thrown in the other direction by him and then the newcomer grappled wildly with Martin.

Silas placed an arm about her as the two men struggled on the edge of the platform. There were wild shouts from the onlookers as Martin lost his footing and with the scream of one doomed toppled back and fell under the wheels of the engine. The warning bell on the engine sounded loudly, there was a great puffing of steam and a screeching of brakes as the engineer battled to halt the train.

The young man who had rescued Fanny turned towards her with a face pale from this shattering experience. He was hatless, with brown curly hair, and like Barnaby Samuels wore a cape of some black material.

The young man came over to her anxiously and asked, "Are you all right, miss?"

She nodded and in a faint voice said, "My thanks to you!"

"You saved her life, young man," Silas Hodder told the sturdy youth. "That man was a murderer who intended to kill this girl."

Barnaby Samuels came up looking shaken, as he said, "It appears we are to know drama even before we reach a theatre. I thought for a minute I was going to lose you, Miss Hastings."

Silas Hodder said, "This young man saved the day!"

"He is also a member of my company," Barnaby Samuels said. "This is David Cornish, our leading man. David, Miss Fanny Hastings and Mister Silas Hodder."

This exchange of introductions was interrupted by the arrival of the railway guards, the police and a physician. The railway men busied themselves with directing the removal of the mangled body from the tracks. Fanny and the others turned their backs on the fearful scene.

The departure of the train was held up as a result of accident. The police talked with Fanny and David Cornish, and also questioned Silas Hodder. It was established in a short time that Martin had attacked Fanny and brought his fate on himself. When the guard signalled that the train was ready to leave, there were a flurry of goodbyes, and Fanny crowded on the train with the others as Silas Hodder, top hat in hand, waved farewell from the platform.

Fanny found herself sitting in a compartment with Barnaby Samuels, Miss Hilda Asquith, the character woman, and David Cornish. She still felt weak and ill from the dreadful experience she'd undergone.

A little while after the train was under way she glanced at the handsome young man at her side and told him, "I can't really begin to thank you."

His smile was radiant. "I'm glad I was there and saw what was happening."

"It was sheer Providence that sent you along," she said.

"I'd say it was my need to catch this train and join the company," he said.

She gave him an awed look. "Are you truly the leading man?"

"That's what I was hired for," David Cornish said. "I have been playing repertory leads for several years now."

"You must have started early?"

"My parents were both in the theatre. I have been on the stage since my parents first carried me on as a baby."

"So the theatre has been your life!"

"It has," David agreed. "I know no other. I lost my parents when I was fairly young. I've been on my own ever since."

"I'm also an orphan," she told him. "My father was an actor but my mother wasn't in the theatre."

"If you resemble her, she should have been," he said. "You are a lovely young woman."

"You flatter me," she said.

"I'm not the flattering type," he assured her. "I mean it."

"This is my first true acting work."

He nodded. "You're in good hands. Barnaby is a fine actor and director even if he has been sorely pressed for funds these last few years."

"Oh?" she said. "I didn't know."

David said in a low voice, "He stranded his last two companies but I took a chance on him because there was no other job to be had and because I believe if his luck turns we might have a long season."

The news that Barnaby Samuels was not financially sound worried her. But it was encouraging to know that he was competent as far as his theatrical ability went. She would also have to hope, like David Cornish, that this time the old man's luck would change.

She said, "This is going to be an adventure for me. My first time with a professional company!"

"What were you doing before this?" the young man asked.

She decided to ignore her period at Brenmoor and tell him only about her apprenticeship at the Emporium of Wonders. He listened to her account of being a mermaid with delighted interest as the train noisily made its way through the darkness. Opposite them both Barnaby Samuels and Hilda Asquith had drowsed off.

• • • •

Rigby turned out to be a small town in an industrial area, an ugly, gray, soot-ridden maze of narrow, mean streets with the tall smokestacks of factories rising above the roofs on every side. The company arrived there in darkness and were transported to the local theatrical lodging house by a wagon with seating provided on plank benches installed on each side. They sat facing each other, most of them befuddled with sleep and a few with drink, as a light shower played on the canvas covering over their heads. Another wagon was bringing their luggage.

Fanny found herself sharing a room with the elderly character woman, Hilda Asquith, each having a cot in an attic room more sparsely furnished than any of the servants' rooms at Brenmoor. That night she learned that the character woman snored loudly until she was in a deep sleep. It was something she managed to endure.

However unprepossessing Rigby might seem at first glance, it did have a lot of factory people starved for entertainment. This time Barnaby Samuels had chosen well in a place to begin his tour. The Opera House was shabby and ratridden, and in the wintery weather backstage was cold beyond enduring. But huge stoves in the rear of the auditorium managed to keep it fairly comfortable and so the place was filled for almost every performance.

The aged impresario of the small company knew the sort of fare the factory people liked and so he put on a series of blood-curdling melodramas in quick succession. They opened with "The Forged Will" in which Fanny enacted the small part of the hero's sister, with the hero played by David Cornish. Barnaby Samuels himself played the wicked lawyer and Hilda Asquith was the befuddled rich woman being tricked into making the wrong will.

This play was followed by "Lady Dudley's Secret," "The Squire of Fynwood," "Done to Death" and "In the Nick of Time." Fanny proved herself an apt student and under the coaching of the director, along with help from Hilda Asquith and David Cornish, she was soon promoted from small roles to more important ones.

Business continued so good at Rigby it was decided the company would remain there over the Christmas and New Year period, and perhaps throughout the winter. Each member of the company, including Fanny, was receiving a pound or more each week, and it seemed that the luck of Barnaby Samuels had finally turned for the better.

Then the leading woman left without notice to join her husband who was in another touring company. There was general dismay until Barnaby Samuels announced that Fanny would be the new leading lady. In "A Bitter Secret" she starred as the widow with an illegitimate child who hesitates to marry the wealthy man she loves for fear of disgracing him. It was a tear-producing drama in which all turned out well and Fanny for the first time felt at ease in a leading role.

After the first performance David Cornish, who had made love to her in his role of the wealthy man on the stage, embraced her in private and said, "You are truly an actress! Tonight you have proven it!"

She smiled up at him. "I have much to learn yet."

"The technique will come easily," he promised. "You have mastered the basics in a surprisingly short while."

And it was true. She was no longer an amateur. When she moved on to other companies, and eventually, as she hoped, to London, she would be an actress with some experience. She found memorizing long new parts and making them come to life on the stage an arduous task which kept her busy all her waking hours. The company had to change bills quickly to keep the interest of their patrons.

The bad food and cold rooms of the theatrical lodging house were accepted philosophically by the members of the company. Most of them had lived under similar conditions all their lives. Even David Cornish did not seem aware how inadequate their living standards were. The important thing was that the season had turned out successfully and in this period of many touring theatre companies there were a disastrously high rate of failures.

Because of the demands of her roles Fanny had small chance to worry about such things. Nor did she ever more than briefly think back to her days at Brenmoor and her romance with Viscount George. Memory of the handsome man always brought some pain but the pain became dulled as time went on.

There was also another factor in the fading of her memories of George. A romance of a different sort had developed between herself and her handsome leading man. It was more a staunch friendship than a passionate affair, since she and David were in the same line of work and had identical ambitions.

Yet, they were male and female, and since they made love every night on the stage it was not surprising that they should sooner or later find themselves in each other's arms in private. David Cornish, like herself, spoke and behaved like a member of the upper classes because of his stage training. His formal education had been limited but he was self-educated. In many ways he was as much a gentleman as Viscount George had been, and even more considerate and tender in his treatment of women.

Fanny found herself thinking of David more and more. And she noticed that he was paying extra attention to her. She was aware of the looks exchanged by other members of the company when they saw them together in their offstage time. Gossip among the players no doubt had them dubbed lovers, but this was not true…as yet.

Fanny had a burning desire to become a star. This desire had been only whetted by her minor success in Samuels' company. Her career on the stage was more important to her than anything else. David Cornish had the same ambition to progress in their profession. She had seen the forlorn state of two of the supporting players in the troupe who had five children living with grandparents.

They sent almost every penny of their meagre earnings home for their children's support. She saw clearly that she was not ready to be a wife or mother. Perhaps she would never marry.

When Christmas came they gave a special performance of Charles Dickens' fine Christmas play, "The Cricket On The Hearth." There were rumors among those in the know that Charles Dickens did not like the dramatization of his story but it made a good vehicle and the simple folk of Rigby were just as pleased with it as the audiences in London had been.

For the New Year, Barnaby Samuels devised a special musical entertainment with Charlie Fitzroy, the comedian of the company, doing comic songs and monologues. One of the other members owned a magic lantern and showed scenes of Europe while the soubrette played accompaniment on the pianforte. David Cornish and Fanny performed a series of skits, both comic and dramatic. The elderly Hilda Asquith sang in a high voice which cracked frequently, but the good-natured crowd applauded as if she'd been a prima donna at Covent Garden. Fanny ended the show by doing her song and dance routine. It was a side of her the audience hadn't seen before and she was the favorite of the evening.

The company had a feast of goose, pork, pudding and port on the stage following the show. Though they had to wear their overcoats and cloaks against the cold, it was a festive occasion.

Barnaby Samuels, with a smile on his classic, emaciated face, offered a toast: "To the New Year and a new season of success!" They all drank to this most happily and then trudged back through a light snowfall to their lodgings.

As they walked slowly along in the falling snow, their arms linked and their bodies close together, she and David talked about their good fortune and the prospects of the new year ahead. So young and happy were they that the dreary aspects of their lives did not bother them at all. The small salary, the poor lodgings, the inadequate theatre, and their provincial audience seemed to them merely steps on a ladder which would ultimately lead them to fine theatres in the West End and distinguished patrons!

Fanny was dreamy from the evening's work, having had her fill of goose and perhaps too much port. Looking up at David, she said, "I don't think I have ever been so happy before!"

"Nor I," he said.

"You saved my life the first time we met," she said. "And ever since you have made my existence more pleasant for me."

"I would be lost without you," he told her.

She smiled at him. "We shall keep on working and one day we shall star together in London in a fine play!"

"Perhaps!" David said. "London is a long way off. Many are lost along the way."

"We don't be," she said. "I feel it!"

He said, "I have some brandy in my room. I want you to stop by and drink to our always staying together." David was one of the few in the company with his own room. It was small, but he did not share it with anyone.

Something warned her that if she accepted his offer she might find herself facing a greater involvement than she desired. But she liked him and didn't want to hurt his feelings. David meant a great deal to her. So she decided to take the risk.

She went to his room with him. He lit the single candle on his dresser and then gently helped her off with her cloak. With a smile, he said, "Welcome to my area of the castle! It is rather chilly, but mine own!"

"You're doing a lot better than I am," she reminded him. "Old Hilda Asquith snores most mightily!"

He had produced a brandy bottle and glasses, and pouring the amber liquid into the glasses, gave her one. "To us!" he said. "And to our success in the new year.

"To us!" she said, her pretty face shining in the glow of the candle light.

They drank and he said, "I know how you can cure that snoring problem."

"How?"

"Move in with me!"

"David!"

"I mean *marry* me and move in with me," he said, placing his glass on the table, then taking her into his arms.

She gazed at him with affection. "Please, David!"

"I mean it," he said with intensity. "These last few weeks I've been tormented with my longing for you!"

"I care for you, David," she said softly. "I care so much! But marriage is not for us! We're just at the beginning. To be a wife and mother might be the end for me!"

"Others have married and succeeded on the stage!"

"A very few," she reminded him. "Look at Forester and his wife. They take miserable jobs and lead awful lives so they can pay the way for their children!"

"They don't seem to mind," David protested.

"We would," she said. "Or at least *I* would!"

"I don't care!" he said, pressing her close to him. "I'm willing to take any risk to have you as my own."

"Dear David!" she whispered.

He looked down into her face and in a troubled voice told her, "I think you have deceived me. Not told me all about your past. That you have loved someone else and are still in love with him!"

She shook her head. "No!" But she knew it was very close to being the truth.

"I believe you have kept many things from me! There is a man somewhere to whom you are still faithful!"

She smiled ruefully. "That sounds like a line from one of our plays."

"I mean it," he went on. "I long for you. I adore you! I'm willing to make any sacrifice for you, but you hold back. It must mean you do not care as much, or that you are in love with someone else."

Fanny stared at him in silence for a moment. Then quietly she said, "Do you want me to begin this new year by giving myself to you?"

"I can think of no gift that would make me happier," he replied.

Fanny sighed. She knew that she had made an initial error in coming to the room to drink with him. But she also knew she had weighed this risk and decided to take it. She had come to feel so close to this man, been given his friendship, and had responded so warmly that he had fallen passionately in love with her.

She had to face that in many ways she had encouraged his passion. She realized this. Still in his arms, she said gently, "I do care for you, David. And I will lie with you. But I will not allow you to enter me."

His handsome face showed a shadow. "What sort of loving will that be?"

"I cannot risk being with child at this point in my career," she said simply.

"You will not!"

"How all-knowing you are!" she mocked him. "Certainly *you* will not bear a baby! I can be surer of that than you can about my fate. Do you wish to make me miserable?"

"No," he said, unhappily. "You know I don't!"

"Then let me arrange this my way," she said. "I will show you my love and relieve your longing."

David stood there in confusion as she moved away from him and began to unbutton the front of her dress. She placed her things carefully on a chair and when she finally turned to him completely naked in the cold room he was still standing there dressed.

She shivered. "I'm cold! Take off your clothes and get into bed with me!"

"Fanny!" he said, a tremor in his voice as his eyes feasted on the supple young lines of her nude body.

Fanny moved to him and began to unbutton his shirt and help him undress. In the end he was feverishly discarding his clothes. Then he lifted her in his arms, lay her on the bed and joined her.

They stretched out together in close embrace. Their kisses were warm and moist. She could feel the firmness of his lithe body next to hers. Then his hands explored her breasts and lightly touched the rest of her body, finding her most itimate places. She felt her own passion rising and she was grateful to George for the diversity he'd shown in his lovemaking!

In David's arms she was able to remember those other moments. And now she would call on them to show her fondness for this man who in many ways was closer to her than George had ever been. She moved her lips down to his hairy chest and slowly down his body. She gently kissed his thighs and then made love to him in the way which George had taught her.

David's soft moaning ended in a sudden cry of ecstasy. She lifted herself up and pressed her long red hair against his chest again, kissing him over and over.

He lifted her up to the pillow and staring at her in wonder said, "You minx! And what did that do for you?"

"I manage well enough," she said. "Do you doubt that I care for you, David?"

"No," he said. "I doubt it no longer. But I also know I was right. That there *was* someone before me. Someone who taught you things you'd never have known otherwise. I want to hear about him! I demand it or I shall be forever jealous!"

She snuggled close to him. "All right," she said. "I shall tell you about George." And she did, explaining it was a first love entered into without thought and with much passion. She finished with, "I know now we had to part, if only so I could meet someone like you."

David kissed her with tenderness. He said, "You have told me all and I shall never again be jealous of you. I feel for the first time you're truly mine!"

And so on that cold New Year's night in that bleak room they entered on a new phase of their relationship. She felt they were as close as most husbands and wives, perhaps closer than many, and they both agreed that when they had achieved their ambitions they would marry. They worked together with a new interest and understanding and it seemed that this simple life they were leading would satisfy them for a long time to come. But some unexpected happenings were awaiting them in the wings.

In February the company moved on to Parkington, which did not receive them as well as Rigby. They remained there only three weeks and were in Wenside for early March. David and Fanny were starred in all the performances now, and they spent most of their offstage time together. It was accepted by all in the company that the two talented young people were lovers.

Wenside was as hospitable to Barnaby Samuels and his company as Rigby had been. Also, the theatrical lodging house was larger and better kept. Fanny now had her own room, which offered her two premiums; she did not have to suffer the character woman's snoring, and David could come to her bed for their love-making.

They were doing a new play, "The Wicked Countess," when Barnaby Samuels came down with gout. While he could still direct the plays, his left foot was too painful for him to take part onstage. It became imperative that another character man be hired. He sent an urgent appeal to London and by the next train an elderly actor named Ernest Hansom came to join the company.

From the first rehearsal Fanny found herself liking the rather pompous, dignified actor. He had iron-gray hair and a stern, brick-red face which showed few lines though he was well along in middle-age. Before he arrived, Barnaby Samuels quietly warned the company that Ernest Hansom had been a leading West End actor who had come to bad times through bouts of drunkenness.

The actor-manager had explained, "He is one of those men who can remain sober for weeks and then vanish for the same period on a drunken debauch. Because of his failing, he is now forced to work in small companies such as this. I pray that you do not offer him drink and avoid accepting any invitations he may offer to have you drink with him."

At the time David Cornish had grumbled, "That sounds like bad news to me. I'd say Barnaby is making a mistake hiring the fellow."

"But if he is truly a fine West End actor we can benefit by his experience," she suggested. "And he may remain sober with us."

"From my experiences with drunken actors he'll slip sooner or later," David predicted.

But now that Ernest Hansom was lending his presence to their company even David Cornish was lost in admiration of his talent. The red-faced man was a much better actor than Barnaby Samuels and the company gained in strength from his acting.

When Fanny was first introduced to him the old actor had seemed rather startled. He had quickly covered his surprise but she had noted it and wondered about the reason. She did not mention this to David as she did not think it important.

Several weeks went by and they continued doing repertory in Wenside. The weather became pleasanter with the coming of spring, but Wenside was another factory town as gray and grim as Rigby. However, this meant little to the theatrical company since the audiences were enthusiastic and attendance was nearly at capacity in the old Opera House.

They were preparing a comedy, "The Caretaker's Bride," and Ernest Hansom and Fanny were not in the last half of the first act which was being rehearsed. So they sat together in the rear of the dark auditorium watching Barnaby direct David Cornish and the comedian in a long scene.

Ernest Hansom had been completely sober thus far and knowing his weakness, Fanny admired him for this. The company had been careful in the use of alcohol in his presence but this alone would not have stopped him from getting drunk if he wished.

As the rehearsal went on the old actor turned his stern face to her and said, "David Cornish has a lot of ability."

"That praise is meaningful coming from you," she said. "We all respect your talent."

"Thank you," the gray-haired man said with a bleak smile. "Though I fear I have not made the best of myself."

"You are doing so well here."

He gave a deep sigh. "This has been good for me. But only the London stage satisfies me now. That should be the goal of all actors wishing to prove themselves. It should be your goal."

"I do want to play in London," she said. "My father was an actor. I'm sure he must have played there. I have been told he had great ability."

"What was his name? Perhaps I may have met him," the old actor said.

She blushed and shook her head. "I cannot tell you his name."

"Oh?"

"No," she said. "You see he deserted my mother and me not long after I was born."

"A cruel fellow," the old actor said quietly.

"I have tried not to hold it against him," Fanny said. "My mother never did. She taught me to revere his memory."

"I would have expected her to have been bitter."

"So would I," Fanny said. "At least, I would have until I came into the theatre myself. Now I understand better why he left us. It was because the theatre meant so much to him. I wish to follow in his footsteps and give my life to the theatre."

"Your talent warrants your wanting to do that," Ernest Hansom said. "Yet you are treading dangerous ground. It is known by all the company that you and David Cornish are lovers."

Again she blushed. "I do not deny that. I'm fond of David. I believe in him also."

"Yet this liaison could end by wrecking both your careers."

"I will not let it," she said firmly.

He stared at her. "You almost convince me."

"I mean it. I take every precaution," she replied, without attempting to explain more.

"Drink has been my compelling passion," Ernest Hansom said bitterly. "I can never be certain when it will drag me down again."

She reached out a hand and touched his arm. "We are fond of you, indeed proud of you. I'm sure you will not let it happen!"

"Not willingly," the character actor said. He stared at her a moment and said, "Do you recall that on our first meeting I stared at you for a long moment in a most unseemly way?"

"Yes," she said. "I do remember. And I wondered about it."

He nodded. Then he said, "It was because you looked so remarkably like someone I knew long ago."

"Really?"

"Someone with your lovely face and coloring," he went on, then paused. "May I ask, was your mother's name Mary?"

It was her turn to be shocked. She stared at him and in a small voice said, "Yes."

"I was sure of it," he murmured.

"How do you know this?"

"Because I am your father," he said gently.

Seated beside him in the darkened theatre she studied Ernest Hansom in confusion. She thought she was going to faint. Her head reeled and she could not collect her thoughts sufficiently to make any sort of reply.

He reached over and placed a comforting arm around her. "Do not hate me! I have lived a long life of regret for deserting you and Mary! I tried to convince myself she had probably married someone else and you were being brought up well. I never dreamed that one day I would find you again!"

She took a deep breath. "You are certain you're my father?"

"Yes," he said. "I knew it when I saw you. I gave up the name of Hastings when I became involved in financial troubles. I left Bristol as Ernest Hansom and I have been Ernest Hansom ever since."

Gradually she accepted what he was telling her as the truth, astonishing though it seemed. When the rehearsal ended they went to David Cornish and told him the news. The handsome young actor listened and placed his arm protectively around Fanny.

He said sternly, "You realize that in deserting Fanny as you did, you gave up all claim on her?"

Ernest Hansom looked hurt. "I wish to make amends as best I can."

"You should not interfere in her life," David said. It was obvious to Fanny that he was jealous of her new-found father.

She quickly told David, "Mr. Hansom—that is, Father is not the sort to do that. And it gives me great joy to know him to be such a talented and kindly man."

David said, "He was not kindly when he deserted you and your mother."

She pressed her fingers to David's lips. "Enough," she said. "That is all in the past."

The young actor still glared at her father. "I am in love with your daughter," he said. "I don't care whether you approve or not!"

"Everything will be the same!" Fanny promised her jealous lover.

Ernest Hansom's brick-red face was sad as he assured David, "I do not ask for rights which I forfeited long ago. It is enough to have found my daughter. I will allow her to make her own decisions as she has done up to now. I desire only success for Fanny and you."

This promise on her father's part appeared to placate David. But Fanny sensed there might be thorny problems ahead between this young man who loved her so much and her newly-found father. For the moment she put these concerns to the back of her mind in her joy at finding her parent.

When the news made the rounds of the company the emotionally inclined actors and actresses were stunned and touched. As old Hilda Asquith said, "It might be the sort of thing dear Mr. Dickens writes! The reunion of father and child! So unexpected! So satisfying!"

This was the way the entire company felt, all except David who kept a suspicious eye on Fanny and her father. His jealousy of her new-found parent was apparent in all but their love-making. Only during those passionate moments in bed did he seem to forget about Ernest Hansom.

In truth he had reason to worry about the old man's influence on Fanny. For while he did not attempt to interfere with her affair with him, Ernest Hansom did work hard at instilling a heightened ambition and unrest in her.

Her career was a favorite subject with the character actor. As they sat together in the parlor of the theatrical lodging house one morning, he brought the subject up again.

"You must get away from all this," he said.

Fanny said, "But Barnaby Samuels is a good manager and director! The company is friendly and I have learned all I know about acting from them."

"The point is," her father said, "you have learned enough. You must not remain in the provinces too long."

"Why not remain here and learn more?" she asked.

"Because you will *not* learn more," her father said. "You now need to take your talent and training to London. If you remain here too long you will be tagged a provincial actress and then you will never get a West End job."

Her eyes widened. "Surely that must be true for David as well?"

"That young actor is not my concern, though I agree he ought also to leave the provinces for the city," Ernest Hansom said urgently. "You must make the transfer while you are young and at the height of your attractiveness."

"I do not like to leave Mr. Samuels," she said.

"He will understand it is for your good," her father said. "He plans to leave Wenside in a few weeks. And I have heard he may give up management because of his continued illness. If that is true we can both leave when the engagement here ends."

She brightened. "You will help me gain a foothold in London?"

"I shall," he said. "It will be one way of making up to you some small portion of what I owe. Sir Alan Tredale is a close friend of mine. He has his own theatre, The People's, and he will give you an audition if I ask him."

"Oh, Father!" she exclaimed, throwing her arms around him. And then, she said, "What about David? Will you speak for him as well?"

"If he wishes me to," Ernest Hansom said reluctantly. "I don't know whether that young man will accept my help or not. He is mighty independent and I'm sure he doesn't like me!"

Fanny managed a smile. "Nonsense! I'm sure he'll value your help. And it isn't so much that he doesn't like you, as that he is jealous of you."

"I know," the old man sighed. "He doesn't want to share you with anyone else. And I can't say I blame him!"

"I'm so excited!" she exclaimed. "Think of us all going to London together! It will be a little different from my last experience there! Though most of the folk I met were good to me!"

"So you have said," her father nodded. "That Silas Hodder sounds like an interesting character."

"He was like a father to me," she said, and then quickly amended this to, "I mean, he was as close to being a father as he could be."

Ernest Hansom smiled. "I'm not jealous of him. Don't think me as hot-tempered as David."

"But you do like David, don't you?" she worried.

"Yes," her father said. "I consider him a fine young actor with a great future, if he doesn't allow his stubbornness to spoil it. I think he might have been more considerate of you. But since you were lovers before I arrived on the scene I can say nothing. Granted, if he does the right things, he should make you a good husband one day."

"I feel the same way," she said seriously. "But he is so impatient. He keeps asking me to marry him and I keep putting him off. It is not an easy situation."

"I expect not," her father agreed.

"But we won't think of that," she said happily. "We will think about conquering London! And meeting Mr. Gilbert Tingley again at his Emporium of Wonders! And Moll, who is the mermaid now in my place! It will be so much fun! You'll meet them all and they'll like you!"

"And you will find a place on the London stage," her father said. "Maybe one day Fanny Hastings will be a star. I could ask for no more."

"I will do what you tell me, Father, and work hard. I promise."

"I will also try to do better," he said. "I have not had one drink since I came here. My happiness in finding you has been partly responsible for that."

She kissed him on the cheek. "I know you will not succumb to drink again."

"I hope not," he said, though his tone lacked certainty. And she realized that this threat and this thirst must be with him all the time, a dreadful strain.

"Should I speak to David about the company closing?" she asked her father.

"No," Ernest Hansom said. "I would prefer you didn't, since Barnaby Samuels told me this in confidence. It might hurt the company's morale if the news got out."

"True."

"Also," he said, "I think it might be better not to say anything about our planning to go to London until the very end. If we do not speak of it until then, David will not have time to oppose the plan and brood about it. By offering it as a surprise I think he might be more willing to join in with us."

"Very well," she promised. "I shall not say anything to him until later."

So it was agreed between them. In the weeks following Fanny glowed with an inward happiness from the knowledge of what was being planned. David noticed her excitement and was mystified by it.

One evening on the way home, he said, "You know there are rumors Barnaby is going to close the company. Yet you seem so happy!"

"I don't think his closing the company will be such a disaster," she said. "We are bound to find work."

David gave her a grim look. "I'm not so sure. I haven't a London reputation like your father!"

"You have talent and youth," she said, squeezing her lover's arm. "Father would trade his reputation for those things."

It was a week later and they were doing a revival of "The Squire of Finby" when the skies quite unexpectedly darkened for Fanny. It began when shortly before curtain time a distraught Barnaby Samuels came to the dressing room she shared with old Hilda Asquith to ask, "Have you seen your father?"

She rose from her chair by the dressing room mirror, a small fear gathering about her heart. "No," she said. "What is wrong?"

"He's not in his dressing room," the actor-manager said. "And I can't find him anywhere in the theatre!"

Panic seized her. "The play begins in ten minutes!"

Barnaby nodded. "Yes. I'm afraid…" He didn't finish what he was about to say.

"What will you do?" she asked unhappily.

"He's probably drunk in some tavern," the actor-manager said. "I know his part and my foot isn't aching too badly. I'll stand in for him!" And he hurried away.

Fanny slowly turned to the elderly Hilda Asquith who was finishing her make-up. She said, "What do you think?"

"Too bad," Hilda said with a sigh. "But we were warned, you know."

"I know," Fanny said in a low murmur. But she could not believe it. Then her disbelief turned to anger that her father should do this. Give way to his weakness in this fashion! After all his talk about her having helped him with his drink problem! It had meant nothing! He had let her down before the company.

She made her way backstage and saw Barnaby standing waiting for his cue to go onstage. He was wearing the make-up of the Squire and dressed in his costume. All the company were now aware that her father was absent.

David came by her and said, "So it has happened! He has finally let us down!"

"Don't!" she said in a near sob, and turned from him.

"I'm sorry," David said. "It doesn't matter. Barnaby will do the part. No one will be hurt but your father." They had no further time to discuss the matter as the curtain had gone up and the play was beginning.

Chapter Six

The performance that evening was an ordeal for Fanny. It took all her training and courage to help her carry on in the light-hearted role in which she was cast. She knew the others in the company were sympathetic but this did little good. At last the curtain fell on the last act, she took her bows and then was free to retreat from the stage.

Downstairs she hurriedly went about removing her make-up with the thought of going out and making the rounds of the local taverns in search of her father. Her anger with him had now given away to concern.

Old Hilda Asquith was considerate of her state and said, "Don't take it too badly, my dear. Barnaby won't dismiss your father for this one lapse."

Tearfully, she turned to the old woman and said, "It is just that I hoped it would never happen."

"He has done well all this time," the character actress said. "You must remember that and not be too harsh in your judgement of him."

Fanny rose from her chair and began to put on her street clothes. She said, "I simply wish to find him now and take care of him."

"That is the proper spirit," Hilda agreed.

"Perhaps David will come with me," she said with a sigh as she started out of the room.

She did not get far as she was met by Barnaby Samuels in the doorway of the dressing room. She saw at a glance that the old actor-manager had bad news for her. His worn face was solemn.

In a tight voice, she asked, "Some news?"

"Yes," the kindly old man said. "Word has just been sent me. We were wrong in blaming your father for not arriving in time for the performance. He did not give way to his weakness again."

"Thank goodness!" she said. "But what detained him?"

Barnaby Samuels placed a hand on her arm. "You must be strong, dear girl. Let your belief in the Almighty sustain you in this sad twist of fate!"

"What is it?" she demanded, frightened.

"Your father was run down by a lorry as she was making his way to the theatre," Barnaby Samuels said. "He had not been drinking. It was just that the lorry rounded a corner suddenly. Your father was killed in an instant!"

"No!" she said brokenly and began sobbing bitterly. The manager helped her back into her chair and Hilda Asquith came to tend to her.

Everything that followed was confused in Fanny's mind. David and the other members of the company came and offered their sympathy, and it was David who saw her home to their lodgings in a carriage. Barnaby Samuels made the funeral arrangements with the local undertaker, sparing her that sad duty.

The body was laid out in the parlor of the lodging house. Happily, Ernest Hansom's upper body showed no sign of the injuries which had taken his life. He looked sternly noble and serene as he lay in his casket. And Fanny was touched by the number of townspeople who came to offer their respects to the veteran actor who had entertained them so well.

Barnaby Samuels stood with her at the end of the room as they watched the line of townspeople paying their last respects. The actor-manager said, "He could not have been afforded a better farewell in London! These people had come to truly know his worth!"

Fanny stood there in sorrowful silence, thinking of the plans she and her father had made. How happy he had been at the prospect of returning to London and his desire to help her and David with their careers! Those plans were completely shattered now.

She said, "It was his dream to appear in London again."

"He might have known disappointment," Barnaby Samuels pointed out. "He had lost his reputation for reliability there. To have returned and not been accepted could well have put him back on the road to drink. Perhaps this way it is best."

Fanny did not attempt to argue with the kindly old man. She maintained a calm demeanor in her sorrow. And when she attended the funeral service in the Wenside Anglican Church and saw him buried in the small cemetery next to it she preserved her dignity. David was at her side as the last sod was turned over the grave. Then they left the cemetery together.

Back at the lodging house Barnaby Samuels sat with her and David over glasses of port. Barnaby said, "My dear, I gather you know I'm giving up management at the end of the month."

"I know there have been some rumors," Fanny agreed. She did not intend to reveal that she and her father had discussed this along with their plans for the future.

"I am too old for touring," Barnaby went on. "I have saved enough to retire. I plan to return to Rigby and live at the inn there."

She said, "That is suitable, since Rigby saw the start of your last successful season."

"Quite so," the actor-manager, agreed. "I have had some concern about breaking up this fine company. Never has a manager known more loyal co-workers."

"True," she said. "But you have operated the company in a manner to warrant our loyalty, as I'm sure David agrees."

The handsome, brown-haired David nodded. "That is so, sir. I have never known a more contented company."

"Which made my decision to put them out of work all the more difficult," the old man said. He beamed at David and went on, "Happily this young man, this fine actor, has brought an end to my dilemma!"

"David!" she said in surprise.

David smiled at her modestly. "It is true, Fanny. I have enough savings to carry on the company. That is what I propose to do. From now on it will be my company, headed by you and me."

"What do you say to that?" Barnaby Samuels asked happily, fully expecting her to be pleased by the news. "I hope this will lessen the sorrow of your father's passing. He would be delighted that you will be starring in this new company."

She was at a loss for words. How could she explain what she and her father had been planning and make David understand? He would be bound to think she and her father had been plotting behind his back. And he was obviously so pleased with this new project that she did not have the heart to show no enthusiasm for it.

She turned to David and said, "I'm proud of you, David. I'm sure you will make a success of the company."

David reached out and took her hand in his. His eyes met hers. "It will be *our* success!"

She sighed. "Yes. I'm certain all the company will be delighted at the news."

David said, "I will have to find someone to replace your father. I will not be able to get anyone of his ability but Barnaby has kindly given me some names."

"And I shall continue to play your father's roles in the new company until another actor arrives," Barnaby said. "There is nothing I won't do to ensure the happiness of you fine young people."

"Thank you, sir," David said. "It is my intention, soon after we begin with the new company, that Fanny and I should be married. With her father gone, I can think of no one whom we would rather have give the bride away than you."

"I shall be delighted," Barnaby Samuels said with obvious emotion. "Fanny has become dear to me."

She smiled in a wan fashion, appalled at her feeling of suddenly being fenced in. These two men were happily going about making plans for her future, indeed for her whole life. And they were not what she and her father had decided upon. Not at all. She had the frantic apprehension that if she married David and went on acting with him in the provinces it would be the end of both their careers. Children would come and they would put off changing their way of life and neither of them would ever set foot on a London stage.

They left Barnaby Samuels to enjoy another glass of port and went out to stroll in the sun of the warm April afternoon. David walked with her silently for a little. Then he halted and stared at her.

"You don't seem pleased with this new turn of events," he said. "I can understand it under the circumstances. You are bound to be mourning your father for a while. But I would like to have your approval of what I'm embarking on."

She felt it was her chance to try and place her father's plan before him. She said, "David, I would like the company to continue. But do you really think we should remain in the provinces?"

He frowned. "What do you mean?"

"Isn't it about time we tried London?"

His face darkened. "I know where that idea came from. Your father was forever talking to you about London. He put those notions into your head."

"What is wrong with them?"

"I don't think I'm ready," he said. "Nor are you! Let me gain some experience with my own company. Then we shall move on to London."

"After we are married?"

"Yes."

"And before I have children," she said. "We should make the break and go to London now before we have any encumbrances."

David looked astounded. "I can't believe you mean it!"

"I do. Most truly!"

"What will happen to the company?" he asked.

"We can remain until Barnaby finds someone else to take it over," she said. "It shouldn't take more than a few weeks. The company is a paying proposition; there should be a lot of interested parties."

"There won't be any," David declared. "I am going to buy it and that's that. Forget this London business for a while."

She was let down by his decision and his tone. "You won't even consider my plan?"

"No," he said firmly. "I'm sorry, Fanny. You know I love you and want to do what is best for you. And I'm sure this is best."

"I see," she said with a sigh.

He placed an arm around her. "Think about the wonderful days ahead with our own company. We shall become the favorites of these industrial towns. Make a triumphant tour each year. The crowds should grow every time we return!"

She resumed walking. "I can see it is your dream."

"Only because I have you to share it," he told her.

On that afternoon a desperate plan was born in Fanny's mind. She knew that she must leave David and the company. There was no other way for her to survive as an individual. Her father had shared her dream of a career in London. David would put it off forever, until London was a lost opportunity for both of them.

Her choice was to follow her father's idea. Now she began her most difficult acting, but it was done off-stage. She made a pretence of going along with David's plan at the same time as she coached one of the new girls in the company, who showed a special aptitude, in her roles. The girl's name was Maude Lyons and Fanny worked with her in secret.

When she had first invited Maude to her room one morning and suggested coaching her in the parts she played, the girl had shown surprise. "But why, Miss Hastings?" she'd asked.

Fanny said, "I do not have an understudy. Father's accident and death have taught me what slim threads hold our existence together. I could be injured or become ill and no one could take over quickly."

The girl began to understand. "But have I the ability? I'm so new in the business!"

"I have chosen you," Fanny said, "precisely because you have the talent. I do not want jealousy from any of the others, so we must do this in secret."

"Very well, miss," Maude Lyons said with an excited look on her pleasant face. "But I hope I never get to play any of the parts since it would mean you were ill!"

Fanny smiled and pointed out, "There could be other reasons. You know there is talk that Mr. Cornish and I are to wed. I would not wish to work during our honeymoon."

"I hadn't thought of that," the delighted young actress said. "I shall labor very hard at learning the parts."

"Good!" Fanny said. "Let us begin at once!"

• • •

Maude proved an apt student. She also had more than average ability. Within a fortnight she had learned all Fanny's various roles. The time had come for Fanny to put her plan into operation. She chose a mid-week so that David would have to remain on the stage and make no attempt to follow her.

The night before she left he came to her room for their usual lovemaking. She catered to him with a passion born of knowing they would not be together again for a long while, perhaps never.

She saw him to the door when it was over and he kissed her tenderly. He said, "All those London notions out of your head, dearest?"

Fanny nodded. "We can worry about that later. I'm so terribly fond of you, David. You mustn't ever forget that!"

He touched his lips to her temple. "Our lives together will be perfect. I promise you!"

She closed the door after him and, still nude, stood there leaning against it. A wry look passed over her lovely face with her tousled red hair falling about her shoulders to accentuate her beauty. A shaft of moonlight shone in through the window and she stared at it. She could almost see Ernest Hansom standing there in the blue light.

Aloud, she murmured, "Do not worry, Father. I have not turned traitor to our dream!"

That night she slept little. The following day she made a trip to the Wenside Railway Station and bought a ticket to London on the train which left at seven-thirty that evening. It would be eight before her disappearance was discovered and by that time she would be well on her way to the great city.

Because of the secrecy of her plan she could only take one small valise with her. In a way it was a repeat of her first visit to London. Only this time she hoped she would be more fortunate. She at least knew something of the city and would not end up wandering the streets as she had that first time.

She wrote a farewell letter telling David that she was determined to follow through with her father's dream and conquer the London theatre world. She warned him not to try to follow her but to continue on his own way. She again told him how much she cared for him, but that she did not want to marry him at this time in her life. She explained that Maude Lyons could immediately step into her roles without the company suffering in any way.

During the late afternoon she stopped by the Opera House and gave the sealed message to the porter there. She instructed him not to deliver it to David Cornish until eight o'clock. When she was sure he had her instructions clearly in his head she gave him a shilling tip.

Her excitement grew as the evening approached. David always went early to the theatre to check on the box office and other matters of business. Sometimes she walked there in company with Hilda Asquith, but tonight she told the older woman she was leaving early. She had hidden her valise downstairs and when she left she had it with her and went directly to the railway depot rather than to the theatre.

She wondered if the porter might have forgotten her careful instructions and given the farewell letter to David early. As she waited on the wooden platform by the rails with several other passengers she worried that at any moment a seething David might show up and demand that she return to the theatre with him. She kept looking in the direction of the street but no one came.

At last the train arrived and she stood in line to board it with the other passengers. Fortunately there was no one in the compartment she chose who recognized her. There were two travelling salesmen and a lady who had been to Wenside to attend the funeral of her sister. Fanny engaged in a conversation with this woman, saying that she had just come from the burial of her father, and with this common bond they became quite friendly.

The journey to London was a tense one for Fanny since she was still by no means sure that David would not try to follow her. When they reached the bustling, dirty London railway terminal she made her way directly to the hackney cab stand where she parted company with the other woman.

After a porter had helped her into the cab she told the driver the name of a hotel which Silas Hodder had once mentioned as being most respectable and reasonable, which was how Fanny came to spend the first night of her return to London in the Strand Hotel.

Once again she slept little. But by the next morning she was much more her own woman. She ate an early breakfast and then hired a cab to take her to the bakery where Silas Hodder had said he might be given a room. By a stroke of good fortune she found him there at the same table where she had eaten with him so often, looking his same, shabby self with his long gray hair still drooping on his shoulders and the battered old top hat crowning his skull-like face.

With a delighted smile he rose to greet her. "How clever of you to find me!" he said.

"I was almost certain you'd be here," she said with a smile, seating herself beside him at the plank table. "You said they were going to give you a room."

"And I have earned it," Silas Hodder told her. "A few weeks ago thieves tried to enter and I scared them off. They seemed to think I was a spectre, due to my long sojourn in the tomb, no doubt!"

"No doubt!" she laughed.

"So now I have a free room and meals here," he said. "I still ply my beggar's trade in the taverns and all is well with me. What about you?"

"It is a long story," she said with a sigh. "For one thing I found my father!"

"By Jupiter!" Silas Hodder said with surprise.

"And I fell in love again, though this time I handled it rather differently."

"I must hear it all," the gaunt man said. And he signalled for one of the boy helpers. When the lad came up to them, Silas ordered him, "Another pot of tea, my boy. And bring an extra cup for the lady."

They sat over their tea while she told him all about her adventures with the company. She relived the happy excitement of finding her father and told of her romance with David. She ended with, "I have learned how to act now and I've come to London to find a proper job on the stage."

Silas Hodder nodded and tapped the side of his thin nose as he considered. Then he said, "I think we should go to the Emporium of Wonders and repeat all this for Gilbert Tingley. He is the expert on matters theatrical."

"Have you seen Moll lately?" Fanny asked. "I wonder if she is still employed as a mermaid."

"I have no idea," Silas admitted. "I have not been there since the day you left. But we shall go at once."

Despite his protestations she insisted on the luxury of a hackney cab again and in a short while they were deposited in front of the ramshackle three storey building which housed the freak show.

Silas Hodder led the way and knocked on the door of Gilbert Tingley's private office. From inside that worthy's high-pitched voice came in reply, "If you're a bill collector slide it under the door and go away! No payments until next Friday!"

Silas showed an amused expression on his skull-face and pounded the door again. "Open it, you miser! It's your friend Silas Hodder and Miss Fanny Hastings, come to see you!"

There was a shuffling from inside and the door was opened instantly by the little man. His mustache quivered with joy as he embraced Fanny and shook hands with Silas. He said, "I thought I should never see either of you again. Do come on in!"

He led the way and she saw he was wearing the same vest and brown trousers which she remembered seeing the previous year. He sat at his rolltop desk and indicated chairs for them.

The little man told Fanny, "My dear, you've bloomed into a greater beauty than ever!"

"Thank you," she said, blushing. "What about Moll, is she still your mermaid?"

The little man shook his head. "No. Moll proved a terrible disappointment. She did well in the show but a soldier came along who took a fancy to her, fishtail and all. Soon they were walking out together and then she informed me they were getting married. She's off with him to India or some other awful place!"

"I'm sorry," she said. "I liked her. I was looking forward to seeing her again."

"I have another mermaid but I'll give you the job back in a minute, if you'll take it. This one has poor skin. There never was a mermaid like you!" Gilbert Tingley said.

Silas Hodder held up his hand. "You're rushing ahead too fast, my friend. This young woman has a story to tell. Suppose you hear her out before you begin making suggestions."

"Very well," the freak show owner said. "Let us enjoy some port along with the story." And they did.

Fanny repeated all the salient points of her adventures and ended with, "If my father had lived he would have been a great help. He knew all the London theatre people."

Gilbert Tingley sighed. "Great tragedy, his being killed like that!"

"It was," she agreed. "But I'm determined to make my way on the London stage because it was what he wished."

Silas Hodder said, "A sincere tribute to your late parent. What do you think, Tingley? We need your advice."

The little man twitched his mustache as he so often did when in the grip of a deep emotion. He said, "It would seem to me the friends of your father would remain his friends even though he is dead."

"That is true," she said.

Tingley went on, "Now, if you could recall some of the names he mentioned, that might help."

She thought for a moment. Then she said, "There was one person he seemed to count on more than anyone else. The owner of the People's Theatre. His name is Sir Alan Tredale."

The little man showed immediate interest. "Sir Alan Tredale is one of the most famous actor-managers in London. He stages his productions in his own theatre. I've seen him act. He plays fine gentlemen most splendidly."

Silas Hodder said, "Then the way is clear. The little lady should present herself to Tredale with the least possible delay."

"I agree," Gerald Tingley said. "And if he is half the gent I think him to be, and if your father really was friendly with him, I see no reason why he shouldn't want to help you!"

Silas said, "I knew a chat with Tingley would be most helpful."

"Call on me at any time," the freak show owner said. "I don't forget my friends either. And if you find yourself in a London play, Fanny, I want you to let me know. I'll be there along with Silas for the opening performance!"

She stood up. "I'll surely let you know. And I'll be back to see the Fat Woman and the Thin Man if I may."

"Why not come back and stay here?" the freak show owner suggested. "I have an empty room. It would be like old times."

"How kind you are!" Fanny exclaimed, kissing the little man on the cheek and delighting him.

So it was settled. He showed her up to a room at once and she left her valise there. Then she and Silas departed the building on their way to the theatrical district and a meeting with Sir Alan Tredale. This time they took a horse car at the behest of Silas who told her she mustn't spend too freely.

"It may be a while until a suitable part comes along," he warned her. "And you don't want to end up wearing that fishtail again!"

This chastened her enough to make her accept his idea of using the cheaper form of transportation in preference to the hackney cabs to which she had become addicted. They arrived in the bustling theatre district and got off at the regular stop in Piccadilly Circus.

A few enquiries brought forth the information that the People's Theatre was located in St. Martin's Lane. She and the gaunt Silas made their way to the building which housed the theatre. It bore the theatre's name in large letters and there were broadsheets at either side of the entrance, announcing a production of "The Knight and The Lady" a new costume drama by Sheridan Knowles starring Sir Alan Tredale.

Silas studied the broadsheets with interest. "It would appear the eminent gentleman has a production under way," he said.

"I'm frightened," she said, realizing she was trembling and suddenly wishing she were back in the provinces with David.

"None of that!" Silas Hodder told her. "This is not the time to give way to nerves."

"Suppose he won't see me!" she worried.

"He *will* see you," the gaunt man promised. And he strode up to the box office and accosted the somber-faced man in charge saying, "This young lady wishes to see Sir Alan. Her father was an old friend and fellow actor of his!"

The clerk glared at the odd-looking Silas over his square steel-rimmed spectacles and said, "Sir Alan is inside rehearsing his new play. He cannot be disturbed."

"But this is urgent!" Silas said with a show of outrage. "This young lady's father was an eminent man. Sir Alan will wish to see her."

"I don't care if her father was Prince Albert himself," the sour-faced man in the ticket booth stated. "Sir Alan will not see anyone now!"

Fanny went up by Silas and tugged his arm. "Please! We can come back later when he's not busy!"

The skull-faced Silas turned to her and with a gloved hand of which one finger of the glove was missing he waved at her airily. "My dear Fanny, you do not understand these things! Men like Sir

Alan always have flunkies for protection! They never allow anyone inside unless they are forced to!"

The sour-faced ticket seller snapped, "Let me assure you, sir, that you are not forcing my hand!"

"There will be no more fol-de-rol with you, my friend," Silas said grandly and he grasped Fanny by the arm. Unwillingly she allowed herself to be propelled through the doors into the theatre.

It was no surprise to her that the outraged ticket seller threw the door of his cage open with a loud bang and came screaming after them. Silas, in the meantime, dragged her on into the theatre itself. They entered the back of the dark auditorium, a weird trio, with the shouting ticket seller in the rear.

The pandemonium in the theatre temporarily halted the goings-on behind the footlights. Onstage a stout man and an attractive young woman halted in declaiming their lines to find out what the disturbance was. Silas continued down the aisle towards the stage with an unhappy Fanny in his grasp and the irate ticket seller on his heels complaining loudly.

At this moment a tall, distinguished figure rose from one of the seats and turned to shout out, "What the blazes is going on, Crimmins?"

Near tears, an upset Crimmins dashed down the aisle and sputtered, "I warned him, Sir Alan! I *warned* him not to bring this young lady into the theatre! But he wouldn't listen! He came anyway!"

The tall, thin man said, "Silence, Crimmins. I shall handle this." He came a few steps up the aisle, an annoyed look on his patrician face. "What sort of conduct is this? Will you two leave or shall I call the police?"

Fanny was too embarrassed to say anything; she leaned next to Silas, trying to hide behind him and thinking she might at any moment faint.

Silas assumed his most dignified manner and said, "Sir Alan, this young woman is the daughter of a fellow actor and friend of yours. A fine man who has recently passed away!"

"Indeed!" Sir Alan said studying him with suspicion. Then sudden recognition came to the patrician face. He pointed an accusing forefinger at Silas Hodder and in his fine, cultivated voice declared, "I remember you!"

"Do you, sir? I'm not sure I've had the pleasure!" Silas said, taken back.

"You were at my club. You somehow managed to get in and sit among the members soliciting alms for yourself in the guise of a former member fallen on evil days! You did very well among us until the manager discovered you, and knowing you were a faker, threw you out!"

"The incident escapes my memory!" Silas said nervously.

"Well, it doesn't escape mine," the distinguished actor replied sternly. "What is your game this time? From what I heard you always have some trick up your sleeve. Where does the young lady fit in?"

"She doesn't fit in at all!" Silas said. "I've brought her here because she is the orphan daughter of an old friend of yours! A matter of common kindness on my part, Sir Alan, for which I ask no payment!"

"It has to be the first time you haven't had your hand out," Sir Alan declared. "What was the name of my supposed friend, this young lady's father?"

Silas looked distressed. "Blast it, sir. All this confusion has sent the name clear out of my mind. But he was close to you and a dear friend of the novelist, Charles Dickens!" Fanny cringed at this. She had never mentioned Dickens to Silas; it was his own invention.

At the mention of Charles Dickens, a shorter man, who had been standing in the background now stepped forward and said, "I'm Charles Dickens. You say this girl's father knew me?"

Silas gaped and could not reply. Thoroughly distressed, Fanny came out from behind him and, nearly weeping, said, "I'm *so* sorry about this! Silas meant well but he went about it the wrong way! My father was an actor who knew you, Sir Alan. His name was Ernest Hansom!"

"Ernest Hansom!" Sir Alan Tredale said. "You are Hansom's daughter? I didn't knew he had one.

"We met shortly before he was tragically killed in a lorry accident," she said unhappily. "He told me shortly before he died to come to London and look you up."

"I'll be dashed," Sir Alan said, turning to the other man. "What do you make of this, Dickens?"

The shorter man with a fine, sensitive face said, "A most unusual situation. But the sepulchral fellow with the gray hair is right. I did know your father, miss. A fine actor. He played leading roles with Macready!"

"Bless me! I must have had a message from the spirit world," Silas Hodder gasped.

"One minute," Sir Alan Tredale said sternly. Then he turned to the people gathered on the stage and told them, "All right, company. Rehearsal is postponed until three this afternoon. No sense trying to go on after this melée."

The figures melted slowly away from the stage as the man told a troubled Crimmins, "Go back to your office, Crimmins. And next time you attempt to keep order, do so less noisily!"

"Yes, sir," the unfortunate Crimmins said in a near whisper and slunk off.

Sir Alan then spoke sternly to Silas. "It would seem you have done your work well enough, sir. You have brought the girl to my attention. If you will be good enough to leave her in my care, I shall talk to her."

"Thank you, Sir Alan," Silas Hodder said with a smile. "Actually, I must be on my way. I'm already late for an important engagement."

"At one of the taverns or clubs, I have no doubt," Sir Alan said with irony. "Good day to you then!"

Silas turned to Fanny. "You'll do well enough now, my dear. I'll see you later at Tingley's place." And lifting his hat to one and all he marched grandly out.

Charles Dickens laughed. "That is a most remarkable fellow!"

"The nerve of a Prime Minister," Sir Alan said, with a chuckle. He stared at her, "How did Ernest Hansom's daughter happen to become associated with a vagabond like that?"

Fanny managed a faint smile. "He is not all that bad! In fact he is a kind person. He has helped me more than once. I cannot repudiate him."

"Then I shan't ask you to," Sir Alan said. "Dickens and I are about to have lunch at a nearby pub. Would you think me bold if I asked you to join us so we might discuss why you came to see me?"

"It would be kind of you to take me to lunch, Sir Alan," she said. "But I don't wish to be a bother to you!"

"A pretty girl like you is never a bother to susceptible chaps like Dickens and myself," the distinguished actor said. "So come along!"

The pub was only a few doors distant and a friendly waiter showed them to a quiet corner of the busy place. Dickens at once asked for a sherry, and Sir Alan Tredale ordered one for himself and for Fanny. When the sherries were served she told the two men her story.

"So that is what happened to poor Hansom," Sir Alan said with a sigh. And he asked her, "You knew, of course, that the only reason he wasn't working in London was because of his drinking problem?"

"I was told that," she said. "He was frank about it himself. But in those last months he was free of the liquor and he gave many fine performances."

Charles Dickens offered her a friendly smile. "I like the sound of your company. It has always been my ambition to tour widely with a theatrical company. But the writing of my novels robs me of the opportunity."

"We did your 'Cricket On The Hearth,'" she told him.

"A miserable adaption," the novelist said promptly.

"Even so, it was well liked," she assured him.

Sir Alan told the novelist, "It was the same in London. Even though you didn't approve of the adaptation it was well received by the audiences."

"One day I shall adapt it myself," Dickens said.

Sir Alan studied her and said, "You say you have had good provincial training."

She said proudly, "Barnaby Samuels was a good director and I played opposite a fine, young actor named David Cornish. My father also coached me and he told me I was ready for London."

Charles Dickens said, "If Ernest Hansom told you that it meant something."

"I agree," Sir Alan said. "If you have a small portion of your father's talent along with your lovely face and figure, you should go far."

"I'll take any sort of work to get started," she said. "If you'll only give me a chance."

Sir Alan smiled at Dickens and pondered aloud, "I wonder if we haven't miraculously found the girl to play Lady Jennifer."

Dickens smiled in return, "I'm pressed for time. But if you'll give her a reading I'll go back to the theatre for it."

"She shall read the part directly after lunch," Sir Alan said. "I owe poor Ernest a debt or two. He gave fine performances in my company and when he was down I'm ashamed to say I turned my back on him."

"You were not alone," Dickens said. "So did Macready. I lectured him for it."

Sir Alan gave Fanny one of his charming smiles. "When we go back to the theatre you will read a scene with me."

"Is it an important role?" she asked.

Dickens laughed. "It's the lead, no less! Alan hasn't been able to cast it! I say, why not start at the top, young lady!"

Sir Alan then ordered lunch and Fanny sat silently, only able to pick at her food. She was too nervous to join in their conversation. But they did not seem to mind this as they had much to talk about. Charles Dickens spoke of a new novel he was doing which he called *David Copperfield*, while Sir Alan went on at length about the trouble and expense of staging one of his huge costume dramas.

At last the luncheon ended and the two men accompanied a thoroughly tense Fanny back to the theatre. She worried that in her nervous state she might not be able to read opposite Sir Alan at all. Her throat would constrict and the words wouldn't come out.

In the theatre Sir Alan went up on stage to get the scripts for the scene and to explain to the stage manager what he was about to do. Charles Dickens smiled at her as he prepared to take a front aisle seat.

He said warmly, "The best of luck, my dear."

"Thank you, Mr. Dickens," she managed.

Sir Alan called out, "On stage please, Miss Hastings. We are waiting for you."

"Yes, sir," she murmured and hurried up to join him.

"Take off your bonnet and cloak," he told her. She did so and the stage manager took them. Then Sir Alan gave her the Script and explained the scene to her. "I play the knight and you are the young lady. I am leaving for the Crusades and this is our parting moment. Before I go, I reveal that I know you have been in love with a younger man who is joining me on the Crusade. You admit you had some friendly interest in him but deny you loved him. You ask me to watch out for him and not hold the business against him. I tell you that I was perhaps too old to make you my wife and so am partly to blame. You swear that you love me and tell me that if I do not return you will place a dagger in your heart. I hold you in my arms and caution you to do no such thing, and I thank you for removing the dagger of suspicion from my own heart which has until now been torturing me without cause! You understand?"

"I think so," she said, studying the script.

"You must first suggest to the audience my accusations against your faithfulness are true. Then in a few minutes you must convince both them and me, that I was wrong. The big emotional moment is when I accept your words as truth and thank you for sending me to the Crusade with a whole heart. That is the crux of the scene."

"I'll try," she said.

"Very well," Sir Alan said firmly and spoke the first line.

In that moment Fanny's training came back to save her. All her nervousness ended as she concentrated on the lines she was reading. She gave them the touches of emotion she felt were right, the slight pauses and the proper emphasis, and she lost herself in the character she was playing. Suddenly the scene was at an end. There was a long silence on the stage and in the theatre.

Then from his seat down front Charles Dickens applauded. "A magnificent first reading!" he told her.

Sir Alan was smiling as he said, "Wherever he may be, your father must be proud at this moment. You have the part!"

Chapter Seven

The opening night of "The Knight and the Lady" began a new phase of Fanny's life. She was given a thunderous ovation by the fashionable audience and in the newspapers the next day the various critics gave praise to her remarkable talents. Nor were Sir Alan Tredale and the play ignored by those gentlemen of the press. It was agreed that the play was one of Sir Alan's best productions and that in Fanny he had offered London a new star.

Fanny's success opened to her a different kind of London, the London of the wealthy and privileged! She moved into a smart flat not far from the theatre and hired a maid and housekeeper-cook. Her new companions were people like Charles Dickens, Lucy Vestris, Charles Matthews and Sir Alan Tredale. It was a gay, romantic world which she had often dreamed about but which she'd hardly dared hope to attain.

However, she did not forget her old friends. She still occasionally paid a visit to the eccentric Gilbert Tingley at his Museum of Freaks and he considerea her his greatest success.

He never missed a chance to take her around the museum and introduce her to his current freaks and tell them, "What this young lady accomplished under my training, any one of you can do!"

The gaunt Silas Hodder was quite disgusted by this. One day as Fanny left the museum in his company, the skull-faced man said with scorn, "To hear him tell it you'd think you'd received all your training playing a mermaid for him! It is your acting in the provinces and especially the coaching by your late father which brought you success!"

"That is true, Silas," she said sadly, thinking of those good days and wondering what had become of David Cornish from whom she'd heard nothing since she ran away from his company. Then brightening, she squeezed the arm of the odd, old man and told him, "Still, if it makes Gilbert Tingley happy to think of me as a protegée, I confess I don't mind!"

"Aye," the thin man lamented. "Trust you to be too tender-hearted. You have conquered London, my lass. But you must be made of stern stuff to keep your footing in this city!"

She gave him an amused glance as they walked along the narrow sidewalk of the grubby street. "*You* have managed very well, it seems!"

He snorted with derision. "I'm what you might well call a confounded failure! A beggar who torments gentlemen to give him alms! Not much to be proud of there! Meeting you is the best thing that ever happened to me!"

"And my meeting you was a turning point in my life," Fanny insisted. "Had you not handled things so well that first day at the theatre I should never have got in to see Sir Alan."

The gaunt face showed modest pleasure. "It was a small business, but I did manage it with a certain flair!"

"I've mentioned it because I have an offer for you," she said as they walked along, she in an enchanting brown taffeta and matching bonnet and he in his somber black suit and tophat.

"What sort of offer?" he wanted to know.

"Sir Alan Tredale needs a new stage door manager for the People's," she told him. "And he favors you. He admires your way of handling people. He asked me to broach the matter to you."

The tall, gaunt man halted and stared at her, his deep-set eyes moist with tears. "You are actually offering to restore me to a place in society?"

"I'm not sure it's what you want," she said. "You have so long made your way by your wits."

Silas Hodder said bitterly, "A way which will certainly see me in paupers' prison if I continue to pursue it." He squeezed her hand. "You are a dear girl! I'm certain you have spoken to Sir Alan on my behalf!"

Fanny smiled. "I *did* bring up your name when he mentioned the position would soon be vacant."

"I shall take it, my girl," the gaunt man said excitedly. "It is my one hope of not losing touch with you!"

"That will never happen! You are too good a friend!"

"It will! It must!" the old man insisted. "You are now part of a London society which tolerates me only on occasion to enjoy me as a freak! I'm as odd to them as any of the displays in Tingley's museum! Gradually they will drop me and I will no longer be part of your circle. But this solves everything! I shall guard your stage door every night!"

"I'm so happy you've accepted," Fanny said. And then she added, "There is just one thing more."

"And what, pray is that?"

"Your…appearance," she said, warily. "I know it is helpful to look weird as a professional beggar. But Sir Alan will demand that you properly shorten your hair, dress a bit less somberly, and present a more normal facade. Do you mind?"

Silas Hodder hesitated for a moment, causing her to think she had offended him. Then he burst into laughter and said, "I declare, child, Sir Alan asked you to approach me because he feared to say such things himself."

"True," Fanny admitted.

"I don't mind sprucing up in the least!" the gaunt old man said happily. "And I shall lose none of my dignity in the doing of it. I shall still make a first class guardian of the backstage area!"

"That is why Sir Alan wants you for the post," Fanny assured him.

He patted her hand and they resumed their walk. "Consider that I have accepted!"

And so it came about that a new-born Silas Hodder arrived to serve at the backstage entrance of the famous old theatre. The transformation in him was satisfyingly complete. He donned a fresh brown frockcoat with yellow checkered trousers and a fawn vest. His battered, black tophat was replaced by one of dark glossy brown. A golden watch-chain graced the fawn vest and he stood at his post with a dignified air. His short gray hair gave his face a less macabre appearance and he soon became a favorite of all the company.

Fanny would have considered this new life on which she'd embarked the happiest time of her existence, had it not been for some memories which haunted her. She had never truly been able to forget her first love Viscount George Palmer. And she felt pain whenever she thought of David Cornish. She knew her running away had caused him unhappiness and she had cared for him greatly and believed in his talent.

But her promise to her father to strive for success on the London stage had been more important to her than anything else. She had deserted David because he'd wanted to tie her to acting in the small towns and cities of the provinces. Her father had warned her that this could easily be a dead end for her, and had urged that she try London. He would have shared the adventure with her had it not been for his untimely death.

As for Viscount George, the old Marquis had soon made her realize that this perfect love was one which could never be. So she had come to think of this early romance in that way, even though she knew she would never forget the handsome young man. For his sake, and her own, it was a dream to be forgotten.

There was no reason why this should be difficult since she had been caught up in the theatrical excitement of the London Stage. Discounting Lucy Vestris and her husband, Charles Matthews, there were no more gifted actor-managers on the London boards than Sir Alan Tredale. She was sure she might have fallen in love with the aristocratic, older actor if he had not been a happily married man with a family of three girls not much younger than herself.

As it was, he became a sort of foster-father to her in addition to being her co-star. There was no question that she would continue to be his leading lady and that her popularity would grow with each new play in which they appeared. Meanwhile she was making many important friends in the world of London's upper classes. The fantastic events of her first descent on the city seemed to belong to a dark world which no longer existed. Though one of her new friends, Charles Dickens, told her in his solemn way, "Do not be deceived by your good fortune, Fanny! Behind the facade of this world of fashion we know there exists a sewer of dangerous slums!"

"I had some experience of them when I first came to the city," she assured him. "But I have hoped that things are better now."

The famous novelist's handsome face was bitter. "Not so!" he said. "The other evening I toured some of these slums with Inspector Field of Scotland Yard. I confess I was sickened. We opened the door of a dilapidated house and were stricken back by the pestilent odor issuing from it! Field held held up a lantern to show ten, twenty, thirty—it was hard to tell—men, women, children, for the most part naked, heaped upon the floor like maggots in a cheese! Poor souls evicted from their homes so that we might build New Oxford Street and other fine streets without regard to where these unfortunates whom we clear out are to find shelter!"

"Must it always be like this?" she lamented.

"That is a question I often ask myself," Dickens said with a sigh. "I have used my pen to fight such conditions but I begin to fear it has been too feeble a weapon!"

"That is untrue! Your writings are not only popular but they have shown up many social evils."

"To what avail?" the famed novelist asked. "I begin to wonder about my purpose in life. What has it all meant and how much is it worth? My domestic life is no longer happy. I find escape only in my friends in the theatre like Sir Alan, Forester and Macready!"

Fanny was all sympathy for her friend. "You must not feel so! You are a success and doing much good!"

This discussion ended when Sir Alan and some friends came to join them. They went on to supper at a favorite restaurant in the Strand. Fanny sat a distance away from the novelist at the long table heaped with fine food and wines, but she watched him during the lively conversation and revelry and saw him to be more restrained and sober than the others.

• • •

Months went by and it seemed that this new life on which Fanny had embarked would continue forever. Sir Alan scheduled new plays and they all were successful. Offstage, Fanny led a quiet life in her small flat near the theatre. And it was there one day in February of the following year that she had an unexpected visitor, none other than the elderly character woman with whom she'd worked in the provinces, Hilda Asquith!

The aristocratic old actress wore a shawl over her thin coat and her lined face under a black bonnet looked more gaunt than when Fanny had last seen her. The two embraced on this gray, winter afternoon and then sat together over tea and cakes provided by Fanny's housekeeper.

"But what are you doing in London?" Fanny asked the old actress.

As if in answer Hilda Asquith coughed, a deep, hacking cough. "I have been ill," she confessed, after the seizure passed. "I'm not longer well enough to travel. David Cornish gave me two months salary and urged me to rest until I regained my health."

Fanny smiled her approval. "David always had a kind heart."

"That he does," the old actress agreed. "But I grew weary of my small room in Manchester. And feeling better, I decided I would come to London."

Fanny took the old woman's thin hand in hers and said, "I'm so glad you're here. You must live with me until you're completely well!"

Looking embarrassed, the old actress protested, "I could not dream of that! Imposing myself on you!"

"I'd like to have you here! I'm lonely!"

"With all your new friends and your success? We have heard about your London triumphs!" Hilda Asquith said.

Fanny smiled ruefully. "To be truthful, my success hasn't made me all that happy! Though I do admit I have been more fortunate than I deserved."

Hilda eyed her fondly. With emotion, she said, "That is not so! You have worked hard for your success! And you inherited much of your dear father's talent!"

"Thank you," Fanny said. "My father will always be a guiding force in my life."

"He dearly loved you!"

"I know," she said, her eyes blurring with unshed tears. "He wanted me to become a star of the London stage, and I have."

Hilda agreed, "He would be so pleased."

Fanny smiled at the old actress. "As soon as you are well again I shall have Sir Alan find a role for you in the new play. Then you can work without having to travel."

"You think me talented enough for the company?"

"I say you have much more talent than many playing with us now," Fanny assured her. "And what of the others? Has David made a success of his touring group?"

"He has done remarkably well," the old actress said. "He is now a respected name in the provinces. He has his choice of the best theatres in all the towns."

"I'm so happy for him!" Fanny said fervently.

Hilda gave her a knowing glance. "He took your leaving us hard."

"I was afraid of that."

"He was in a black mood for weeks after," the character actress confided. "We all tried to help him. I talked to him and tried to make him understand you'd left to carry out your father's wishes. In the end I think he came to terms with your decision."

Fanny bit her lip. "I hope so," she said in a small voice. Her eyes met the bleak, faded, blue eyes of the old actress. "In a way, I loved him."

"And he had eyes for no one but you!"

"It made it doubly hard for me."

"And for him," the old actress sighed. "But then life is never easy, is it? He has achieved success and so have you."

Fanny said, "Has he ever mentioned my being on the London stage?"

"He spoke of it one day when I was alone with him, after I became ill and he had come to my room to visit me. He had read a review of your latest London appearance and he was proud of you. He came close to saying that you had done right in leaving us."

"But he did *not* say it?"

"You know David Cornish. His pride would not allow that. Yet I feel he now realizes you followed the right path. The bitterness has passed."

"I pray so," Fanny said.

"It has, I'm sure!"

She asked, "What about him? Has he shown any interest in anyone else?"

Hilda Asquith smiled bleakly. "It is a question I expected you to ask. For a while it seemed that girl whom you trained to take your place, Maude Lyons, would win his affections. I can promise you she tried hard enough."

"And?"

"It didn't work," the old actress said. "Maude did well enough as leading lady but he showed no interest in her off the stage. In fact he treated her so coldly she left at the first opportunity and David had to find a new leading woman."

Fanny felt both pleasure and sadness in the news. It was warming to know that David's love for her had been so true, but troubling to think she might have turned him into a bitter bachelor.

She said, "I wish he would find someone to love and who would love him. He needs someone."

"What about yourself?"

Fanny blushed. "I have been too busy for romance. I have many male friends to escort me about, but I have made no romantic friendships."

Hilda nodded. "I think it has been much the same with David. He has worked hard to become a provincial star. And if I'm not wrong, one day he'll make his mark here in London."

"I hope he does," Fanny said sincerely. "I'm sure he could be a success here if he tried hard enough. My complaint was that he could not see beyond the provinces."

"He does now," Hilda assured her. "I think you have shown him the way."

Fanny hoped this was true. She could think of no happier development than David Cornish coming to London and gaining a reputation in the great city. They could be friends again if only he could find it in his heart to forgive her. But would it ever be the same? Would they resume as lovers? She was not sure. Still vivid in her mind and heart was the image of Viscount George Palmer. Though she hadn't seen or heard of him in a long while she knew that he was still the great romance of her young life!

With the arrival of Hilda Asquith life in the London flat became less lonely. And as soon as Hilda was well enough she took her place in the company with Fanny and Sir Alan.

Silas Hodder, secure in his position of stage door manager, was much impressed with the old actress. He privately told Fanny, "Miss Asquith is not only a talented actress but a fine woman! It is my intention to invite her out to supper one night!"

And to Fanny's amusement, he did. Hilda accepted and the two became close friends. The company appeared before enthusiastic large audiences every night and it seemed that nothing would change this pleasant world.

True, there were ominous rumblings of approaching trouble in the Crimea. There were some who went so far as to predict war with Russia! And the miserable poverty of many in the city and countryside in this era of growing industrial prosperity and the making of a new wealthy middle class did not appear to distress young Queen Victoria or her Consort, Prince Albert.

Then, without warning, a troublesome rivalry began in the London theatre world. Sir Alan Tredale was too much of a gentleman to initiate any such thing, and the other noted stars of the London stage, Charles Matthew and his wife Lucy, were close personal friends. It was from a much less exalted section of the theatre managers that the ill-will sprang.

There were a group of cheap companies presenting lurid dramas of a type gradually losing appeal. They blamed their vanishing audiences on the prosperity of Sir Alan and his company. These theatres south of the Thames presented such thrillers as *Gloomy Dell* and *Suicide Tree*. One of the gaudiest managers of these cheap drama houses was Tobias Wall, who had been pointed out to Fanny at several London restaurants.

Tobias Wall was a stout, red-faced man with graying side-whiskers and a florid manner both on stage and off. He wore frockcoats of atrociously loud plaids and his bad manners matched his poor taste. But he did have a following among the rabble and he became the chief among the trouble-makers for the People's, Covent Garden, Drury Lane and Haymarket theatres.

He sent bully boys to annoy patrons lining up at these theatres to purchase tickets and also had these same roughnecks shove their way past the ticket takers to pass out handbills of the current Tobias Wall play in the theatres. Appeals to the police did little good; the bullies were dispersed only to return soon again. The London police could not be at the theatres constantly as they had other calls on their services.

Silas Hodder had several run-ins with the bullies trying to force their way in the stage door and though he and the other backstage crew had managed to repel the thugs, he was gloomy about the developments.

As Fanny paused to talk with him on her way out of the theatre one evening, the gaunt-faced man told her, "I don't like it, Fanny! I don't like it at all! Sir Alan is taking this too lightly! I say Tobias Wall and his lot are out to cause us serious trouble!"

She sighed. "I know others who agree with you. I will talk to Sir Alan and urge that we take more precautions."

But when she approached the gentlemanly stage star he only showed pain on his handsome face and spreading his hands, asked, "What can I do? I will not stoop to the methods of these villains. I can only depend on the police and hope they will soon tire of baiting us."

The hot summer came and some of the hooliganism ended. It appeared that Sir Alan had been correct. The worst of the conflict seemed to have passed. One August afternoon when there was no performance at the theatre Fanny accepted the invitation of a young admirer, Simon Frith, to accompany him to the races. She agreed on the condition she might bring Hilda Asquith along as chaperone. The charming, blond, young Simon was the son of a wealthy London brewer and had the reputation of being a rake, so she felt she must be especially cautious with him.

To her surprise, Simon cordially agreed that Hilda should accompany them in his carriage. And so they all three drove out to Ascot.

It was a hot afternoon and both Fanny and the elderly actress had worn light dresses of cotton lawn and carried parasols to protect them from the sun. Simon Frith in light gray frockcoat and gray tophat was perspiring fiercely as they arrived at the racetrack. The circular track was surrounded by the carriages of the gentry and the less affluent strolled about between the carriages.

"I vow it is the warmest day of the season," Simon said, after he'd found a place for the carriage and a groom had taken his horses off to a shady spot. He stood beside the carriage wiping his forehead with a large white linen handkerchief. "My apologies for bringing you out on such a day."

"I do not get to the races very often," Fanny smiled. "So I'm bound to enjoy myself. And so is Miss Asquith."

"It is all quite thrilling!" Hilda Asquith agreed.

Simon replaced his hat on his head and glanced about bleakly. "I'm afraid it is all too familiar to me." The races had not yet begun and vendors were going about hawking cold drinks and food items. Itinerant acrobats and other entertainers were giving the crowd gathered there a sample of their talents. Later one of their number would go from carriage to carriage with a tin cup for donations. Jockeys were also appearing on finely-groomed horses and it presented a colorful spectacle.

Simon Frith told them, "If you will excuse me, I have a favorite bookmaker whom I must find before the horses run!" And with a bow he left them and vanished in the motley crowd.

Old Hilda Asquith smiled. "It would appear young Mr. Frith is more interested in betting than in female companionship. I fear my being here is hardly necessary."

"You are wrong in that," Fanny told her. "I need company while Simon attends to the races and there is always afterwards to consider. I have heard some distressing stories about our charming host."

"At any rate I'm enjoying it," the elderly actress said. "I have never attended such a grand affair before."

Fanny was about to make a reply to this when a young man in the red and gold jacket and blue breeches of an army officer came up to their carriage. Removing his black hat with its gray plume he addressed himself to her.

"Well, Fanny, don't tell me you've forgotten me so soon!" he said.

She stared at the pleasant-faced, fair-haired young man for a moment before she recognized him. Then she exclaimed, "You've grown a mustache, Captain Charles!"

"I have but I can't imagine it has made so much difference in my looks," he teased her good-naturedly. "I'm afraid I made so little impression on you, you've forgotten me!"

"Not at all," she said with a small laugh. "You remember you were always a favorite with us downstairs."

The young army officer said, "But it's downstairs for you no longer, Fanny. I've seen you on the stage playing opposite Sir Alan. You've become a star of the London stage."

"You've seen me at the theatre?" she asked, pleasantly surprised.

"Several times," Charles Palmer assured her. And with another of his amused looks, he added, "And I'm not the only one. Another member of my family whom you must remember a lot better than you do me, has also watched you on the stage."

Fanny felt her cheeks burn. "Really?"

"I have much to tell you," Captain Charles Palmer said.

"The races are about to begin," she told him. "Miss Asquith and I are awaiting the return of Simon Frith."

"Simon?" Charles raised his eyebrows. "You are mixing in fast London society, my girl. Do you think Simon would excuse you if you joined me for a short chat and left Miss Asquith here to entertain him?"

She smiled in confusion. "I'm not sure he'd approve."

Hilda Asquith had taken in the situation and at once spoke up, saying, "Go on with your friend, Fanny. I will explain to Mr. Frith when he comes back. I'm sure he'll understand."

"There you are!" Charles said warmly. "Miss Asquith is on our side!"

She turned to Hilda and said, "Tell Simon I won't be long." Then she allowed Charles to help her down from the carriage and lead her a distance from the track.

As they walked, a cry rose up from the race track, and people began hurrying by them in the opposite direction, anxious not to miss the first race. Charles glanced at her, "You don't mind missing the race, I trust."

"No," she said. "I'd rather talk."

"And so would I," he agreed. "So many things to say. There is a big oak tree back here which will offer some shade."

They reached the huge tree which was within sight of the race track. The area surrounding it was deserted and so they were able to sit together on the grass and talk without interruption.

Charles studied her with admiring eyes. "I must say you've grown a lot move lovely! And you were a beauty at the start!"

"No flattery, please," she said.

"It's not flattery," the young officer protested. "You know I've always been in love with you!"

"Charles!" she reproved him and touched his hand gently with hers to show that she was indeed very fond of him.

His pleasant face shadowed. "I know. It has always been George hasn't it?"

Fanny blushed. "What about George?"

"You should have married him. He was eager to marry you, he told me so himself."

She shook her head. "Your father made me see how disastrous that would have been for both of us. And he was right."

"You are a star of the stage who mixes with high society. You could marry him now," Charles said. "Unhappily for both of you, it is too late."

Fanny's head swam and she said faintly, "Too late?"

He nodded. "He married Virginia. You knew father was determined to make the match. He succeeded. George and Virginia have a son and a daughter."

She fought to recover herself from the shock of this news, telling herself it should not be important to her. She had not seen George for years. They lived in different worlds.

Looking away she said in a taut voice, "I hope Virginia has made him a good wife. I trust they are happy."

"They are not."

She turned to stare at Charles' sober face. "Why do you say that?"

"Virginia was never right for George," he said. "We all knew that. Even before the marriage there was the rumor of her drinking."

"Has it gone on?"

"Worse than before. She disgraced George on several important occasions. Now he has stopped making social engagements altogether and devotes himself to his political career."

"And Virginia?"

"Continues to drink and there is talk of her having affairs with other men behind George's back." He hesitated. "I might say one of those named is your escort of today, Simon Frith!"

"No!" she cried in dismay.

Charles shrugged. "You need not be upset by it. Virginia is to blame for her own conduct. She doesn't even properly run the house for George or look after the children. Our cousin, Dora, has had to move in with them and take charge of the youngsters."

This mention of Dora Carson made Fanny think fondly of the warm-hearted, poor relation of the Palmers. She said, "Dora was so kind to me. I hoped that George might marry her."

"She would have made him a better wife than Virginia. But, again, father opposed George showing any interest in Dora. And to be truthful, George did not care for her enough to marry her. You were his single great love."

"A downstairs maid!"

"That did not matter," Charles said, looking at her directly. "I know you gave yourself to him. I do not think it wrong. What was wrong was your leaving the way you did."

"What else could I do?"

"You might have discussed it with George," his brother said. "He might have agreed to wait. To have tried to help you get a start on the stage."

"I was too confused and frightened to wait," she said. "The Reverend Kenneth had already labeled me as a harlot. To that, your father added that I was also a fool!"

"Father is a stubborn old man," Charles said. "And as for brother Kenneth, he has always been a little mad. He has made a fetish of his religion. Last year he became so mentally ill he had to give up his post as assistant to the Bishop. Now he has recovered and has a small church of his own."

She stared down at the grass. "It's all past history. I only wish thing's were better for George."

"And I wish that they were better for you," Charles said with urgency. "Simon Frith is no sort of man for you to be going about with."

"He is only a casual acquaintance," she countered.

"He has a bad reputation."

"I know," she said. "That is why I was careful to have Miss Asquith chaperone us."

"You showed wisdom in that," he agreed. "George thinks you have great talent."

She smiled wistfully. "He gave me my first big audience the night he forced me to entertain Prince Aran!"

Charles chuckled. "Of course! That studgy Indian chap! And the bounder fell in love with you and wanted to take you back to India with him as his concubine!"

Fanny corrected, "As an instructress for his children."

"No one believed that for a minute," Charles said. "Not even father. George soon put an end to it!"

"Perhaps I should have gone," she sighed.

"It would have been an experience," Charles agreed. "I understand the Prince's father died shortly after he returned to India and so he is the Maharajah now."

"Has he returned to England since?"

"No," Charles said. "And according to my father he has not answered any correspondence sent to him by the family firm. One gathers he does not forgive easily. He blamed the family for not turning you over to him."

She pictured her last encounter with the Prince and recalled the lean, grim face of the brown-skinned man. She said, "I'm sure he is a vindictive type."

"I quite agree," Charles said. "But enough of him. What about you?"

She told him of her adventures in provincial theatre and of meeting her father. She was careful not to mention David Cornish in describing these adventures and her coming to London and finding fame. She ended with, "I find a dedication to my stage career enough."

"That can never be enough for a woman like you," Charles argued. "You are sure there is no one else?"

"No one," she said soberly.

"No use waiting for George," he warned her. "Virginia comes from a long lived family of hard-drinkers, and she needs her marriage to George to cover up her drinking and her affairs."

"What does the Reverend Kenneth think about her?" Fanny asked.

Charles sighed. "He visits her every so often and tells her she is headed straight for Hell. She, in turn, tells him to take the same destination. We're truly a comfortable family," he said acidly.

"It will work out," she said. "There is Dora to solace George, and the children."

"I'm not worried about him," Charles said. "I'm concerned about you."

"You needn't be."

"Marry me," Charles pleaded, moving closer to her.

"Charles, I'm terribly fond of you," she said, "but I can't marry you."

"Because of your feelings for my brother."

She closed her eyes and sighed. "Because I'm so completely confused." She stood up. "It's time I returned to Simon's carriage."

Also on his feet, Charles restrained her, saying, "I think fate made us meet here today."

"You do?"

"Yes. Otherwise I might never have seen you again."

"What do you mean?"

"My regiment is sailing for the Crimea in a day or two. Trouble is expected there."

She frowned. "I've heard rumors. I didn't know that English troops were being sent."

The young officer said, "Nothing official yet! We are being sent ahead to the area as a precautionary move, as are some of our largest naval units."

She gave a tiny shudder. "Another war! I had hoped they might be at an end."

"Never believe that," Charles said. "So even though we have met there is no time for us."

Fanny looked up at the crestfallen Charles. "I shall pray for your safe return!"

He smiled. "And I shall try jolly hard to keep out of danger since I want to see you again."

"Come back soon and safe," she said in a soft voice.

"Dear Fanny!" Charles said with emotion and he took her in his arms and kissed her long and lovingly. When he at last let her go, he said, "If I get back will you think about my offer?"

She protested, "Don't ask me for promises, Charles! I don't want to make any I can't keep."

"Then don't," the young officer said. "And when I return I have the feeling you'll be more sure of what you want. And I'm going to try and make sure you want marriage with me!"

Fanny smiled ruefully. "You're very persistent!"

"Always!" he said, taking her by the arm and escorting her back in the direction of the race track.

When they reached the carriage Simon Frith was seated there with Miss Asquith, watching the race through binoculars. When Frith saw them coming towards the carriage he gave the binoculars to Hilda Asquith and came down to greet them.

Simon eyed the pair coldly. He said, "I did not know you and Charles were friends."

She said quickly, "We're old friends."

"That is obvious," Simon said in the same icy vein. "Since you chose to miss most of the racing to be with him."

Charles spoke up, "We had a lot of catching up to do. We've not seen each other in years. I took more than my share of Fanny's time as I'm being shipped out East in a day or two."

This seemed to cheer Simon up. He said, "Are you? What luck! I wonder you don't go on half-pay and let someone else take your place. It's a fairly common practice, I'm told."

Charles looked resentful. "Not for those who take the service seriously, though I hasten to agree there are only a few of us who do. I prefer to serve the Queen where needed and win my promotion rather than buy it."

"Admirable!" Simon said with sarcasm. "Then we shall just have to carry on without you."

"Not for long," Charles said. "I have an idea the trouble out there will be settled shortly."

"No need to rush," Simon said with a sour smile. "I can promise to look after Fanny in your absence."

Charles took this with good humor. "Since she is the darling of London I have no doubt there will be many to watch out for her." He turned to the carriage. "Good day, Miss Asquith." Then to Fanny, he said, "Remember all I have said." He took her hand and lifted it to his lips. Then he nodded to Simon and turned and went on his way.

Simon watched after him. "I say, he has a nerve!"

Fanny gave the young man a reproving glance. "If you wish me to continue being your friend you must not speak any evil of Charles."

Simon expressed amazement. "You are so serious about him?"

"He is like a brother to me."

"A brother," Simon said mockingly. "That I can endure. And I assure you I shall leave his name unscathed!"

Fanny said, "Good! If you'll help me up into the carriage I'd like to enjoy the rest of the races."

"By all means," Simon said, helping her. "There is just one important race to be run now."

Hilda Asquith removed the binoculars from her ancient eyes to joyfully inform Fanny, "Would you believe it? Because of Mr. Frith and his very obliging bookmaker I'm the winner of a full five pounds!"

"Wonderful!" Fanny said, amused.

At her side Simon said, "You see what you've missed. Not to mention the pleasure of my company as well."

"I do regret that," Fanny said.

Simon eyed her warily. "Thank you, though I doubt that you mean it. One tends to not take actresses too seriously."

"Then you're making a mistake," Fanny frostily assured the young roué.

"So you and Charles Palmer are friends," Simon mused. "Do you know his brother, George?"

"The Viscount?" She hoped she was not blushing again.

Simon said mockingly, "Knowing the family as you do I would suppose you would be familiar enough with him to call him George."

Fanny could not help giving him an impish glance and saying, "Just as I understand you are 'intimate' enough with the family to call his wife, Virginia."

This time it was Simon's face which reddened shockingly. He rushed to grab the binoculars from Miss Asquith and hold them to his eyes as he said, "I believe the horses are lining up for the final race now!"

Chapter Eight

It was January 1855 and the shadow of the war in the Crimea hung over all England. Opinion was divided as to whether the war had been justified and whether Britain and her Allies were winning it. One thing was certain; despite all the government propaganda it was not a popular war. There were ominous rumblings among the common people as they learned from war correspondent William Howard Russell's eye-witness stories in the *London Times* the truth about the miserable and meaningless affair.

Most deaths among the British troops were not from battle but from disease, starvation and exposure. Battles were planned by incompetent and stupid generals which led to the senseless slaughter of their men. There were few heroic bright spots such as MacMahon storming the Malakov redoubt and Florence Nightingale holding aloft her lamp to comfort the wounded and dying in the crowded, stinking wards and corridors of makeshift hospitals in Scutari and the Crimea.

And there was the Charge of the Light Brigade, the gallant legion which rode to doom in the "Valley of Death" at Balaclava. The full facts of this affair were not yet revealed to the British public. So it was a grim irony that the incompetent Lord Cardigan who had indeed led the Light Brigade in the charge was received with all the adulation due a war hero on his return to London. He was greeted by cheering mobs and his picture was displayed in shop windows. The Queen and Prince Albert invited him to stay at Windsor where he described the charge with becoming modesty. Bands met him at railway stations to serenade him with "See the Conquering Hero Comes."

Fanny Hastings was among those who suspected that Lord Cardigan was neither a hero nor a conqueror. Captain Charles

Palmer was one of the few who had made the ride into the Valley of Death and survived with only a minor injury. His letters to her had been bitter and revealing. He could not wait for the meaningless war to end. He spoke longingly of returning to England and seeing her again.

• • •

One evening in February following the performance, Sir Alan Tredale came to visit Fanny in her dressing room. The lean, distinguished actor was still in his dressing gown and he had an engraved invitation in his hand.

Sir Alan had heard her express her views about the war and the folly of the sacrifice of the Light Brigade. So now he stood by her with a somewhat troubled expression on his aristocratic face.

Clearing his throat, he said, "Fanny, an invitation has been left in my dressing room. It is for both of us, so I have come to discuss it with you."

Seated before her dressing room mirror in her robe, she gazed up at him with raised eyebrows. "And who has sent us this invitation?"

"Lady Grace Smedley," Sir Alan said. "You know she has been most generous in her patronage of our theatre."

"Of course," she said. "What is the affair?"

"I know you will not approve," he said, apologetically.

She at once stood up. "I trust it is not anything to do with honoring Lord Cardigan! Surely London has had enough of that lunacy! Charles Palmer was in the charge with him and he claims it was a senseless slaughter!"

The distinguished actor sighed. "I'm afraid it is an affair in Lord Cardigan's honor. Lady Smedley is holding it in her home and she has requested that we attend following the performance on Friday night."

Fanny said, "Soon the facts will out and the country will know the truth about that man! And what fools they have made of themselves!"

"I quite agree, Fanny," Sir Alan said wearily. "Yet I do not wish to offend Lady Smedley since her support is so important to the theatre."

Fanny's pert face showed grim resignation. "You want me to attend?"

"I plead with you to join me there for at least a little while," the actor said. "We need not remain long since we'll be arriving late in any case."

She hesitated, thinking about the problems they had been having lately. She could not help but sympathize with the man who had made her career possible and carried the burden of the company. So she said, "Very well, I'll go. But do not expect me to pay any compliments to the guest of honor."

Sir Alan smiled a thin smile of relief. "I do not ask that. Just that you appear with me so Lady Smedley will know we are not ungrateful for all she has done for the People's Theatre."

Fanny found herself in the crowded ballroom of the mansion in Lionel Square the following Friday night. She wore a yellow silk gown that bared her white shoulders and bosom. On the chill February night she had draped a heavy cloak over it to protect her against the cold. On Sir Alan's arm she was introduced to the vapid Lord Cardigan.

Fanny did no more than acknowledge the introduction. She was happy there were others in line so that she and Sir Alan were able to move on quickly. Then they mingled with the other guests at the glittering soirée which represented the cream of London society. A string quartet played at one end of the huge ballroom with its painted ceiling of blue clouds and cherubic figures. Under the crystal chandeliers the elegantly clad men and women chatted.

Sir Alan was, as usual, at once surrounded by a number of elderly female admirers. Fanny, her auburn hair coiled in the latest fashion, stood back to let these women surround her co-star, while she watched with a cynical smile on her lovely face.

A voice spoke in her ear, "Knowing your views of our military hero I'm surprised to find you here." It was the dandy, Simon Frith, elegant in blue frock coat and ruffled white shirt.

She gave him a rueful glance. "I'm here on the orders of my superior."

"Sir Alan?"

"Yes. Lady Smedley is one of our loyal patrons."

Simon nodded. "You theatre folk do have to consider that, don't you?" He glanced around. "In any case you'll find many of your friends here."

"Will I?"

"Yes," he said. "In fact, one of them is coming towards us now. And if you don't mind I'll move on. I've had a slight difference with the fellow" Simon smirked at her and vanished in the crowd almost instantly.

At the same moment Fanny found Viscount George Palmer standing before her. His sudden appearance left her speechless as she studied him. He looked much older than she remembered him and his handsome face wore a drawn expression.

His serious eyes met hers and he took her hand and kissed it. "Fanny," he said. "After all these years!"

She nodded and found her voice at last. "So much time has passed!"

"You have grown into true beauty," he said, his eyes never leaving her.

"It is good to see you again."

"I have often attended the theatre," George went on. "Your talent has improved along with your looks."

"You are too generous!"

"It is true," George said soberly. "Charles told me of his meeting with you before he left for the Crimea."

"Yes. It was good to see him again," she said. "We had only a brief time together."

"Who did you come here with?"

"Sir Alan," she said. "Is your wife here?"

George's lip curled in scorn. "I went to her bedroom to get her and she was already too sodden with drink to be able to leave the room. I instructed her maid to help her undress and came here alone. I have to do much of that these days."

"I'm sorry," Fanny whispered.

"I was wrong and weak," the handsome Viscount said. "I ought never to have married Virginia. I was so disconsolate when you ran off. It was father's idea."

Her smile was sad. "You were always too much the romantic! There was no future for us!"

"You listened to Father! And Father was wrong! He had no right to interfere!"

Fanny said, "His judgement was better than you think. I had to make a place for myself. We were far from being equal in those days."

"It is different now," George pointed out.

"Now you are married to Virginia," she reminded him.

"It is no marriage!" he said angrily.

"Perhaps she will reform as she grows older, conquer her weakness for drink and make you a proper wife."

"I do not see it," George said. "If it were not for Dora my children would be brought up by servants. Dora has kindly taken over my household for me."

Fanny gave him a knowing look. "Dora has always cared for you deeply."

"I know," the weary-looking George said. "And I greatly admire her. But I do not love her. I have always loved only you!"

She lifted her fan to silence him. "You must not say such things."

George took her by the arm and said, "Let us find a place where we may have more privacy."

Fearful of allowing herself to be with him alone and yet unable to resist him, she let him lead her across the crowded room to a winding flight of stairs. They ascended the stairs to a balcony which surrounded a large part of the ballroom and gave a view of it. He led her along the balcony until they came to a deserted area and drawing her behind a draped column which would hide them from anyone in the ballroom below he took her in his arms.

Fanny had often considered what she would do when and if this moment came. Since meeting Charles she had thought much of his brother who had once been her lover. And she had rehearsed how she would act if they met and she found herself in his embrace. She had promised herself to draw away from him and repulse his advances.

But she had not counted on the intensity of her own feelings! Once she felt his lips on hers and their bodies close together she was overwhelmed by the memory of their passion. Trembling, she discovered herself responding to him with ardor to match his own. Her behaviour shocked her even as she knew she could not control it.

"Dear Fanny!" George breathed in her ear and held her tight to him.

"This is wrong! We mustn't!" she protested in dismay.

"It cannot be wrong that we love each other," he rebuked her. "I refuse to believe that!"

"It's too late!"

"Not for us to be together," George said. "I have a flat I often use when things become too dreadful at home. We can go there now!"

"No, George!"

"I beg you," he said huskily. "I'm completely lost. If you turn from me I swear there is nothing left. I shall take my life!"

"Do not talk so wildly!"

He stared at her, his face grim. "I mean it! It is not wild talk!"

"George!" she sobbed, resting her head on his chest.

"Is there someone else?"

"No!"

"Then we must help each other," he said. "You prepare to leave and I'll tell Sir Alan that I'll take the responsibility of seeing you home."

She closed her eyes and gave a deep sigh. "Even though we know our love is genuine this can only lead to trouble! I'm sure of it!"

"Being together once more, if only for a little, will be a touch of Paradise for both of us," the young Viscount assured her.

They went back downstairs and while she crossed to the ladies' cloakroom to get her things, George sought out Sir Alan and let him know he was taking Fanny home in his carriage. Fanny knew Sir Alan would not be surprised at this since he realized she did not wish to remain long at the soirée.

Within a short time they were in George's carriage on their way across town. She insisted that the driver take a message to Hilda Asquith at her apartment, so the older woman would not worry about her not returning. She simply wrote a brief note saying she was spending the night with a friend.

The flat which George had rented was not far from the Houses of Parliament. As Fanny left the carriage and mounted the outside steps with their light covering of snow, she was trembling, not from the cold but from the knowledge that she and George were embarking on a path which they would find it hard to depart from, even though it might well lead to their destruction.

This knowledge was confirmed a little while later as they made love on blankets before the blazing fireplace. It seemed their desire would never be satiated, and when the glorious climax came for them, they lay for a long while in each other's arms, light of the flames flickering on their naked bodies. Fanny gazed at the expression of content on her lover's face and knew that she could not desert him again.

It was on that winter's night that their romance was resumed. It went on throughout the year. Fanny confessed the truth to no one but Hilda Asquith, so the elderly actress would not be concerned at her being absent from their flat on certain nights.

The old woman was troubled for her. "I do not like it," she said. "He cannot marry you. And sooner or later your affair will come to light and you will be disgraced."

Fanny shrugged. "I know all that, Hilda. I realized it from the start. But I love him!"

"He has a wife!"

"You can hardly call her that."

Hilda's lined face showed distress. "Better you had married David Cornish. I'm sure he loved you as much as any man could."

"Please," Fanny begged. "Don't bring David into this. It is difficult enough as it is."

The war in the Crimea was coming to a slow, unhappy end. Charles wrote that he hoped to be sent back soon to England. Then the old Marquis died suddenly and George was at once the inheritor of the title and his father's seat in the House of Lords. Fanny begged him to give up their affair, fearful of what a revelation of it might do to his political career.

George was stubborn in his resistance to the idea. He told her solemnly, "I would rather face any sort of disgrace than lose you!"

So her furtive visits to his flat continued. Several times when she was leaving the house to get in the carriage to take her home she thought she saw a black-clad male figure standing partly-hidden in an alley across the street.

She mentioned this to George but he did not take her warning seriously. She said, "I think it may be a detective spying on us. Someone your wife has hired."

"Nonsense," George argued. "Virginia is in such a sodden state these days she would never be able to think out or organize such an action against us."

"Are you so sure?" she worried.

He took her in his arms. "You must not think about such things," he said, silencing her by pressing his lips on hers.

Still, she continued to see the same figure watching from the alley on several other occasions. Once she asked the driver to turn the carriage around so she could get a closer glimpse of the mystery man in the alley. But when the carriage went close by the alley entrance the figure moved back into the shadows to remain just as obscure as ever.

In October there was another outburst of theatre rivalry. Tobias Wall again hired thugs to annoy the People's Theatre patrons. They also plagued old Silas Hodder at the stage door. He complained of this to Fanny and warned her to be cautious in arriving at the theatre.

"Never leave your carriage if any of those ruffians are around," her good friend said.

"I'll keep that in mind," she agreed. "Hilda is usually with me. If I see any figures lurking by the stage door we'll go around to the front entrance of the theatre."

"That would be wise," Silas said. And then he added, "I have another question to ask you. Are you acquainted with a minister? There has been a man in clerical garb appearing at the stage door lately. I do not like his appearance. He has a strange gleam in his eyes."

It was natural that she should at once think of George's brother. She had not seen the Reverend Kenneth Palmer in years, though she knew he continued to preside over a small church in the London area. All at once she began to wonder if his might be the mysterious figure in the alley watching her leave George's flat, as well as haunting the stage door. Knowing his history of mental instability it was not a pleasant thought.

She longed to discuss this possibility with George but he was suddenly plunged into a grim argument in the House of Lords about the conduct of the Crimean War. As a chief critic of the party in power he had a great responsibility and so she did not dare to add to his worries by telling of her fears concerning his brother. Whether the Reverend Kenneth knew about them or not, it was unlikely that he'd try to expose them, since this would bring disgrace on the family. She counted on this and planned to tell George about her concern as soon as the parliamentary crisis was over.

One murky autumn evening when she and Hilda arrived at the stage door of the theatre a dark figure suddenly sprang out of the shadows to confront them. Although Fanny had not seen the Reverend Kenneth for a long while she at once recognized him.

His thin face was a venomous mask as he cried out at her, "Whore!"

"Please!" she begged him.

"I have seen you repeatedly leaving my brother's flat," the Reverend lashed out at her. "I know what is going on!"

"Who is this dreadful person?" old Hilda quavered and stepped back.

"Go inside," Fanny told the elderly actress. "I can deal with him!"

"But …" Hilda hesitated.

"Please!" Fanny shoved her towards the stage door. Then she turned to face the malevolent priest, saying, "You do not understand! Please try to be charitable in this!"

The emaciated man in the black dress of an Anglican priest fairly spat at her. "I have no mercy for whores! You are blood guilty!" And saying this he drew a pail out from behind him and hurled its contents at her. Then he turned and ran off just as an aroused Silas Hodder came out the stage door to aid her.

"He's gone!" she said in a faint voice.

The old stage door man gazed at her in consternation. "What did he do to you, Fanny? You're all splashed with blood!"

She collapsed at this point and when she came to again she was on the floor inside, near the stage door. Sir Alan, Hilda, Silas Hodder and some other members of the company were gathered around her in an anxious state.

Sir Alan knelt by her. "Are you all right?" he asked.

She rose up from the floor on her elbow. "I think so!" Then she saw her blood-stained clothing. "The blood?"

"Is happily not yours," the actor said. "Someone hurled animal blood of some kind on you. If it's another trick of Tobias Wall to harrass us I shall make him pay dearly. The police shall hear of this!"

She shook her head in protest. "Don't call the police! You mustn't!"

"Why not?" Sir Alan asked in surprise.

"Wall shouldn't be allowed to get away with such things," Silas Hodder agreed.

Fanny struggled to her feet with the help of one of the actors. She said, "This had nothing to do with Tobias Wall. I know who it was and why it happened."

"You do?" Sir Alan was amazed.

"Yes," she said, unhappily. "I'm not hurt. So please just forget it happened."

The distinguished actor asked, "Is this enemy of yours apt to attack you again?"

"I think not," she said, though she was far from convinced.

He still showed reluctance to let the matter drop. "I do not like it at all," he said.

Hilda and she shared a dressing room and the elderly actress helped her remove the blood-stained clothes. As Fanny sat pale and ill-looking before her dressing mirror, the old actress hovered about her worriedly.

"Do you feel able to go on tonight?" Hilda asked.

She nodded. "Yes."

"Better to use your understudy than have you collapse on the stage!"

"I won't collapse," Fanny said. "I will manage.

The lined face of the character woman studied her. "You said you knew it wasn't anyone hired by Tobias Wall. Why were you so certain?"

She glanced up at the old actress. "I knew who it was. It was his brother!"

"George Palmer's brother?" Hilda gasped.

"Yes," she said. "He's always been a little mad and he has always hated me!"

"He came here to frighten you from seeing the Marquis," Hilda said.

"He's been watching me coming and going from the apartment. I suspected it but I haven't had a chance to tell George."

Hilda said grimly, "You must tell him now. I'd say his reverend brother is mad!"

"I'll tell him tonight," she said. "I'm meeting George at his flat after the show."

"Not tonight!" Hilda lamented.

"I promised to be there. George would worry."

"Send him a message. That brother of his might be there waiting to attack you again," Hilda warned her.

Fanny gave a deep sigh. "I think not. In any event I must risk it."

The elderly actress said, "Is it worth it?"

She looked up at the old woman's troubled face. "I love him, Hilda. Everything else seems to fade in comparison."

She slowly completed her make-up and changed into her costume. She was still in a nervous state but she bolstered her courage by thinking of her father and what he would expect of her in such a crisis. When she appeared in the wings to make her first entrance she could tell the other members of the company were tense and watching her every move.

Somehow she carried through her long role in the play without a slip. When the final curtain came down to enthusiastic applause Sir Alan Tredale came over to her and placed an arm around her.

"You did magnificently," he said. "It was an example of complete control. You're a true actress!"

"Thank you," she said with a small smile. "You all helped me."

"About that man," the actor went on, "are you certain you don't wish me to report the incident to the police?"

"Quite certain," she said firmly.

It was fortunate that she had some extra clothing in her dressing room. She was able to find enough things to wear from among these items. Her ruined clothing had been thrown away by Silas Hodder.

The gaunt old stage door man summoned a carriage for her and helped her into it. "Take care, Fanny," he said. "That madman is liable to strike again."

It was a dark night and when she reached the neighborhood of the flat she was unable to tell whether anyone was lurking across the street watching her or not. She safely made her way up to George's apartment and used her own key to let herself in. She found him seated in the study, his desk strewn with a mass of papers which he was going over in the soft glow of his desk lamp.

He rose from his work and came to take her in his arms. "A difficult night at the theatre?" he asked. "You look pale."

She managed a small smile. "You might call it an...unusual one."

He waved at the papers on his desk. "I have to be familiar with all these before the House sits tomorrow. I've been working on them for hours."

"I shouldn't have come!"

His weary face showed a smile. "I counted on your coming. I'm finished with these. Make yourself comfortable and I'll get some brandy."

When he returned with their brandies she settled in the big leather chair and told him what had happened. She ended with, "There is no question that it was your brother."

George rose to pace up and down before her in anger. "So he is going to try and cause us trouble again."

She said, "From his point of view we're the ones in the wrong."

He waved an impatient hand. "Kenneth has always been too ready to judge others while continuing with his own demented behaviour. I shall have to see him and lecture him."

"Will he listen to you?"

"He'd better!" George said. "Or I'll threaten to give Virginia grounds to divorce me before she drinks herself to death!"

"What good will that do?"

"He is terrified of a family scandal," George said. "He hopes to become a bishop. He thinks bad family publicity would harm his chances."

She sipped her brandy. Then she raised her eyes to meet his. "George, perhaps the time has come. I've never been happy about all this, though I've been weak enough to go along with you. Maybe we should end it before there is more tragedy!"

The handsome, weary-looking man came to stand before her. "If you leave me I won't have the strength to go on. Things daily get worse at home. I'm under pressure in the House. If I did not have this refuge here with you I would break! I know it!"

Fanny stretched a hand out for him to take. "You managed before we came back together. I have an idea you are stronger than you realize."

He took her hand in his and she felt his skin to be feverish. He said, "When we met that night I was at the end. I was planning to take my life. You have given me a new chance."

She said, "We must not deceive ourselves. The truth is bound to come out. Sooner now, perhaps, with your brother in such a state. When it does, my career and yours are both apt to be ruined."

"I'm willing to pay the price," he said, firmly. "What about you?"

Fanny put aside her empty brandy glass and stood soberly facing him. "Would I be here otherwise?"

He drew her close to him. "Then nothing else matters."

She pressed her cheek against his chest. She said, "Is Virginia's health truly so bad?"

"Yes. The doctor has been to her twice in the past few weeks," he said. "The last time he told me her liver has been ravaged by her steady intake of liquor. He warned her that unless she gave up alcohol she is doomed to die shortly."

"And she has not stopped?"

"I've tried everything," George said unhappily. "She bribes tradesmen to bring her supplies. And she has friends like Simon Frith who think it a joke to bring her liquor. Dora keeps a constant watch on her and she still manages to wind up drunk nearly every day."

She sighed and drew back to gaze up at him. "How unhappy she must be to do this to herself!"

George reminded her, "Virginia was addicted to alcohol before I married her. When she realized she'd made a mistake in marrying me it didn't make things better. I tried to be a good husband but she sensed I did not truly love her."

"My father was a drinker," she said. "But he managed to get over it before his death."

"I cannot hope that will be the case with Virginia," George said. "If she's bound to do it I wish she would finish it quickly so we might be free to marry honorably."

She shuddered. "Don't say such a thing!"

"I cannot help it," he said. "I hate this being so unfair to you!"

She studied his worn face; already he had aged prematurely. She said, "What about Dora?"

"She is my chief support, other than you," he said. "She is wonderful with the children."

Fanny asked him. "Does she know about me? That you are seeing me again?"

He hesitated, then in a low voice said, "Yes. I felt I had to tell her."

"Why?" she asked in despair. "You are expecting too much from her. You know she also is in love with you!"

"Dora admits you are better for me," he said. "She is glad I have you to turn to."

"She is so fine," Fanny said unhappily. "I would not wish to cause her pain!"

"Dora understands!"

She shook her head. "Knowing about us still has to be an added trial for her. I feel I should go to her and ask her pardon!"

"Because we are in love?"

"A love that has always been doomed," she said. "Does it justify our causing a widening ripple of hurt to all around us?"

"You're exaggerating the situation because of what Kenneth did tonight," he said, closing his arms around her again. "I promise I will take care of him. In a few days you will have forgotten the whole business and feel much better about everything."

"I hope so," she sighed, with little conviction.

But despite her pessimism he proved to be right. She was busy rehearsing a new play at the theatre. This kept her mind occupied and the incident at the stage door gradually faded into oblivion. George made a speech against the conduct of the war in the House and the newspapers praised him highly and suggested that he was destined to play an important role in Her Majesty's government in the future.

She and George continued to meet but because they were both so busy, they did not see each other as often as before. Fanny felt this was to the good. George had gone to see the Reverend Kenneth and frightened him into submission. He had told his brother that he was prepared to ask Virginia for a divorce if any more attacks were made on Fanny.

• • •

The new year of 1856 dawned with all seeming more hopeful. Fanny continued to receive letters regularly from Charles and with the ending of the war he was now expecting to be home in a matter of weeks. She found herself worrying about this and wondering what complications would ensue when Charles learned she had resumed her affair with George. For Charles still insisted he loved her and wanted to marry her.

Then there was a new and most unexpected development. There was a knock at the door of the flat Fanny shared with old Hilda Asquith one morning and when she went to the door and opened it she discovered the actor, David Cornish, standing there.

"David!" she gasped with delight. "How good to see you!"

He smiled and entered. "I wondered if I'd be welcome." He was dressed smartly in a gray suit and looked elegant and prosperous.

"Of course you're welcome!" Fanny cried. "Hilda will be so happy to see you. She's out doing some shopping just now but she ought to be back soon."

David smiled. "Good old Hilda! She's still acting?"

"An important member of our company," she said, her eyes bright with happiness. "Oh, David, you look so well!" And she threw her arms around him and kissed him.

His arms enfolded her and he kissed her warmly in return. Then she led him over to the settee where they sat facing each other.

Rather shyly, he said, "I was badly hurt when you ran off!"

"I know," she said. "It pained me as well. But by now you must understand. I had to make a try at London!"

His good-looking face brightened. "And you have! No doubt of that! You're a real star!"

"I have to thank Sir Alan for much of my success," she said modestly. "And what about you? I have heard such grand reports of your tours in the provinces. They say you had to extend your stay in Birmingham by two weeks last season!"

David looked pleased at this. "True," he said. "And in Liverpool we did an extra week."

"You have conquered the provinces," she said. "You are probably the biggest touring company in the country."

"Perhaps," the young actor said. "In any event, that's over with."

"Over with?"

"Yes. I've decided to produce in London this year. I want to make my name here just as you've done!"

Fanny was surprised but she also was pleased. She took his hands in hers and told him, "You will conquer London just as you have the provinces. I know it!"

"It's a risk," he said. "I must pick out the right plays and the best company possible. I've saved some money and I feel I should take the gamble."

"So do I!"

He gave her a searching look. "You're just as lovely as ever," he said. "What has been happening in your life apart from the stage?"

She found herself blushing. She looked down and said quietly, "Not too much. And yourself? Are you engaged or married?"

"Neither," he said.

She offered him a tiny smile. "Waiting for the right girl to come along."

"She came along a while back," David said. "Trouble is, she didn't stay with me."

"David!" she said with a tone of mild rebuke.

The young actor asked, "Are you still in love with that fellow you met so long ago? Is he still the only one you can think of?"

She sighed. "So many things have happened. The world has changed. We have changed. We can't go back. It's better not to talk about it."

"Which, translated, means he is somewhere about and still holding the key to your heart," David said grimly.

She gave him a fond look. "David, friendship is sometimes better than love. We've always been good friends."

"I'd like to believe that," David Cornish said earnestly. "But I'd still prefer you to be in love with me."

She tried to pass this off with a light laugh, saying, "Perhaps I am and don't even know it. That's the way it always seems to be in plays. And speaking of plays, what do you propose to try in London?"

He at once became the professional manager, which was what she'd hoped for. Frowning slightly, he said, "I'm reading a new comedy. I think I manage best in light things. And with the war ending so badly I think London will be looking for entertainment to cheer people up."

"I fully agree," she said. "I hope your comedy works out."

"One other thing," David said. "What sort of contract do you have with Sir Alan?"

She said, "None really. Just word of mouth agreement on each play. Why?"

"I'd like you to leave his management and join me," David said. "I will pay you double the salary you're getting now to make up for the gamble you'd be taking."

Fanny listened in a confused state of mind. "I don't know, David. I'd love to work with you again. And I'm sure you're going to be a success. But I owe Sir Alan so much. I'd hate to leave him without discussing it with him first."

"Then do it," David said. "I'm not trying to raid his company. But if you and Hilda will join me I'd take it as a good luck sign."

"I'll talk to Sir Alan," she promised. "He might be glad to have a new leading lady. A change might be good for everyone."

David stood up. "I must be going. I have to see a theatre owner this morning about a possible lease. In any event I'll be starting rehearsals in about a month. So see what you can manage with Sir Alan. I'll be in touch with you."

"I promise to discuss it with him right away," she said, seeing the young actor to the door.

He halted to add, "And don't forget to remember me to Hilda and extend my offer to her."

"I will," she said. And, kissing him on the cheek, "Good luck, David!"

He smiled. "Just seeing you and talking to you again has been luck enough for today."

She closed the door behind him with a feeling of unreality. It didn't seem possible that after all this time David Cornish had come into her life once more. She recalled how much she'd enjoyed acting with him and decided she would seriously discuss the matter of joining the new venture with Sir Alan. She knew the distinguished actor-manager would advise her well.

When Hilda returned she told the old actress of David's plan and they were both filled with excitement. But before she was to have the opportunity to discuss the matter with Sir Alan there were to be other, darker happenings which she had not anticipated.

She was resting for the evening when Hilda came in to her bedroom to inform her that she had another caller. The old actress said, "A young woman."

Fanny got up and donned a dressing gown and went out to see who it was. Standing there nervously waiting for her in a dark blue gown and matching bonnet was the attractive Dora Carson!

Fanny hurried over to her and embraced her. "Dora! What a surprise! You've hardly changed at all!"

"Thank you," the dark-haired girl said quietly. "You must forgive my coming here!"

"Not at all," she said. "I've been wanting to see you."

Dora eyed her solemnly. "I'm afraid I'm the bearer of bad news!"

Chapter Nine

Not until that moment did it strike Fanny that this was more than a mere social visit. Her first thought was that there had been some sort of accident, that George was perhaps injured or even dead. Fear rose up in her and her throat became taut. She took several steps away from the subdued Dora.

Tensely, she asked, "What is it? What dreadful thing has happened?"

The lovely girl's dark face was sad and frightened at the same time. She said, "It is difficult to tell you!"

Fanny reached out a pleading hand. "George? Is he all right?"

"Yes," Dora said. "Please don't fret about him. He is at least all right for the moment."

"What do you mean?" This came from her in almost a wail.

Dora's eyes met hers solemnly. "It's Virginia! She is dead."

A great part of the weight of her fear left her. Though still shocked she felt this was something she could cope with. No doubt George had been too stunned by the death he'd predicted to come to her himself with the news. Also, it was much more discreet for Dora to be the bearer of the sad tidings.

Fanny said, "Poor thing! So it has happened at last! George told me it would."

The other girl stared at her. "What did he tell you?" she asked in a shocked voice.

"That Virginia was drinking herself to death. The doctor had warned her that she would not live a year if she went on. And so his words have proven to be true."

Dora said, "It was not drink that killed her."

This was a second shock. Fanny's eyes widened as she asked, "*Not* drink?"

"No. She died of poison!"

"Poison!"

"Arsenic poisoning to be exact," Dora went on grimly. "I found her dead in her bed early this morning."

Fanny gasped. "How dreadful! She had come to such a point that she took her own life!"

Dora's face was an expressionless mask. "That is the question."

"What do you mean?"

"It is not known whether she took the poison deliberately or whether it was placed in her drink. She had been on another of her drinking bouts!"

Fanny listened in confusion. "Who would put poison in her drink?"

"The doctor called in the police when he discovered traces of arsenic still in her glass," Dora said. "There will be an investigation. A coroner's jury will decide what really happened."

"How awful for George," she said, worriedly. "This is bound to be a dreadful time for him. There will be publicity and the shame that goes along with a suicide."

Dora said, "I don't think you fully understand. There is a possibility that George may be involved."

"Involved?" Fanny echoed.

"In Virginia's death."

"That's preposterous!" Fanny cried, anger replacing her fear. "George is not that sort of man! He would never do such a thing!"

"I know that and so do you," Dora said quietly. "But there are many who do not have the same knowledge of him. He is a Peer of the Realm now, and the public are often suspicious of those in high places."

"I'm sure George can somehow clear himself!"

"I pray so," Dora said. And then she revealed the most shocking news of all, adding, "You see, it is no secret that George made the purchase of the arsenic from a chemist a few days ago. It was in the form of ant paste which he'd bought at the request of the housekeeper."

The room reeled around her. She saw the other girl move quickly to her and offer her an arm in support. Fanny moaned, "It can't be! George would not do it!"

"I agree," Dora Carson said leading Fanny across to the settee and easing her down into it, then taking a place beside her.

Fanny said, "He hasn't been charged with the crime?"

"No. But I fear he may be," Dora said. "The Doctor knows there was no love between Virginia and George; the housekeeper will testify about his buying the ant-paste. And the police found the remains of the ant paste hidden in a corner of a closet in the hall on the same floor as Virginia's room. I could tell by the manner in which the Police Inspector talked to George that he believed the matter to be a grave one."

Fanny closed her eyes and tried to straighten it all out. "George told you to come to me!"

"Yes, he was anxious that you should know," Dora Carson said.

Realization of the shocking position in which she was in now came to her. "And he could not come here himself!"

"Hardly! If his close relationship with you became public information it might truly tie the noose around his neck!"

"Don't say such things!" Fanny implored her, even as she knew this to be true.

"Forgive me!" Dora said, chastened. "I only wish to be of help to you both."

Fanny bent to the other girl and kissed her on the cheek. "Dear Dora! What a saint you have been all these years! I vow I could not match your goodness. Now you are risking involvement in this dark affair by acting as messenger to me."

Dora gave her a look of encouragement. "You must not accept the worst. He has not yet been charged with the crime."

"From what you say he will be."

"That depends on the result of the inquest," Dora said. "It may well go in his favor. Even though the doctor was friendly to Virginia he cannot conceal the truth of her grave weakness for drink and the dreadful life she gave George! Until a year or so ago, she even entertained other men!"

"George told me all that."

"She knew her own life was in ruins and she wanted to destroy him," Dora said bitterly. "I never would have remained in the house but for the children."

"You have shown him such devotion," Fanny said. "He ought to have married you!"

"How can you say that! You know you are the only one he has ever loved!"

Fanny sighed. "Our love has been a tragic one from the start! How many times I wish we had never met, and how many times have I thanked Heaven for sending him my way! I do not know whether such a love has blessed or cursed us!"

"You must not lose courage," Dora said. "If we are all cautious I have a feeling George will not be charged for the crime."

"If they find that I'm his mistress, he is almost bound to be placed in a worse light," Fanny said.

"And your career would be ruined," Dora added. "But I think no one aside from myself knows. So you are both safe in that regard."

She shook her head. "You are wrong! At least one other person knows!"

"Who?"

"His brother, the Reverend Kenneth," she said.

Dora looked worried but she went on to say, "That is not good. But George has strong influence over him, and Kenneth is mortally afraid of scandal which might harm his church career. I cannot see him wanting a brother in the criminal court!"

"George must go to him at once and silence him," Fanny said.

"I'm sure that he will," Dora agreed. "What about the old woman who let me in a few minutes ago?"

Fanny nodded. "She knows. But she can be trusted. She is like a mother to me."

"Good," Dora said. "Is there any incriminating evidence in the apartment in which you met George? Any articles of your clothing, or such, which might be identified with you."

"No," she said. "I have been careful about that. I feared for a while the Reverend Kenneth might break into the place in search of such things."

"That is all to the good, then," Dora said. "George asked me to send you his love and assure you he will somehow see you at the first moment possible."

"No," Fanny said. "He must not think about that! He must keep away! Give no one a chance to link him with me!"

Dora studied her sympathetically. "I'm sure no one outside the few we've mentioned have guessed about you two. You can be sure of my silence. And when this horror is over you and George may be able to marry."

"I dare not think about that at the moment," Fanny said. "All I wish for him is his safety."

"I will be in touch with you if there are any other swift developments," Dora said. "You can count on my playing the role of messenger between you."

Fanny worried, "I do not like to have you further burdened with such a risky duty."

Dora rose and touched a hand to her bosom. She said. "Never fear! Like you, I thrive on challenges. I shall manage this one easily!"

Fanny also was on her feet. She said, "Charles wrote that he expected to sail home from the Crimea at any time. If only he were here now, he would be a strong support for George."

"True," Dora agreed. "Perhaps by some good fortune he will arrive soon. No matter what happens, the next weeks and months are going to be difficult ones for George."

"I realize that all too well," Fanny said.

Dora started for the door. "I must go now."

"Won't you wait to have tea with me?" Fanny asked.

"No," the other girl said. "I must not stay away from the house too long."

"Very well," Fanny said. "Give George my love and tell him I shall pray for him. You may reach me here or at the theatre. I'm seldom anywhere else."

Dora gave her a gentle touch on the arm and in parting said, "Be your own brave self and we shall all survive this storm!"

Fanny saw her out and then came back into her living room and closed the door after her. She leaned against it and began to sob. At the same time old Hilda Asquith came hurrying out to join her.

Fanny managed to ask, "You heard?"

"Enough," Hilda said, placing an arm around her and leading her to the bedroom. "I couldn't help overhearing most of it! What a dreadful business!" She insisted that Fanny stretch out on the bed to rest.

Hilda hurriedly made tea and brought it to her. Then the older woman sat by her bed as they drank it and went over the situation.

Fanny said, "George's wife must have somehow found the arsenic and committed suicide."

"I expect so," the old actress said with a frown. "But the young woman mentioned that the remains of the poison were found hidden."

She stared at Hilda. "You think it unlikely that Virginia would administer the poison to herself and then go to the trouble of hiding the balance of it?"

"If I were the police I would wonder about it."

"And you would be right," Fanny said, badly upset. "It will make things worse for George."

"A point against him," the elderly actress said. "But you know he is not the sort to commit such a crime."

"He'd never do it!"

"Maybe then, she was crafty enough to think of this and go to the final effort of hiding the poison to cast suspicion on her husband."

"Yes," Fanny agreed. "It is what might be expected of her in her hatred against him. She would do it purposely."

Hilda said, "If the police are intelligent, that possibility should also occur to them."

"George's character will stand in his favor." Fanny paused. "Unless his affair with me is dragged into it."

"A man may have a mistress and still be incapable of murder," Hilda said.

"That is surely so," Fanny said, "but any black mark against George at this time will hurt him."

The old actress suggested, "Could it have been someone else in the house who poisoned her?"

She frowned. "I suppose so. Though I can't imagine who, and I'm inclined to go along with the suicide theory."

"An abused servant?" Hilda said.

"I know little about the household," Fanny admitted. "Or how many servants were employed. I would expect quite a few."

"Or another member of the family; this Dora Carson, who brought you the bad news. Could she not be the culprit?"

Fanny shook her head. "Never! Dora is an even more unlikely suspect than poor George. I think we must consider it a suicide."

"You must not try to see the Marquis again," Hilda warned her. "It will be a temptation but you must fight it."

"I will," she promised. "And I pray that George will also behave with reason. He must not be seen coming here."

"There should be no need of that so long as his cousin acts as his messenger," the old actress said.

Fanny put aside her empty teacup and lay back against the pillows. She worried, "There's one person involved who frightens me. The Reverend Kenneth! If he should decide to talk there is no telling what harm he may do!"

She was to live with these worries for some time. The following morning the newspapers carried the story of the mysterious death of the wife of a member of the House of Lords in headlines. It became the latest scandal on the lips of Londoners of every class. At the theatre the next night there was much discussion of the scandalous affair backstage. Fanny tried to avoid being dragged into the talk but she could not help overhearing some of it. And she was appalled at the number who nodded their heads wisely and decided George had killed his wife.

They were doing a new play, "The Lost Island," about a group of people shipwrecked on an island in the Pacific. The play was filled with action, with Sir Alan playing the courageous captain and Fanny a noble lady among the passengers stranded on the island. Much special scenery was used, including scenes of the shipwreck and the island. Backstage was crowded with the special effects and the large crew needed to provide them.

Fanny was standing in the shadowed wings backstage ready to make her entrance when she heard a commotion from the rear of the backstage area and then the dread shout of, "Fire!"

The cry rang out above the words of the actors onstage and they halted in consternation. At the same instant there was the strong smell of smoke. Fanny hurried to the rear of the stage setting and saw clouds of smoke and flames rising from a distant corner where extra scenery was stored. Stagehands were desperately trying to battle the fire, seemingly without success.

She ran to the wings again in time to see Sir Alan Tredale, who was onstage, advance to the gas footlights and calmly announce to the large audience, "We have a small fire backstage, ladies and gentlemen. I ask that you retire slowly and in good order from the theatre until the danger is over, at which time you may re-enter and we shall resume the performance."

The audience reacted speedily and in a panic rather than in good order. The frightened voices of men and women rose in a clamor as they scrambled, fought, and shoved their way to the nearest exits. It was a scene to strike terror in the soundest heart.

Above the din Sir Alan called out vainly for order as smoke swirled around him on the stage. The other actors made coughing exits while he knelt down and begged the orchestra to remain in place and strike up some lively tune to calm the audience. Fanny saw the stricken face of the orchestra leader as he hesitated over the request, and then saw him give way to his fear completely, throw down his baton, and join the maddened patrons in racing for the outside and safety. Needless to say the other musicians followed him, the violinists and horn-players clutching their instruments under their arms.

Sir Alan came stumbling out to where she was standing and glimpsing her, cried, "Come along, my girl! If we remain here we'll be burned to death or suffocated!"

She allowed him to guide her to the stage door and out into the wide alley where other members of the cast stood huddled together in despair. At the same time the black autumn night was lit up with the flames shooting up through the roof of the backstage area of the theatre.

"The People's is doomed," Sir Alan said grimly. And he turned to those who had escaped with them and asked, "Are all the company and crew out?"

Silas Hodder staggered over to them, his head cut and bleeding. He said, "All out and accounted for, sir!"

"I fear those in the audience will not fare so well," Sir Alan said grimly. "They are in full panic and trampling on each other!"

Silas Hodder said, "It was arson, sir. A masked man came running in and struck me down. I was stunned for a moment! By the time I came round he had set the fire and made his escape!"

"No doubt one of Tobias Wall's thugs," the actor said angrily. "I did not think the opposition would sink to such a despicable thing as this!"

Fanny heard the sounds of fire engines clanging and tugged at the distinguished actor's arm. "It will not be practical or safe for us to remain here! The fire fighters are arriving and they will need to work from here. There is also the danger of the building collapsing!"

"Quite so!" Sir Alan said and he called out to the grim, frightened actors and crewmen to move out of the alley and away from the danger. Then he led the way with Fanny at his side. The melancholy group straggled along, knowing their jobs and many of their material possessions were being destroyed by the flames.

When they reached the street and mingled with the maddened patrons, it became evident this was no minor calamity. People were still jammed in the exits and the screams of those trapped inside could be heard. Many had already been trampled to death underfoot or suffocated in the panic-stricken flight from the burning theatre.

The fire engines with their teams of strong horses pulled up. The bright red and brass trucks and the firemen in their red uniforms and brass helmets added to the color and clamor of the scene.

Fanny watched as they went about battling the fire with an orderly precision born of experience. These stalwart fellows in their shining helmets and red jackets had the trucks drawn close around the burning building, the pumpers working and the hoses streaming water to stem the flames within minutes of their arrival.

They also helped to clear the jammed exits and carry out those who had collapsed or had died. Despite their valiant efforts the flames continued to spread until the entire huge wooden structure was ablaze. Doctors had been summoned and surgeries set up in near-by pubs and shops. Dazed survivors of the blaze stood staring blankly at the flaming building or went about frantically crying out the names of relatives or companions who had been in their company and were now lost.

A fireman in high rubber boots, his clothing black with soot and smoke, his face as dark as that of any Ethiopian went over to shere the company had gathered and warned them to move further up the street.

"The walls will burst! Get away while you've time!" he cried, moving down the line of spectators with his warning.

They took heed of his words and saw that the fire trucks and engines were being moved. The horses pawed the cobblestones and neighed in terror as they waited to be led from the danger area. Ladders were retrieved and some left behind as frantic warnings circulated among the firefighters. These last brave ones to move from near the doomed structure barely escaped before the front wall bulged out with a puff of smoke and flame and rained rubble on the street.

Sir Alan's noble face was highlighted by the reflection of the fire as he sadly watched his theatre collapse in a flaming ruin. His arm around Fanny and in a tight-lipped voice, he said, "It is the finish for me! I shall retire! After what has happened here tonight I never wish to step on a stage again!"

"You will feel differently later," she comforted him. "You will find another theatre, begin once more."

"Too late," Sir Alan said sadly. "I have been thinking about retirement to a quiet cottage somewhere in the country. Now I know the time has come."

She did not attempt to argue with him. After a while the crowd began to disperse. Police had arrived to take charge. Already thieves and pickpockets had joined the crowd to make a miserable profit on the tragedy.

Silas Hodder found a carriage to take Fanny and Hilda to their apartment. The old woman was in a state of shock and near collapse. Silas Hodder decided he should come along with them to help Hilda up the stairs.

By the time they made the short journey the old actress had recovered herself sufficiently to require hardly any help, but they both invited Silas up for a brandy. The stage door man did not refuse.

He sat in a high-backed chair, gaunt and shattered, as Fanny tended to his cut head and tied a bandage neatly around it. She asked him, "This arsonist. Did you get a good look at him?"

Silas shook his head. "He was masked, just as I told Sir Alan! But I do know one thing. He wasn't a big man, he was of no more than medium size!"

"So you do recall something," she encouraged him. "If you keep trying you may remember more details."

"What he was wearing?" Hilda Asquith suggested.

The gaunt-faced man frowned. "He struck me with a club of some sort. I only had a quick flash of him! But I think he was wearing dark clothing!"

"Likely," Fanny mused. "He would be least noticed if he wore dark things. If Tobias Wall was behind what happened tonight he has more than one death on his conscience!"

"I'll warrant that," Silas Hodder agreed. "The last count the firemen and police made were over thirty dead and three times that many injured."

Hilda Asquith said, "I'm only thankful all the company escaped. But now they have no work."

Fanny reminded her, "It does not matter for us. You and I have an invitation to join the new company David Cornish is forming."

The old woman brightened. "I was thinking it might be the workhouse for me! But if David wants me I'm willing to join him as long as my old body allows it."

"I, too, am cast into the depths again," Silas Hodder said lugubriously. "No doubt I shall soon be back to begging and sleeping in cemetery crypts once more."

Fanny put an arm around him fondly. "I think not! When I have told David Cornish what a fine stage door man you are I'm sure he'll be begging you to work for him!"

Fanny slept little that night. The next morning she and Hilda sat long over breakfast talking about the fire and their future. For a short while she forgot all about George and his plight. Then it came back to her. It seemed that misfortunes arrived in parcels.

Their first visitor of the day came at noon. It was David Cornish and he brought copies of all the London morning newspapers with him. The young actor was warmly sympathetic.

He hugged Fanny and then old Hilda, saying, "You might have died in that fire last night!"

"I'd be no great loss," old Hilda smiled mirthlessly. "A noisy old bag of bones. But it would have been different if Fanny had gone, with all her future before her!"

Rather morosely, Fanny said, "I wonder if my future will be worth having?"

"Of course it will!" David said. "Dreadful as last night was you must not let it allow you to lose your zest for life. We theatre people, above all others, need that."

She said, "Sometimes it is hard to cling to. Sir Alan has decided to retire. He told me last night he will not attempt to start over."

"Then the theatre has lost a fine and gallant old actor," David said with sincerity. "He will be missed. But it does solve one problem. You no longer need hesitate in joining me."

Fanny smiled ruefully. "That is true. Hilda and I will be glad to accept your offer. And there is the stage door man whom I can recommend. He has been a good friend to me. I'd appreciate your finding a place for him."

"I shall have need of a stage door man," David said. "If he is a friend of yours, send him along. In fact, I'd like the names and addresses of all the company. Sir Alan surrounded himself with good actors. I'd consider it a privilege to hire as many of them as I can use."

Hilda Asquith said, "I'm sure Silas Hodder can supply you with a list. If not, you can go directly to Sir Alan for it. I'm certain he'd be glad to help."

Fanny was studying the headlines. She said, "Thirty-seven killed and nearly a hundred injured! What a terrible thing!"

David nodded. "According to the *Times* it is suspected that a thug hired by a rival theatre manager started the fire. Do you think that possible? Can their be such villainy and rivalry among theatre managements in this city?"

"Yes," she said. "You must keep that in mind when you start your company. Some of the cheap theatres south of the Thames are solid against the new and better companies who are taking away their business. Yet I did not think even they would do such a dastardly deed as was committed last night."

David said, "I shall maintain extra guards at my theatre. A tragedy like this must not be allowed to happen again. I would expect it to go hard with the criminal if he is found."

"The chances are he won't be," Fanny said with a sigh. "There are so many evil men in London willing to take on any criminal task for the right payment."

David gave her a knowing look. "I'm sure of that, just as I'm sure that the evil in London is not confined to the lower classes. Have you read of the mysterious death of Marquis George Palmer's wife?"

Fanny was taken by surprise at his sudden reference to this matter. She tried to maintain a calm facade, calling on all her skill as an actress. She said, "I read about the case but I gave it scant attention."

David, who happily seemed to be ignorant of her having had any relationship with the Palmer family, or who had forgotten if she'd mentioned it, said, "I've read the accounts carefully and I think it's plain this fellow has poisoned his wife. I'd be willing to bet he'll be arrested for the crime."

"Well, that should settle it," Fanny said hollowly. "Let the police decide his guilt, not the press."

David looked surprised. "You think I'm being unfair to the fellow?"

Hilda Asquith spoke up quickly from her chair by the window, "I don't think Fanny is in any fit state to talk about such grim matters today. She should be in bed resting."

"I'm sorry," the actor said at once. "You are right, Hilda. You both have gone through too much to talk idly about possible murders and the like. I apologize and I'll take my leave."

Fanny said, "You need not hurry away."

He lifted a hand. "No. Hilda is right. You both need quiet. I shall call again tomorrow when you will have had more time to recover from the shock of all this."

Fanny saw him on his way and then returned to collapse into a chair across from the one occupied by Hilda. She moaned, "It's really too much! I don't think I can bear it!"

"You will," the old actress told her. "You must! If only to save the man you love."

And this was true. Somehow Fanny managed to get through that day and night and the next. On the third day after the fire Dora Carson came again. This time Fanny guessed the worst before the dark girl said anything. She could tell by Dora's pale, worn face.

Dora's hands twisted nervously as she sank down in the chair which Fanny had offered her. She bent her head and said, "They came for him this morning!"

"Oh, no!" Fanny protested.

"The Inspector and two officers," Dora said. "I stood by while the Inspector read the charge. He was most kindly in his manner!"

"How can they think George a murderer!" Fanny said, her eyes brimming with tears.

"The inquest indicated he should be placed on trial," Dora replied, looking up at her for the first time. "I was afraid it might. The circumstances seem to be all against him. The housekeeper can't recall asking him to buy the ant paste. The remnants of the paste were found hidden! The servants heard Virginia in her drunken tantrums warning George that she knew he was plotting to kill her. These all add up to placing him in the shadow of guilt."

Fanny sat on the divan, trying to adjust to this latest bad news. Although she had expected it, it still was a blow. What had been a fearful possibility was now a reality!

Dora went on, "There was no fuss. George accepted the news very quietly. He asked for a few minutes to get some possessions together and time was granted him. He said farewell to the children and to me, and then he left with the Inspector and his men."

"What can we do to help him?" Fanny worried.

"Very little. He has the best legal advice available. He anticipated all this happening and has been in touch with his solicitor. I had only to notify him."

Fanny asked, "When will he be tried?"

"I don't know that yet," the other girl said. "We can hope it will not be too long delayed. In the meantime, George will have to languish in prison."

"If only I could see him! Talk with him!" Fanny said.

Dora said, "You know that would not be wise."

Fanny rose to her feet and began to pace slowly back and forth. "I feel so frustrated!"

"The fire at the theatre must have been a terrifying experience," Dora said. "George was frantic until he had word that you were safe."

"This last week has been like a hideous nightmare," Fanny said, still pacing.

"At least you have been relieved of the strain of being on stage every night," the other girl said. "Feeling as you do that surely had to be a great burden."

"Not really," she said. "I think it was better for me to be working. At least I could lose myself in my part while I was onstage."

"I must confess my knowledge of such things are limited," Dora said. "I know how you must be tormented about George's fate. I share that torment with you."

She was moved by the dark girl's words. Crossing to her, she patted her on the shoulder. "You have been too kind to me, Dora, coming all the way here to keep me informed. You have more than enough to occupy you with looking after the children and the house."

"It is better now that the funeral is over," Dora said. "Virginia's parents were extremely cold towards George at that time."

Fanny frowned. "They knew their daughter to be an unstable alcoholic before she married George. Everyone knew it!"

"Of course they want to conceal that."

"It should not be hidden. It ought to be an important part of George's defence!"

"I'm sure his solicitors will take that in consideration," Dora said. "I will make it a point to mention it."

"How did the Reverend Kenneth behave at the funeral?" Fanny wanted to know.

"Not like a loving brother, I can assure you of that!" Dora said with bitterness. "He barely spoke to George, but fawned on Virginia's parents. And he was most abrupt with me."

"Surely he will be kind to the children!"

"He did not seem to be aware of them," Dora said with a frown. "I'd say that he's on the edge of madness! A righteous madness in which he sees himself a saint and everyone else as sinners!"

"That is the form his madness has always taken," Fanny said ruefully. "I'm sure that becoming a clergyman was the worst thing for him. He has become a fanatic in his zeal!"

"He may wear a clerical collar but there is little of true religion in him!"

Fanny nodded. "I must agree. I'm surprised that he has not further hounded me."

"You must be careful. There is always that possibility. It is hard to say how he will react to George being changed with Virginia's murder. I'm inclined to think it will please him."

"Could he be so cruel?" Fanny wondered.

"I'm sure he could," Dora said. "If only Charles would get here, he could act as a counterbalance to Kenneth."

"His last letter said he was leaving the Crimea," Fanny said. "He must be on his way."

"I hope he arrives before the trial," Dora said.

Fanny hoped for the same thing. She had great faith in the good-natured Charles and knew he would have a good effect on George. In time of trouble George was too prone to give way to despair. Charles had an exuberance about him and would help to instill the confidence George must show in his appearances in court.

Dora left after promising to keep Fanny in touch with the rapid turn of events. Fanny found the empty hours of waiting endless. Once more she was reminded how important the theatre was to her. Her dedication to the life which her father had wanted for her was an integral of her pattern of living which she needed badly.

•••

She was grateful when a few days later David Cornish came in a carriage to take her to see the theatre he'd leased near Covent Garden. He invited Hilda along as well, but the old actress elected to remain in the apartment in case any messages arrived. So on the brisk autumn afternoon Fanny rode in the closed carriage to the Windsor Theatre which he had rented.

On the way they had to pass the ruins of the People's and he had the driver halt for a moment so they might gaze at the charred wreckage. Fanny felt a great sadness well up in her, for it was in this lost theatre she had first had billing as a London star. Here the dream her father had treasured had come into being.

It was the end of an era for her! Yet the world of London seemed to have taken the tragedy in its stride. The street was filled with people who went their various ways with only a quick, curious glance at the charred ruins. Venders shouted their wares, street gamins laughed and ran recklessly between the carriages and the great wagons which lumbered along the cobblestoned street.

Finally the carriage halted before the Windsor which she saw was a building of brick and stone, with modest columns in front. It was smaller than the People's but would be large enough for the audiences David would attract with a new company.

As they stood on the sidewalk admiring the building, he said, "It will be just about right in size. Better to turn away than to have empty seats. And best of all, it is near to being safe from fire."

She sighed, "After what has happened, that is an important consideration."

"We must view the theatre from the stage," the young actor manager said, taking her by the arm and leading her along the narrow alley to the stage door.

Her first pleasant surprise was having Silas Hodder greet her. The old man had on a new gray frock coat and gray top hat and looked much less forlorn than when she'd last seen him. He opened the stage door to them and removed his hat.

"Welcome, Miss Fanny," the old man said. "You see, thanks to your good services, I'm already on duty!"

"Wonderful!" she exclaimed.

David's pleasant face held a smile. "I've managed to be in touch with many of the actors from Sir Alan's company. You will almost think you're back with the same group again."

"With you as leading man and director," Fanny said, looking up at him fondly. "It is like a dream come true, David!"

"It is only the beginning," he promised. "Come take a look at things from the stage."

They wandered out onto the stage of the shadowed theatre and she was dimly aware of the seating arrangements which included a good-sized dress circle and balcony. She saw how proud and happy the ambitious David Cornish was, and knew that one of her wishes had been fulfilled. David had at last seen the wisdom of making a name in London.

She turned to him impulsively and threw her arms around him and kissed him. "Good luck, David!"

He laughed. "How can I have anything else with you at my side?"

These words brought her back to the grim reality of her life once more. David Cornish did not guess her true state of mind, did not know that the man she loved was shortly to be tried for murder. If George were convicted and sentenced to be hanged, could she force herself to go ahead with this new stage project? Fanny much doubted it!

Chapter Ten

Fanny spent as close to a pleasant afternoon with David as was possible in her troubled state of mind. When he said goodbye to her at the door of her flat, he invited her to dinner that evening and suggested that he call for her around seven. Reluctantly, she agreed, thinking it would help occupy her mind. When curtain time came and she had no show to do she was always restless.

David returned to the carriage in high spirits and she waved to him as he was driven away. She stood there watching wistfully after the vanishing carriage for a little. Several times during the afternoon she had been at the point of being completely honest with him. She felt in fairness she should tell him about George and her relationship with the titled young man. Should the trial go against him, she might not be able to serve as leading lady in David's company. In fact she didn't know what such a turn of events would do to her.

She went inside and began mounting the stairs to the rooms she shared with Hilda Asquith. Perhaps tonight she would find the opportunity to tell David her dilemma and get his reaction. She feared it might not be a pleasant one since she was aware that David continued to have a romantic interest in her. It was all terribly confusing!

Fanny found the key to the door in her purse and fitted it into the lock and opened it. As she entered the flat she found the elderly Hilda there ready to greet her.

There was an anxious look on the old woman's face as she said, "You have a visitor, Fanny!"

Fanny looked beyond her and at once cried out her joy. For it was none other than the stalwart Captain Charles Palmer who rose from the high-backed chair and crossed the room to her.

"Charles!" she said with deep relief. "How good to have you safely back!"

"Dear Fanny," the young man said, taking her in his arms and kissing her gently. Then releasing her, he said, "If you could guess how many times I dreamed of this moment when I was in that Godforsaken Crimea!"

"Let me study you!" she exclaimed, standing back and holding his hands in hers as she looked at him. His frame had filled out and his skin was bronzed. His heavy side-burns matched his mustache and the entire effect was one of more maturity. He looked at least ten years older than when she had last seen him only a little more than two years earlier.

He smiled grimly, "Well, tell me the worst!"

"You look older but more rugged. I should say from the female point of view you are much more interesting."

Charles laughed in his good-natured way. "That is most pleasant to hear."

She led him by one hand to the settee, saying, "I don't know anyone I wished to see more. I've been praying for your return this last week."

The young man at once became sober-faced. In a quiet voice, he said, "I have seen George."

"You know everything, then," she said tensely.

"Yes," he hesitated as he glanced around. "Can we talk quite frankly?"

She saw that Hilda had discreetly withdrawn to the bedroom and closed the door. She said, "You may. Hilda is to be trusted completely." And she sat down.

He sat across from her, his pleasant face shadowed. "As you know, it is a bad business."

"I don't dare think how bad it may be," Fanny said. "From the moment of George's arrest I have known no peace."

Charles surveyed her in silence for a moment. "Poor Fanny!" he said. "You will remember that I long ago warned you against falling in love with George."

She felt her cheeks burn and she stared down at her hands, nervously clasping and unclasping. "Unhappily one is not able to control one's feelings in such matters."

"So it would seem," he said dryly. "In fairness, I warned you long ago when you were a servant in our house. And I again warned you before I left for the Crimea. Yet you began seeing him soon after that."

"It was not planned on either of our parts. We bring each other as much pain as happiness," she said wearily. "Yet we do not seem to be able to live apart from each other."

"I deeply regret that," Charles said. "And I'm surprised that George spoke of your affair in almost the same tone as you. He feels you are fated for each other, though you may not be fated to bring each other any lasting good."

"That about sums it up," she said. "He had no life with Virginia. And I have never truly loved anyone but him."

Charles sighed. "And all the while I wrote you letters from the front, I had the sincere hope that you were coming around to my point of view. That you were gradually falling in love with me."

"I am so fond of you, dear Charles!"

"But I do not stimulate the torment of love in you my brother does," the young man in the red and blue uniform said bitterly.

"Do not be cruel to me, Charles," she begged him.

He patted her hand. "I have no wish to do that, believe me. But I was shocked and hurt when I heard from George that you two had become lovers again."

"I'm sorry."

"His plight is desperate enough as it is," Charles said. "If his affair with you came out it would prove such a strong motive for his murdering Virginia that I'm sure any jury would convict him."

"But that kind of violence was never in our minds!"

"A jury might find it hard to believe," the young officer said dryly. "Thank goodness you have kept it a secret. The newspapers would make much of it."

"I don't care what it might do to my career but I worry that it might hurt George's defence," she said.

"And you are quite right in that," Charles told her. "I have talked a long while with George and he is concerned more for you than himself. He is resigned to whatever fate may have in store for him."

"That is his weakness," she exclaimed. "He is not the kind of fighter you are. You must give him support and help him find the courage he needs to win his case!"

"I will do all I can," Charles said. "I have talked to Dora. She mentioned her visits to you. I can take over the task of messenger now. In fact, it might be wise if we were publicly seen together. Let your name be linked with mine."

"To throw any who might suspect off the track?"

"Exactly."

"I can see the sense in that," she agreed. "And yet it will keep me in as close touch with George as is possible, since you will be in constant daily contact with him."

"True. Dora is doing a fine job with the youngsters." He paused. "You will not mind my saying this, but *she* is the one whom George should have loved and married. Neither you nor Virginia could supply him with the kind of support offered by Dora."

Fanny grimaced. "You may be all too right in that. I have thought of it myself."

He nodded, then started on another theme, saying, "I'm happy to tell you that George has the best possible defence in the person of Mr. Charles Williams, Mr. Montagu Matthews and Mr. W. S. Robinson."

"I know little of such matters so I do not recognize the names," she said. "I'm glad that in your view he has a good firm of solicitors."

"I'm fully satisfied," Charles said. "I have talked most with Montagu Matthews whom I like the best. The trial has been set for Thursday morning, November 8th at ten-thirty."

"So soon!"

"Better to get it over with," he said. "The longer the wait, the more time the papers have to write sensational stories."

"I can see that," she said.

"The Judge will be Mr. Justice Hawkins, who has the reputation of being severe in cases of this sort."

"Who heads the prosecution?"

"The Solicitor-General himself," Charles said grimly. "None other than Sir Alan Norville. So the public may be sure that their peers are being prosecuted by the best talents and shown no special favors."

Fanny said, "The fact that George has a title will go against him, if anything."

"I'm afraid so," Charles agreed.

"I must be there in court," she insisted.

"It will not be a pleasant experience."

"I must be there with him!"

Charles gave her a warning look. "It also might be risky."

"Not if I come with you," she said. "Especially if we carry out our plan of being seen in public places together. It will only look as if I have come as your lady friend."

"I suppose we might take the chance," Charles said with caution. "I think we ought to begin by having dinner at the Holburn House tonight. Enough people will see us there."

Fanny hesitated, remembering her promise to have dinner with David Cornish. She said, "I'd like to, but—"

"But what?"

"I have already promised to have dinner with an actor friend who has asked me to become a member of his company."

Charles wrinkled his brow. "Surely you can cancel that. Our being seen together is urgent now. I heard about the theatre burning and realize you must consider your career. But which is more important to you—George, or your future in the theatre?"

She said, "There can be no question. At this moment George urgently needs my allegiance."

"So that must solve it," the young captain said. "Leave word with the old lady that a friend has unexpectedly returned from the Crimea and you could not refuse him the pleasure of your company on his first evening in London."

Fanny hesitated only a moment more. "Very well," she said. "I'll do it. But we must leave before seven. That is when he is coming for me."

"We can leave whenever you are ready," Charles promised her.

They dined together in the Grand Salon of the Holburn Restaurant in view of what seemed half of fashionable London. An orchestra played sedately at one end of the room and the food and drink was as elegant as the company. Fanny selected quail as her main dish while Charles decided on salmon. It was one of her first appearances in public since the fire and she was aware that many eyes were on her and her handsome soldier escort.

Charles smiled across the table at her and said, "I can hear the whisperings about us gathering like the in-coming waves of the ocean."

"I'm not sure I enjoy it," she told him.

"But you are used to being in public view on the stage. I'm a modest soldier normally exposed to only a small band of my fellow officers. The ordeal is bound to be worse for me."

"I contradict that," she said. "Being on display here has little in common with appearing in a role behind the guarding footlights."

"You must give a light-hearted performance. Show no worries or the whole purpose of our little excursion on the town will be defeated. You wouldn't want that!"

"No, I wouldn't want that," she said, managing a smile. All the while she was filled with concern about George and feeling guilty for having broken her engagement with David Cornish. David did not deserve such treatment.

The evening went well. Several theatre-goers paused by their table and asked Fanny when she would be appearing on the London stage again. She mentioned the opening of the David Cornish company and said she hoped to be the leading lady in his productions.

It was past ten when Charles saw her to the door of the flat. He said, "This evening has meant a lot to me, apart from what we may have done to help George. I shall keep in touch with you and we must be seen together often."

Standing in the shadowed hall with him, she begged him, "When you see George, give him my love!"

"I shall," he promised. "And do you not have even a single chaste good-night kiss for his brother?"

"Goodnight, Charles," she said gently. "And thank you!" Her kiss was brief and surely chaste but seemed to satisfy him.

Inside she consulted Hilda, who had gone to bed. She roused the old woman from her sleep and asked, "How did it go? What did David say?"

Hilda, in her nightcap, blinked sleepily at her. "What do you expect? He was hurt and angry!"

She sank down on the side of the bed. "I knew he would be!"

"Can you blame him?"

"No."

"I stressed the fact that Captain Palmer was a war hero but it didn't make much difference to him," the old woman said. "He left with the promise of coming to ask you for an explanation in the morning."

"I see," Fanny said dully.

"What are you going to do?"

Fanny looked down at the carpet. "I shall have to tell him the truth. In fairness, I can do no less. Now that Charles has returned I shall be seeing him a lot. He will be my link with George."

Hilda gave her a concerned look. "You have another course! Desert this unhappy love and lover. Refuse to see the soldier brother as well! Give your future to the theatre and David. It is what you were born for!"

Fanny could not help but be startled by the old woman's impassioned words. And she knew well that Hilda Asquith might be right. This was her last chance to free herself from George. She was not sure that he would allow her to return to the stage even if he were acquitted and they eventually were married. He might refuse to let her return to acting.

And acting was her life! She knew that now just as her father had known it long ago. But her sense of loyalty and her love for George would not let her desert him in his desperate hour of need. She must stand by and see the outcome of the trial before thinking about her own future. And she must be frank in explaining all this to David Cornish.

She broke away from these sobering thoughts to tell the old woman, "I may be making the wrong choice. But I cannot see that I have an alternative. Tomorrow I shall be completely honest with David."

Following an almost sleepless night she felt little prepared for her confrontation with the young actor-manager. She put on her favorite rose moire gown and tried to bide her pallor and weariness by spending time on a flattering new hair-style.

David arrived promptly at eleven as he had said. She bade him to sit with her on the settee but he refused, and insisted on standing through her long and uneven explanation. Somehow she managed to tell it all. Then she looked up at his stern, young face and waited for his reaction.

It came soon enough as he said angrily, "So this is the man you have loved since your girlhood! This titled murderer!"

"George is not that!"

David Cornish made a dramatic gesture of disgust with his hand, thrusting away her protest. "The court seems to think so since they are putting him on trial for the murder of his wife!"

"He must be declared innocent!"

"That remains for a jury to decide," David reminded her.

"I cannot help my love for him," she said, a sob in her voice.

David knelt by her and took her hand in his. "You have foolishly given yourself to this man long enough. And what have you received in return? A few furtive rendezvous and the total loss of your peace of mind. You've even threatened your career."

"I had no choice. Neither did he. Our love was too strong for us to cope with!"

"That sounds like a line from a badly-written melodrama," David said scornfully. "Now his brother is using you. Between them all they will ruin you. Give up this senseless love and dedicate yourself to the theatre where you belong!"

She looked at him sadly. "A woman needs more than a career. I want love and affection as well."

"I offer you that," David told her. "I will marry you tomorrow if you say the word, or you can ask me to wait until you are ready, and I will. In the meantime you can go on to further glory on the London stage under my guidance."

"I do not question your genius for the stage," she said. "Nor do I know a better friend, than the one I have in you."

David's sternness vanished a little. "In that case the matter should be settled."

"It's not that easy!" she protested. "You must be patient a little longer. Wait until the trial is over. Then I shall give you my answer."

His face shadowed again. "And if he is acquitted? Will you marry him?"

"I'm not sure how I'll feel then," she said. "Or what his feelings will be!"

"And if he is convicted?"

"The conviction must be appealed," she said. "I know him to be innocent."

"Either way you are throwing your lot in with him and turning your back on me and the real people in your life!" David said angrily. "Do this and you will live to hate yourself!"

"There is hatred in my feelings now!"

He got to his feet again. "I find it hard to believe. You are so intelligent in other ways. In this you are a hopeless case."

She looked down. "I'm sorry, David."

"I wonder about that," he said bitterly. "And I promise you I'm going ahead with my plans, with you or without you. I shall begin rehearsals on the fifth. If you are not at the Windsor for the first rehearsal I shall find a replacement for you."

"I understand," she said quietly. "You are justified in all that! I ask nothing of you!"

He sighed. "The sad thing is, you could have anything I have to offer. Everything that is mine! But nothing that I offer balances your love for that murderer!"

She broke into sobs at this but he did not attempt to offer her solace. Instead he angrily picked up his hat and cane and strode out of the apartment, slamming the door after him. In effect, she realized, he was walking out of her life.

• • •

The days and nights which followed were not easy ones for her. The news concerning George would be good one day and bad the next. His attorneys were filled with confidence about their case on Monday and by Wednesday morning would find some weakness in their argument. In the meanwhile she continued to see Charles and he gave her all the support he could.

They went out together enough for the gossips to note their friendship. Yet he never embarrassed her by trying to press his own case while the fate of his brother hung in the balance. Fanny did not know which bothered her most, her concern for George or her estrangement from David Cornish.

Hilda had begun rehearsals with the actor-manager and she brought daily news of what was happening at the theatre home to Fanny. David had selected a new comedy for his first play and when she had not shown up he had found another young actress of talent to take her place.

Hilda told her, "I'm sure he'd chuck her in a minute and make her understudy if you were to join us. This girl is not a quarter the actress you are."

"You know it's impossible, Hilda," she said wearily. "The trial begins Thursday and I must be there."

"You should be in the theatre and not a courtroom," the elderly actress said. "The theatre is where you belong!"

Fanny put her arm around Hilda. "I'm sorry, dear Hilda. I do hate deserting you all!" But she knew nothing would change her mind.

It was bitterly cold the morning of the trial. For the first time in several years London had a dusting of early snow. Fanny feared it might be a bad omen for the trial ahead but hoped the foul weather might keep the courtroom less full. Great crowds usually attended sensational trials of this sort.

Charles arrived early with a carriage to take her to the Central Criminal Court. He pressed her arm, and said, "Now we show all our courage, my girl!"

She needed his reassurance. When they reached the court it was filled despite the weather. They were buffeted by throngs of people as they sought a seat near the front. The morbid-minded were out in strength and some were even standing outside the brick walls of the court waiting for the proceedings to be relayed to them.

Charles whispered to her, "Apparently this is a case not to be missed by members of the Bar; the Court is positively white with their wigs."

Gazing around she saw this was true and in turn, she whispered to him, "It might be a garden party or a fashionable at-home' considering the number of fashionably dressed ladies here!"

The trial was set for ten-thirty, but it was not until ten minutes later that the familiar rap on the door at the end of the Bench announced the judicial procession. All present in the court rose to their feet, including Fanny and Charles, as the heavy door opened and Mr. Justice Hawkins, robed in scarlet and white ermine, strode majestically into the courtroom. He was followed by other legal notables, with a black clad chaplain bringing up the rear. When they had all lined up, his Lordship beneath the Sword of Justice, the Bench bowed to the Court, the Court returned the salutation and all were seated. As the Judge sat down he placed a little square of black cloth beside him. It was the black cap donned by a judge when giving a prisoner the death sentence. This brought a hush over the courtroom and sent a cold chill down Fanny's spine. Charles gave her a reassuring glance.

Then George appeared and took his place in the dock, a forlorn figure in his drab, gray suit, carefully guarded by warders as if he were a dangerous criminal. His face was white and haggard and he kept his eyes cast. Fanny wanted to sob aloud at the sight of him. But no such demonstration of her feelings could be allowed.

The trial began. To the customary question from the Bench, George bowed respectfully and in a low voice said, "Not guilty." There was another murmur from the audience. Fanny, more and more, had the feeling it was a sort of grim play and not a trial at all.

The prosecution began under the competent direction of florid-faced and white-side-whiskered Sir Alan Norville, a skilled member of his profession. His case against George was summed up in a temperate, impartial and grimly convincing manner.

Sir Alan admitted that, as in most cases of this kind, much of the evidence was circumstantial. But he then stressed that the chain of events was complete and each link neatly fitted together. He ended with the statement that the only missing link was that no one had actually seen George administer the poison to his late wife.

The court recessed before the defence began and Charles took Fanny to a nearby pub for some food and drink, though she wanted neither. He found them a table in a back corner of the crowded place and urged her to eat something.

"You will be faint if you don't," he warned her. "And think of the sensation if you fainted in court. That might be the finish for George."

"Very well," she said. "I shall have a sherry and a small sandwich."

He ordered for them and then asked her, "How do you think it is going?"

"Sir Alan Norville is a master of the courtroom," she said. "He made it seem that he was sorry for George yet at the same time thought him a murderer."

"I know," Charles said with a deep sigh. "Did you notice how he kept repeating the phrase 'wife-poisoner'?"

"It was most sickening. I only hope Montagu Matthews is as good as you believe. George is going to need all the help he can get."

"I have confidence in Montagu," Charles said.

They finished their lunch and hurried back through the cold to the court. The number still standing out in the courtyard astonished and appalled her. They were waiting for the man she loved to be given a sentence of death! They took their seats in the front again and the judge and prisoner took their places.

The defence began. Montagu Matthews was a short, portly man, bald, with an almost jolly, round face. He wore a high collar and had a deep, rumbling voice which appeared to emanate from somewhere in the depths of his considerable stomach. He went over the same ground as the prosecution but pointed out the thinness of the Crown's circumstantial evidence. The trial continued through the afternoon and then recessed until the following morning at ten-thirty.

Charles escorted Fanny home and as they sat in the jolting carriage, he asked her, "Do you think Montagu is making his points?"

"Yes," she said. "But he is taking such a long while!"

"He is playing for time, or so he tells me. He is looking for a missing witness he feels will help his case, a servant discharged just after Virginia's death."

"I can't deny I'm worried," she said. "I feel George is in terrible trouble. Thus far the count is against him."

Charles sighed. "I'm forced to agree."

The next day was equally cold and gray. Once again Charles brought Fanny to the place of the trial. The crowds gathered there seemed larger than the previous day despite the inclemency of the weather. Dora Carson had not attended the first day of the trial but she was present on this second day with a woman companion. Charles was not certain whether the Reverend Kenneth was in the courtroom or not. Fanny glanced around and could not see him.

Montagu Matthews resumed the defence and at once Fanny felt he was about to play a trump card. It came as no great surprise to her when he brought the housekeeper to the stand. There, with tears in her eyes, the woman confessed that she *had* mentioned the subject of ant paste to her employer, though she had not actually suggested that he buy some.

The plump and jolly Montagu Matthews became suddenly stern. He pointed a chubby forefinger at the woman and said, "But, madam, you do admit you mentioned that some ant paste was needed to take care of insect pests in the house?"

"Yes, I did speak to him about the need of it," the woman sniffed.

He frowned at her. "Then it was wrong of you to testify that you had not asked the Marquis to buy the ant paste!"

"I did *not* ask that he buy it," she retorted. "Mr. Malcolm, the butler, usually ordered such articles along with the other household supplies."

"Yet there was a possibility that the Marquis, knowing your need of the item, might have purchased it and brought it home, then for some unknown reason forgot to hand it over to you."

"He might well have done," the woman said, seeming ready to break into tears at any moment.

"Thank you, ma'am" the chief counsel for the defence said with a smirk on his round face. "You may step down."

She left the stand to a swell of murmuring from the people in the courtroom. It seemed for a moment that Sir Alan Norville was going to ask her to return so that he might question her statement. But after a short conference with his associates, he sat back grimly and said nothing.

Montagu Matthews turned to the Bench and said, "I would now like to call an important witness who until this morning was not available, since no one had been able to locate her. I ask that Miss Gladys Huff take the stand!"

Charles whispered in Fanny's ear, "The important missing witness! Things ought to look up for George now!"

She nodded and glanced up at George standing in the box. He seemed to be showing more confidence, and looked much less forlorn than on the previous day.

Miss Gladys Huff proved to be a petite young woman neatly dressed. She pertly took her place in the witness stand, an assured look on her snub-nosed, rather homely face as she was sworn in.

Montagu Matthews questioned her. After he had established that she had been an upstairs maid in the house, he asked her, "Will you tell us why you are no longer in the employ of the Marquis?"

The girl looked annoyed. "It was him, Mr. Malcolm, the butler. He never liked me and when I complained about the room he'd given me being too cold he told me I could pack my things and leave since it wasn't going to get any warmer."

"Aha!" Montagu Matthews said. "And so you left despite the fact you enjoyed the children of the Marquis and his wife, and had hoped to stay on in your job."

"I missed the young ones," Gladys Huff agreed. "But I wouldn't stay and take cheek off that Malcolm!"

"So you went off with a final week's wages in your pocket."

"Yes, sir."

"Did you tell Malcolm where you were going?" Montagu Matthews wanted to know.

"No, sir. I told no one where I was going. And if you hadn't found where my stepmother lived and that I had a stepbrother at whose place I had gone to stay, I wouldn't be here now!"

"Will you tell the Court why you agreed to come?" the stout old lawyer for the defence said smoothly.

"To see justice done, sir!" the maid spoke out loudly.

"Objection, My Lord!" Sir Alan Norville said, jumping up.

"Objection sustained," the Judge droned. "The remark will be struck from the record."

"Your pardon, My Lord," Montagu Matthews said, looking not at all repentant for all this. He asked the girl, "May I ask you to tell the court what you told me, about a happening several nights before you were dismissed from the employ of the Marquis."

"I went of my own accord," Miss Huff insisted defiantly.

"Whatever," the stout man said waving his hand airily. "Let us hear what happened on that certain night."

"The night the missus was took bad and died," Gladys Huff said. "Well, sir, she'd been drinking all day and I'd been told to watch over the youngsters as she was paying no heed to them at all. I was glad to be with the poor little tots. I left them for a little to go down and have a bite below stairs. When I returned I found the boy playing with a package he'd found somewhere. I looked at it and saw the box contained ant paste. Knowing it to be a poison I took it from him and hid it away in a cupboard in the hall."

There was a loud reaction from the observers in the courtroom, so loud that the Judge rapped for quiet and threatened to clear the court unless the clamor ended. The face of Sir Alan Norville evidenced concern while in the prisoner's box, George was looking a good deal brighter.

Sir Alan at once rose to cross examine. But he was unable to change the maid's testimony; she insisted this had taken place on the night Virginia had died and that the cupboard where the poison had been hidden was the same one in which the police had later found it.

The court recessed for lunch. This time it was a more joyous occasion. Over her beef sandwich and ale, Fanny asked Charles, "It will be all right now, won't it? They can't possibly convict George in the face of Miss Huff's testimony."

"I think Montagu Matthews has done well," Charles agreed. "But we mustn't count on anything until the trial is over."

Fanny gazed about the pub in which they were having their lunch and said, "I don't see Dora anywhere. We missed her on the way out."

"I doubt if she will return," Charles said. "She doesn't like to be away from the children long. She mentioned to me she would attend the morning session only."

Fanny was amazed that Dora could be so calm. She said, "I don't know how she can take it all so coolly. I should die if I missed the summing up."

Charles gave her a wan smile. "You have a taste for drama in your make-up which Dora lacks."

"I will not deny that," she said.

It was snowing lightly when they left the pub. They had barely taken their seats in the courtroom when the court assembled again and the trial resumed. There was an expectant air among the observers since all had been thrilled by the revelations of the morning and were eager for some added last-minute excitements.

But there were no excitements, merely the summing up. Sir Alan Norville pointed out the instability of the housekeeper's nature, and her confusion over what she had and hadn't said. He also attempted to darken the character of Miss Gladys Huff, and condemn her as an impudent, vengeful young woman ready to say anything to discredit the rest of the servants with whom she had served.

The jury retired at three o'clock, and the prisoner was taken from the dock. The jury were away a half-hour. At length the foreman returned, looking solemn. George resumed his place in the prisoner's box and the Judge and barristers were in their proper seats.

An expectant hush fell over the crowded courtroom and the foreman rose, cleared his throat and in a loud voice, intoned the words which Fanny had been praying for, "We find the defendant not guilty!"

Bedlam broke out in the courtroom. The Judge, looking displeased, insisted that order be restored. He then made a brief comment on the verdict, thanked the jury, and the trial was over. Charles and Fanny embraced happily and then Charles alone went over to the dock and congratulated George, putting an arm around him. Montagu Matthews and Sir Alan Norville were exchanging pleasant platitudes as the crowd left.

Charles quickly returned to Fanny and escorted her out. He said, "George sends you his love and told me he will see you as soon as he possibly can.

"I can wait," she said. "I have waited this long. He must not rush things. We still have to be careful. It would be wrong to cause scandal after winning the trial."

"Exactly," Charles agreed. "But perhaps he can quietly come to your place tonight."

Fanny made no reply, only hoping that this might be possible. This hope sustained her through the afternoon and early evening as she recounted the happenings at the trial to Hilda Asquith.

Hilda said, "Then all your troubles are at an end."

"I wonder," Fanny mused, standing by the fireplace and staring into the flames with a sudden feeling of desolation which she could not comprehend. She should be elated and somehow she wasn't.

The old actress said, "David can still use you in the play. You should see him."

"No," she said. "Not until I talk with George."

It was nearly ten o'clock and the elderly Hilda, having an early rehearsal call, had retired for the night, when there came a knock at the front door of the flat. Fanny ran to open the door, her heart pounding with deep emotion, ready to throw herself into George's arms.

But when she opened the door it wasn't George who stood there but Charles. He was wearing civilian clothes and a heavy cape against the cold night air.

He looked sympathetic as he said, "I know it was not me you wished to find waiting out here."

She shrugged. "It does not matter. I have become used to disappointments."

"I'm sorry to be part of this one," Charles said.

"Why was George not able to come himself?" she asked.

Charles looked grave. "He is here, waiting in the carriage below in which we both arrived. You're to go down to him as he did not dare venture up here."

She stared at Charles' grim face and in dismay exclaimed, "Something's wrong! Tell me! What is it?"

Charles placed his hands on her shoulders. "You must be brave. A dreadful thing has happened. Opposition members in Parliament have full information on George's affair with you, including a list of dates on which you spent the night together. They hired private detectives to watch you both every minute. They now threaten to give this information to the press and ruin George socially and politically if he does not retire from public life!"

"Oh, no!" she said, closing her eyes. Tears trickled down her cheeks. "After all we have gone through!"

"The worst danger is that it would again cause tongues to wag about Virginia's death," Charles said. "So you understand why he did not dare come up here."

"What is to be done?" she groaned.

"George must resign his seat in the House for the time being. In view of all the business of the trial that might be best anyway. If you were to leave the country, or best of all, marry someone else, there would be little point in involving you. Later on, when all is quiet again, George can resume his political career."

"It's too sudden! Too much of a shock!" Fanny cried, her head spinning, her whole being sick with grief. All her great hopes seemed to be shattered.

"George feels very badly about this," Charles said. "Go down to him."

"Dare I?"

"It should be safe enough. I'll watch from the vestibule. When you have seen him the carriage will take him home."

"I'm not sure I can say goodbye to him," she told Charles brokenly.

He placed a comforting arm about her. "Rely upon your theatre training. You can carry it through and save him. If you persist in this romance you'll both be destroyed!"

"All right," Fanny said in a dull voice and went for her cloak.

It was snowing lightly and the waiting carriage had a mantle of snow on it. Fanny left Charles in the vestibule and went outside to the carriage.

Entering its dark interior she sat beside George. She was shocked by his appearance. If he had looked gaunt at the trial he surely looked ten years older now. He embraced her and kissed her gently. "Dear Fanny!" he said, holding her to him. "What are we to do?"

Steeling herself, she said, "Save what we can! I'll go abroad for a while. You can live in peace. In a few years you can resume your seat in Parliament."

"What about us?" George asked in agony.

She kissed him and caressed his face with her hands. "My dearest George," she whispered, "we can never lose what we have had. A stormy love, yet a rewarding one. Perhaps one day we can be together again."

"I want you now!"

"And you would soon hate me if I remained with you," Fanny told him. "No. We must part. And there is always Dora. She loves you and nothing would make her happier than your asking her to marry you. All this while she has been a dedicated foster mother to your children."

"Dora has been wonderful," George admitted. "But it is you I love."

"I know," she said, resting her head on his chest. "But many people never do marry the ones they truly love. Our case is not so unusual, believe me!"

"How can I go on without you?"

She said, "We have our memories. You'll be surprised how much comfort they will offer. In time, they may even be enough! Goodbye, my love!" They kissed again, embracing passionately one last time.

Then abruptly Fanny drew away from him and literally flung herself out of the carriage. He called after her, "Fanny!" She paid no attention but went inside and joined Charles in the vestibule. They both turned and watched the carriage move away.

"I gave a stellar performance," she sobbed. "The trouble is, I wasn't able to convince myself!"

He placed his arm around her. "Let us go upstairs. You need some brandy."

A few moments later they stood facing each other before the blazing log fire, brandy glasses in their hands. The soldierly Charles raised his glass and said, "I offer a toast to a brave lady."

Smiling wanly through her tears, Fanny replied, "If I may offer one to a loyal brother and a faithful friend."

They drank and then Charles stared at her in silence for a long moment. He said, "I have a suggestion. Let me change that faithful friend to something more intimate."

She said, "What do you suggest?"

"I want to be your husband," Charles said quietly. "I'm not the one you really want. But I have always loved you devotedly. I think in time you might find it in your heart to care for me just a little."

Fanny lay her hand on his wrist. "Charles, you are too kind!"

"Wait until I explain," he said. "My regiment leaves for India within a week. We can be quietly married and you could accompany me as my wife."

"Charles!"

"It will get you out of the country and you will have my protection as your husband," he said eagerly.

Her eyes filled with tears again. She was past fighting the cruel tricks of fate which had so long kept her apart from George.

"Very well, Charles," she said wearily. "I shall be honored to be your wife."

Next morning when the elderly Hilda heard the news she sputtered angrily, "Isn't it enough to ask you to give up the man you love without asking you to leave your country and the theatre?"

Fanny raised a protesting hand. "It is best this way."

"I say it is nonsense and needless," the character actress said. "You love London and the stage! David will find you a part in his new company. You know that!"

"If the yellow press attacked me it might destroy his London venture," Fanny said. "I would never forgive myself for that."

"He wouldn't care!" Hilda said.

"I would," Fanny told her. "The only safe thing is for me to leave London."

Hilda gazed at her sorrowfully. "It will be like losing a daughter! You're positive you don't want me to talk to David about this?"

Fanny turned away from the old woman to hide her tears. "Positive!"

The next development in the mad rush of events came the following day. Fanny had shut herself up in her flat until she received word from Charles as to the time and place of their wedding. When he arrived the next afternoon he was once again wearing his uniform, but she could see by his worried expression he had things other than the wedding on his mind.

"Charles, what is it?" she greeted him.

"My brother—" he began and stopped.

"George? What has happened to him?" There was fear in her voice.

"Not George," Charles said in a grim voice. "Kenneth, the Reverend Kenneth!"

The name of Kenneth brought forth a vision of the evil priest who in his fanatacism lacked any trace of charity in his heart. With dismay, she asked, "Is he going to try to harm George in some way? Use me to harm him?"

Charles shook his head. "No," he said. "It seems the trial completely deranged Kenneth. Last night he hung himself in his room near the Cathedral. He left a note behind admitting he was the one who set the fire in the theatre in which you were playing, the one in which so many people died! He asked forgiveness!"

"I often wondered if it might have been he," Fanny said. And turning away, she asked in a low, anguished tone, "Is the agony never to end?"

"The Palmer family have brought you nothing but grief," Charles said. "George took you from the theatre you loved. Kenneth railed against you and in his hatred wound up murdering many innocents! And here I am, offering you a second-rate love and the doubtful pleasure of living as an army officer's wife in distant India!"

Fanny quickly faced him again. "Yours is no second rate love, Charles. You were always the strongest and best of the three. I shall willingly marry you and go to India. And with God's blessing we shall be happy together!"

"I pray that we shall," Charles said solemnly, taking her in his arms. "I shall return tomorrow at seven. We shall take a carriage out of London and be married in a country chapel whose vicar I know. We shall need witnesses."

"Hilda Asquith and Silas Hodder," she said promptly. "They shall be here ready to accompany us."

"Your last ties with the stage," Charles said with a sad smile. "I'd say they'll make excellent witnesses."

"What about Kenneth's funeral?" she asked.

"It will be private. Tomorrow morning. We hope to keep his suicide a secret, along with his confession that he set the fire. The

Bishop takes the position that he was demented at the time of his death and not responsible for what he wrote. The family are in full agreement, as we've had enough disagreeable newspaper publicity for the moment."

"It is surely for the best," she agreed.

He took her in his arms. "Until tomorrow evening," he said.

At first Hilda Asquith stubbornly refused to take part in Fanny's wedding to Charles Palmer. But Silas Hodder won her over. The old stage door man was extremely persuasive and ready, as always, to do anything to help Fanny.

Seven o'clock chimed on the mantel clock the next evening. Fanny sat ready in coat and bonnet, solemnly awaiting the arrival of Charles. A nervous Hilda and Silas waited in the adjoining room. Suddenly there was a knock on the door. Fanny slowly rose and went over to open it, trying to look happy so Charles would not be hurt.

The door opened and standing there looking handsome in greatcoat and top hat was David Cornish! The young actor removed his hat and came inside. "Surprised?" he asked.

"David!" she stammered. "I'm waiting for Charles. We're to be married tonight."

David shook his head. "No!"

"No?"

"Charles sent me as his substitute," the actor said.

"I don't understand!" Her head was reeling.

David took her in his arms. "Charles realized he wasn't being fair to you. He came and talked with me. He told me it would be best for you to marry and leave London, but that he didn't feel he was the right man. I told him he was correct. That *I* was the man!"

"But David!" Fanny protested. "You're opening your first company here in London!"

He smiled and shook his head. "Not any longer. I've turned the whole project over to Sir Benjamin Fuller. He will head the company and star in my place. I have accepted an offer to play in America. We open in New York in a month. The vessel leaves within a few days. I also have an opening for a leading lady, whom I would prefer to be my wife!"

"David!" she cried out in wonder. Tears of joy filled her eyes, for in that moment she knew this was right. It was what she had truly wanted without ever admitting it! The stage was a fever in her blood of which she'd never be cured. Her father must be smiling at her now from wherever he was, she thought fleetingly. He had known better than she did that she could not desert her destiny!

David's lips were on hers, his arms held her tightly to him and Fanny knew this was the beginning of something new and wonderful which would last for them as long as life itself.

A Sneak Peek from Crimson Romance
(From *The Cowboy's Baby* by D'Ann Lindun)

"Okay, that should be creepy enough."

Cat O'Brien stepped off the ladder and backed up a few feet to admire the orange and black lights she'd strung around Gran's porch. Along with the cardboard witch and ghost cutouts on the door and carved pumpkins on the steps, the blinking lights brought a new level of delicious holiday spookiness to the old house. Luckily, she'd been able to find her Halloween decorations in one of her still unpacked boxes. Although she'd procrastinated until the afternoon of the holiday, the chore was done now.

The trick-or-treaters would love the decor, and just maybe, this year she could create a happy holiday season. If Gran were still alive everything would be close to perfect. Cat fought her fresh grief, and pulled her coat close as a cold wind raced down from Harmon's Peak. She looked up to where ghostlike fingers of snow clouds grasped the top of the jagged mountains. Early snow was common in Granite, Colorado, nestled deep in the Rockies. And by the looks of the swirling gray clouds, a big storm was coming.

Before entering the house, Cat stopped to admire the rows of Gran's bright orange, rust, and yellow chrysanthemums lining the sidewalk. There would be snow on them by morning. She shivered and went inside, draping her coat and scarf over the back of an original Victorian chair she'd found for next to nothing at an estate sale in Telluride. Making sure the candy dish was full, she flipped on the radio to ward off the silence, then moved into the kitchen to fix herself a cup of hot chocolate and some soup.

After settling her gray tabby, Darlington, in her lap, Cat sipped the steaming hot chocolate and stared out the window. Not quite 4:00 P.M., yet almost dark. The towering peaks had obliterated the winter sun. Aspens scraped against the side of the house and a few snowflakes hit the windowpane. She made a mental note to call Franklin DeMato to ask him to drop off a cord of wood in the morning.

She moved Darlington and stood with a heavy sigh. No time like the present to put the empty Halloween boxes back in the attic.

After storing her boxes, Cat hurried downstairs. She peeked outside and the storm had gained momentum. Heavy, wet snowflakes fell in a steady stream. The doorbell rang, signaling her first visitor of the evening. She stood still; amazed she would get any trick-or-treaters in this weather. When the bell rang again she called, "Hold on. I'm coming."

She grabbed the candy dish and peered through the peephole before sliding back the deadbolt. Someone stood on her porch, but Cat couldn't make out any features through the tiny opening. She swung the door open and a gust of snow blew in her face. The storm had picked up to be a regular winter gale, swirling snowflakes all around. Blinking, she looked for small children, but only an adult in a heavy coat and a shawl covering most of the face stood there. Was this a teenager trick-or-treating? If so, as what? Obviously not a ghost or princess.

"Can I help you?"

The bundled-up figure mumbled something, but the words were lost in the wind. Cat struggled to hold the door with one hand, and held out the candy dish with the other. The stranger said something unintelligible. Cat raised her voice to be heard over the protesting shutters. "I can't hear you."

The black scarf again muffled the answer.

Cat shivered in the wind, but she was unwilling to let a total stranger into her house. This might be Granite, population eight hundred, but she had spent too many years in Denver to be careless.

She motioned to the wicker chairs still sitting on the porch. "Step over here and tell me what brings you out in a storm."

Instead of moving toward the chairs, the stranger pulled the scarf from her face and striking blue eyes met Cat's. "Are you Cathleen O'Brien?"

"Yes." A vague unease rose up Cat's back. "Do I know you?"

"No." The girl jutted out her chin in an all-too-familiar gesture and shoved a wad of papers toward Cat. "But you gave birth to me."

"Oh, God." Cat let go of the candy dish and it crashed to the floor, sending miniature candy bars and cheap plastic toys flying across the porch. Her knees threatened to buckle and she grabbed for the door. Was she hallucinating? How could this be? It wasn't possible for the baby she'd given up almost eighteen years ago to be standing in front of her. She stared at the daughter she'd given birth to, but never seen. Her eyes, her nose…his mouth.

She *would not* think about Tanner Burke.

She blinked, dazed. "How did you find me?" She shook her head. "My gosh, you must be frozen. I have hot chocolate. Soup, too."

This wasn't the tearful reunion she'd imagined between her and the daughter she'd never stopped missing. Why was she babbling about food when all she wanted to do was throw her arms around her baby and sob?

"Please come in."

"Okay."

Without removing her snowy biker boots or ankle-length down coat, the girl followed Cat, clomping across Gran's polished hardwood floors. In the warmth of the kitchen, she settled onto one of the chairs and wrapped her arms around her middle. Darlington sniffed one ankle, but the girl ignored him.

With shaking hands, Cat took leftover soup from the avocado green fridge and managed to place the bowl in the microwave.

Then she moved to the stove to make hot chocolate. Not with powder from a packet, but with milk, sugar and cocoa, the way Gran used to do for her.

As the food heated, Cat sat at Gran's old kitchen table and stared at the apparition in front of her. Short, dark hair, much like Cat's own pixie style, but with hot pink spikes. Blue eyes, nearly identical to hers, but circled with makeup so dark it looked ghoulish. High, beautiful cheekbones. A diamond nose stud. Full maroon shaded lips turned down. An ankle length black coat and combat boots. When Cat had taught history in Denver, a girl dressed this way would be called a Goth.

The girl looked intently back at her while Cat wondered what she thought. Cat didn't normally wear much makeup and her clothes were nondescript jeans and a plain gray sweatshirt. So many questions whirled around in Cat's head she couldn't settle on which one to ask first. Her mind spun and when she focused on the snow melting at her daughter's feet, the water took on a fluorescent glow. Her head and ears rang. Was she going to pass out?

The girl picked up Darlington and stroked him. "I know you didn't expect this…"

"It's more than okay," Cat rushed to assure her. She desperately wanted to hug her daughter, but sensing such a move would scare her off, held back.

Staring intently into Cat's face, the girl said, "I look like you."

"Yes." Their facial resemblance was strong, but at five four, Cat was petite, whereas her child had taken after her biological father in height. She stood around five nine, and although not fat, appeared bigger boned than Cat. "And this displeases you?" It shouldn't hurt, but this stranger/daughter's almost disgusted tone sent another arrow zinging into Cat's tattered heart.

She shrugged. "Not really. It's just weird."

"Very."

To have someone you'd never met carrying your genes was unsettling. Cat had never seen her baby. The nurses had whisked the squalling newborn away without allowing Cat even a glimpse, using the excuse that it would her hurt too much. From that day on, Cat looked in the face of every girl of the right age to see if she could recognize herself. The second she turned 21, she had tried to get the courts to let her know who had adopted her baby. But the law was unbending; no information could be disclosed. Cat had managed to get her mother to tell her the family lived in Denver, but nothing more. Candace claimed she didn't know any more than that.

Now Cat drank in every feature, trying to capture each nuance of similarity. Too much makeup, but gorgeous nevertheless, with a flawless, china doll complexion.

"Do I look like him, too?" Cat's daughter blurted out, her face beginning to crumple almost as if she couldn't bear the answer. "My biological father?"

Oh, God. Not yet. Cat's mind raced, trying to find a way to stall. She didn't want to include Tanner in this. Not now. Later, after she'd had time to process it all.

She swallowed hard. "Yes. The shape of your mouth. Your cheekbones. Your height."

Cat's daughter's expression changed, hardened. "Can I meet him?"

"I don't know." Cat stood and dumped her full cup in the sink. Anything to avoid her newfound daughter's hungry eyes. Anything to avoid letting her see the burning resentment that still lingered, even after all these years. Would Tanner want to see his daughter? He had been eager enough to give her up.

It occurred to Cat she hadn't even asked the most basic questions. "What's your name?"

"Eve Sheppard."

Cat whirled around and stared at her in astonishment. "Why, that's the—"

"Middle name you picked out." Eve played with Darlington's tail. "Yeah. I know."

"I called you Noelle Eve…the name chosen for the baby girl born in early spring, not Christmas at all. Cat's throat burned and she fought to speak. "I can't believe your parents kept it."

"Yeah, me neither." Eve's eyes began to tear and her voice filled with pain and anger, emotions Cat had helped put there. Cat's never-ending guilt ratcheted up a notch. She didn't think she could feel any worse than she had all these years, but in less than five minutes that pain had been overcome by new and unexpected cuts to her heart.

Eve's magenta lips twisted. "Eve Daniella. They dropped the Noelle."

"Pretty," Cat commented. "How did you find me? I've only lived here a month. I've looked for so long—"

"Not because my parents helped." Eve's scowl deepened. "They've done everything to keep me away from you…because they've known who you were from the beginning. The priest who arranged the adoption told them."

Cat's throat closed and she fought dizzying waves of nausea. Even though she wanted an open adoption, her mother and Father McCauley both insisted closed would be better for everyone involved. The only way Cat kept her sanity had been by imagining the mother petite and blonde and the father tall, dark and handsome. More importantly, both would be kind and wise. Completely different from her own emotionally cold mother, and her father who'd died in the Sudan fighting an ancient war no one cared about.

"How'd you find me?"

"Mom told me who you were. She said since I turned out like you, I should come here."

"Like me? What do you mean?" Cat dragged her mind back to the present, and for a long moment, tried to make sense of this sudden turn of events. Who cared how it had happened? Her daughter was here! Her child had shown up, a prayer had been answered.

"Never mind." Eve suddenly seemed to find the pictures on the fridge fascinating. She studied the last picture Cat had taken of Gran, one of her standing in the backyard among her beloved flowers, a wide smile across her wrinkled face. "Who's that?"

"My gran." Cat's heart hurt when she thought of her. "You would've loved her."

"Maybe."

"Do you need to call your parents—" her voice caught on the word, "—to let them know you're here and that you're okay?"

"I guess," Eve muttered and picked at one of her black fingernails.

Cat pointed to the old fashioned rotary model on the wall. She'd kept it because it reminded her of Gran. "Use that one while I go stoke the fire. The five o'clock news said I-70 and the road into Granite are closed. Please tell them you're welcome to stay the night."

As she added another log to the fire, Cat tried to calm her racing heart. This wasn't supposed to happen this way. She should be ready with answers for the tough question sure to come. Explaining her love affair all those years ago wouldn't be easy. She closed her eyes and just for a minute remembered the perfect summer she'd found in Tanner's arms. How he had helped chase away her loneliness and fear.

Eve said from the doorway, "My mother wants to talk to you."

"Okay." Cat's stomach tumbled as she hurried toward Eve. What would the woman who has raised her daughter say? Cat motioned to the ottoman in front of the fire. "Sit here, take off your coat and I'll go speak to your mom."

As Eve sank onto the plush green velvet, Cat walked into the kitchen and picked up the phone. "Hello."

"This is Mary Sheppard," a cold voice replied. "Eve's mother."

"Of course." Cat wrapped the long phone cord around her hand and twisted until her fingers turned white. There was no need for Mary Sheppard to stress the fact she was Eve's mother. Cat held no claim to the title.

"She found you then."

"Yes."

"I suppose Eve told you how horrible we are—"

"Not at all," Cat rushed to say. She didn't want to start out on the wrong foot with Eve's mom. Doing so would make it difficult to stay in contact with Eve, and nothing was going to jeopardize their new relationship if she could help it.

Mary snorted. "I suppose she said we're awful because we don't want her to keep the baby."

"Baby? What baby?" Cat stared at the photo Eve had been looking at. What would Gran do in this situation? She'd been so wise. "I don't know what you're talking about. Eve just arrived a few minutes ago."

"Then she hasn't told you she's seven months pregnant? I'm not surprised. Eve came to you because she feels that you will sympathize with her."

Mary's words faded away. Cat's newfound daughter was pregnant? My God. Talk about the past reliving itself. "I'm not siding with anyone, Mrs. Sheppard," Cat managed. "But since adoption worked out so well for you—"

"Adoption hasn't been what we hoped it would be," Mary interrupted. "Eve has been a problem child practically from day one. Skipping school, boys, drugs. This is just the final straw. Eve isn't welcome in our home any longer."

"You don't mean that," Cat said, horrified. Her own mother had said things nearly as nasty. And she had left Cat in Gran's care fast enough when she found out about the pregnancy.

"I mean every word," Mary choked out. "Eve has no place in our family. We have two young impressionable daughters who will glamorize their sister's mistake. If she would listen to reason, live with my brother until after the baby's born and then put it up for adoption, we would allow her to stay. But she insists she wants to keep it, raise it on her own. What she means is that my husband and I would be burdened with an infant. We're near retirement age. Simply too old to raise a baby."

"Why now? Why did you tell her about me now?"

"We didn't intend to, but she somehow figured out where her adoption records were hidden and discovered who you are." Mary's voice turned as cold as the winter storm raging outside. "We gave her a choice—give up the baby and stay with us, or leave our house. Eve made her decision when she decided to find you."

"Mrs. Sheppard, please, we need to talk rationally."

"I just can't do this anymore."

For a moment there was silence, then a man's soft voice came over the phone. "Are you there? This is Bill Sheppard, Eve's father."

"Hello, Mr. Sheppard."

"Mary says Eve is there with you?" His voice shook. "Thank God she's not out on the streets." He sounded genuinely concerned. Mrs. Sheppard apparently was quite overwrought to say the things she had. Cat's own mother had said and done similar things when she learned about Cat's pregnancy. Maybe she regretted them now.

"Yes, Mr. Sheppard, Eve is here in Granite with me. The roads are closed tonight," Cat told him. "There's a terrible storm in the mountains, so Eve can spend the night with me. The roads will be clear by morning. I'll bring Eve home then." Without waiting for an answer, she hung up.

As Cat reentered the living room, she found Eve sitting on the ottoman, staring into the fire. "Are you okay?"

"Sure." Her hunched shoulders and hanging head told Cat differently, but she didn't comment.

"Your mom told me about the baby."

"Yeah. I'm sure you want me out, too." Before Cat could respond, words poured out of Eve. "It was a mistake to come here. Or to think you might want me now. You don't want me around. You made your choice when I was born." Her bitter words raked across Cat like nails on bare skin.

"That's not fair." Eve had no idea how badly she had been wanted. "Turn around, please."

"No, I'm leaving." But she continued to stare into the fire.

Cat stepped forward and put her hands on Eve's trembling shoulders. "There's a raging storm outside. You can't go anywhere tonight. Please take off your coat and stay the night."

"My mother told you she threw me out because I won't give up my baby?"

"Yes. But I'm sure she doesn't mean it." Cat knew all too well how much Mary meant her words. She'd had a similar conversation with her own mother seventeen years ago. Waves of déjà vu washed over her. Her mother's horrified expression, followed by an immediate declaration that Cat 'should just get rid of it.'

Eve finally stood and turned to face Cat. Twin rivulets of black ran down her cheeks and she gnawed on her lower lip until Cat thought she might bite through it. "I want to keep my baby."

Cat prayed not to say the wrong thing—words that would never erase themselves. She tried to choose her words carefully. "It's a big decision. You're very young to raise a child on your own. Adoption might be the best thing."

"They said you'd say that since you gave me away." Eve's lips twisted into an ugly line. "Why would I ever think you'd help me find a way to keep my baby when you didn't even try?"

Her angry words hung between them.

Cat dragged in a breath. "That's not true—" Seeing Eve wasn't buying it, she asked, "What does the father say? Will he be involved?"

Eve's hands cradled her belly in the same protective manner Cat remembered doing even all these years later. "He wants nothing to do with us. No one does. Dad would, but he won't stand up to my mother. You were my last hope."

"What if I agree with them that you're too young to have a baby?"

Cat forced the words past the lump in her throat. Eve was almost eighteen, not sixteen like she had been. This wasn't her fight. She wasn't even involved. Eve had parents who knew what would be best for her. Maybe they weren't the kindest people, but they had to care about the girl they'd raised. "Eve, let's talk some more."

After a long hesitation, Eve pulled off her coat. Under it, she wore a clingy black T-shirt and leggings. For just a moment, Cat's gaze lingered on Eve's swollen belly. A child. Her grandchild. A shudder ran down Cat's back. How could she endure another infant being carried out of her life? Once had nearly destroyed her; twice would finish her off. In spite of her better judgment, she asked, "How would you support a baby? You still have at least another semester of school, I presume?"

Eve turned toward her, hope leaping into her eyes. "Yeah, but I can get a part time job."

"What about college? Don't you want a career?" To her own ears, Cat sounded exactly like her own mother pointing out all the reasons she could not keep her own child.

"I can go to night school." Eve leaned forward, eyes intent. "Lots of people do it."

"Do you know how hard that would be? Getting a college education the regular way is hard enough, but adding a baby and a job, too, well that's a tough road."

"It would be easier than not knowing what happened to my baby," Eve declared with flashing eyes. Again, the unspoken accusation lay between them. That Cat had not cared; had not spent a lifetime grieving for the baby she'd been forced to give away like a stray pet.

Cat sat on the chair nearest the ottoman. "What do you need from me?"

For the first time, some of Eve's bluster faded and her lower lip trembled. She couldn't seem to find words for a minute. "I want to stay with you."

"What? You can't." Cat would have cut off her own tongue to take back the hurt that crumpled Eve's face. She had to make Eve understand how much she would wound the people who'd raised her by turning to her. "Your mom and dad wouldn't go for it. They'd be devastated."

"You heard my mother. She threw me out," Eve said in a dead voice. "I don't have anywhere to go and I'm desperate."

"I'm sure they don't mean it," Cat said. "They're just hurt and angry. Your dad didn't say anything about you not coming home." But Mary Sheppard had been adamant about Eve not being welcome back home. Cat's mind raced, searching for a solution. Did she really want to take in a pregnant teenager? Did she have the skills to pull it off? Would she and Eve try to forge a parent/child relationship? Or be more like roommates?

Cat closed her eyes for a moment. God help her, she stood on Eve's side in this. Only Gran had listened when she pleaded to keep her baby. But not even Gran could stand up to Candace O'Brien when she made up her mind that Cat would give up her child.

As soon as the birth parents took their new baby home, Candace acted as if the whole thing never happened and promptly enrolled Cat in a private all girls' school, pretending everything was perfectly normal. She acted as if Cat's newborn daughter had not been ripped away from her.

"My mother is dead serious," Eve said. "If they weren't, would I have come here?"

Cat flinched. That hurt.

Maybe she *could* help Eve. She hadn't fought hard enough to keep her baby back when she should have. Maybe this was Cat's chance to make it up to her. A chance to wipe the slate clean…"If I agree to this there would be some rules."

Eve's mascara ringed eyes filled with hope. "Anything."

"Most importantly, you'd finish high school and enroll in the community college over in Snow Valley next semester. You'd have to find a part time job and take parenting classes. Would you do that?"

"Yes," Eve cried. She struggled to rise and hugged Cat, her belly wedged between them. "Thank you!"

"You're welcome," Cat managed around the lump in her throat. A ragged tear in one corner of her heart mended a little bit as she held her daughter for the first time. "We'll make you up a bed for tonight. In the morning, we'll drive to Denver because we need to talk to your parents again. I have to be certain that they mean what they say about you not going home."

"They mean it," Eve said.